FIC SAINTCR LI Redempt
Saintcrow, Lilith.
Redemption alle
1st ed.

D0444101

m

We also get federal funding if a paranormal incident is big enough to qualify, or if it crosses state lines.

"Defense spending" isn't only for mundane threats.

Plus, the Church subsidizes training no few apprentices. Even if they do bar us from Heaven, they try to make sure we're funded enough to hold back the tide of Hell. We're usually overworked and just-barely-paid-enough, but that's better than nothing. Resident hunters don't need to worry about rent or their next meal, thank God.

We just have to worry about damnation.

And being psychic has its perks when it comes to investing. Mikhail had done very well for himself. Screw that "not using your powers for personal gain" bit. When you're getting shot, knifed, electrocuted, strangled, dumped in rivers, thrown off buildings, or almost eviscerated protecting the common citizenry, the *least* the world can do is give you a break or two on the stock market.

Of course, living long enough to claim a retirement fund is the problem.

Praise for the Jill Kismet series:

"Jill Kismet is, above all else, a survivor, and it is her story that will haunt readers long after the blood, gore and demons have faded into memory."

—*Romantic Times* on *Night Shift*

BOOKS BY LILITH SAINTCROW

JILL KISMET NOVELS

Night Shift

Hunter's Prayer

Redemption Alley

Flesh Circus

DANTE VALENTINE NOVELS

Working for the Devil

Dead Man Rising

The Devil's Right Hand

Saint City Sinners

To Hell and Back

Dark Watcher

Storm Watcher

Fire Watcher

Cloud Watcher

The Society

Hunter, Healer

Mindhealer

Steelflower

REDEMPTION ALLEY

★

LILITH SAINTCROW

www.orbitbooks.net

New York   London

The characters and events in this book are fictitious. Any similarity to real persons, living or dead, is coincidental and not intended by the author.

If you purchase this book without a cover you should be aware that this book may have been stolen property and reported as "unsold and destroyed" to the publisher. In such case neither the author nor the publisher has received any payment for this "stripped book."

Copyright © 2009 by Lilith Saintcrow
Excerpt from *Flesh Circus* copyright © 2009 by Lilith Saintcrow
All rights reserved. Except as permitted under the U.S. Copyright Act of 1976, no part of this publication may be reproduced, distributed, or transmitted in any form or by any means, or stored in a database or retrieval system, without the prior written permission of the publisher.

Orbit
Hachette Book Group
237 Park Avenue
New York, NY 10017

Visit our Web site at www.orbitbooks.com.

Orbit is a trademark of Little, Brown Book Group Ltd.
The Orbit name and logo is a trademark of Little, Brown Book Group Ltd.

Printed in the United States of America

First Edition: August 2009

10 9 8 7 6 5 4 3 2 1

ATTENTION CORPORATIONS AND ORGANIZATIONS:
Most HACHETTE BOOK GROUP books are available at quantity discounts with bulk purchase for educational, business, or sales promotional use. For information, please call or write:

Special Markets Department, Hachette Book Group
237 Park Avenue, New York, NY 10017
Telephone: 1-800-222-6747 Fax: 1-800-477-5925

To L.I., Because I promised.

Si vis pacem, para bellum.
—Unknown

Bonis quod bene fit haud perit.
—Plautus

1

Right before dawn a hush falls over Santa Luz. The things that live and prey in the night are either searching for a burrow to spend the day in, or looking for one last little snack. *The closer to dawn, the harder the fight,* hunters say. Predators get desperate as the sun, that great enemy of all darkness, walks closer to the rim of dawn.

Which explains why I was flat on my back, again, with hellbreed-strong fingers cutting off my air and my head ringing like someone had set off dynamite inside it. Sparks spat from silver charms tied in my hair, blessed moon-metal reacting to something inimical. The Trader hissed as he squeezed, fingers sinking into my throat and the flat shine of the dusted lying over his eyes as they narrowed, a forked tongue flickering past the broken yellowed stubs of his teeth.

Apparently dental work wasn't part of the contract he'd made with whatever hellbreed had given him supernatural strength and the ability to set shit on fire at a thousand paces.

I brought my knee up, hard.

The hellbreed this particular Trader had bargained with hadn't given him an athletic cup, either. The bony part of my knee sank into his crotch, meeting precious little resistance, so hard something popped.

It didn't sound like much fun.

The Trader's eyes rolled up and he immediately let go of my trachea. I promptly added injury to insult by clocking him on the side of the head with a knifehilt. I didn't slip the knife between his ribs because I wanted to bring him in for questioning.

What can I say? Maybe I was in a good mood.

Besides, I had other worries. For one, the burning warehouse.

Smoke roiled thick in the choking air, and the rushing crackle of flames almost drowned out the screams coming from the girl handcuffed to a support post. She was wasting both good energy and usable air by screaming, probably almost out of her mind with fear. Bits of burning building plummeted to the concrete floor. I gained my feet with a convulsive lurch, eyes streaming, and clapped the silver-plated cuffs on the Trader's skinny wrists. He was on the scrawny end of junkie-thin, moaning and writhing as I wrenched his hands away from his genitals and behind his back.

I would have told him he was under arrest, but I didn't have the breath. I scooped up the handle of my bullwhip and vaulted a stack of wooden boxes, their sides beginning to steam and smoke under the lash of heat. My steel-reinforced bootheels clattered and I skidded to a stop, giving her a once-over while my fingers stowed the whip.

Mousy brown hair, check. Big blue eyes, check. Mole high up on her right cheek, check.

We have a confirmed sighting. Thank God. Now get her out of here.

"Regan Smith." I coughed, getting a good lungful of smoke. My back burned with pain and something flaming hit the floor less than a yard away. "Your mom sent me to find you."

She didn't hear me. She was too busy screaming.

I grabbed at the handcuffs as she tried to scramble away, fetching up hard against the post. She even tried to kick me. *Good girl. Bet you gave that asshole a run for his money.* I curled my fingers around the cuffs on either side and gave a quick short yank.

The scar on my right wrist ran with prickling heat, pumping strength into my hand. The cuffs burst, and the girl immediately tried to bolt. She was hysterical and wiry-strong, choking, screaming whenever she could get enough air in. The roar of the fire drowned out any reassurance I might have given her, and my long leather trenchcoat was beginning to smoke. I was carrying plenty of ammo to make things interesting in here if it got hot enough.

Not to mention the fact that the girl was only human. She would roast alive before I got *really* uncomfortable.

Move it, Jill. I'd promised her mother I'd bring her back, if it was at all possible.

Promises like that are hell on hunters.

I snapped a glance over my shoulder at the Trader lying cuffed on the floor. He appeared to be passed out, but they're tricky fuckers. You don't negotiate a successful bargain with a hellbreed without being slippery. Of course, since I'd caught him, you could argue that his bargain hadn't been *that* successful.

More burning crap fell down, splashing on the concrete and scattering. A lick of flame ran along an oily runnel in the floor, and the girl made things interesting by almost twisting free.

Dammit. I'm trying to help you! But she was almost insane with fear, fighting as if I was the enemy.

It probably messes your world up when you see a woman in a long black leather coat beat the shit out of a Trader, using a bullwhip, three clips of ammo, and the inhuman speed of the damned. Silver charms tied in my long dark hair spat and crackled with blue sparks, hot blood slicked several parts of me, and I'm sure I was wearing my mad face.

I hefted the girl over my shoulder like a sack of potatoes and spent a few precious seconds glancing again at the motionless Trader. Burning bits of wood landed on him, his clothes smoking, but I thought I saw a glimmer of eyes.

She beat at my back with her fists. I sprinted down the long central aisle of the warehouse, hell-lit with garish flame. Fire twisted and roared, stealing air and replacing it with toxic smoke. Something exploded, a hurricane edge of heat mouthing my back as I got a good head of speed going, aiming for a gap in the burning wall.

This might get a little tricky.

Rush of flame, a crackling liquid sound, covering up her breathless barking—she had nothing left in her to scream with, poor girl, especially not with my shoulder in her stomach—and my own rising cry, a sound of female effort that flattened the streaming flames away with its force. The scar—my souvenir from Santa Luz's biggest hellbreed—ran with sick wet delight as I pulled force through it, my aura flaming into the visible, a star of spiky plasma light.

Feet slapping the floor, bootheels striking sparks, back burning—I'd wrenched something when I'd brought my knee up. *Probably still feel better than he does. Hurry up, she can't take much more of—*

I hit the hole in the wall going almost full speed, my cry ratcheting up into a breathless squeal because I'd run out of air too, darkness flowering over my vision and starved muscles crying out for oxygen. Smoke billowed and I hoped I'd applied enough kinetic energy to throw us both clear of the fire.

Physics is a bitch.

The application of force made the landing much harder. I don't wear leather pants because they make my ass look cute. It's because when I land hard, something snapping in my right leg and the rest of my right side taking the brunt of the blow, trying to shield the girl from impact, most of *my* skin would get erased if I wasn't wearing thick dead cow.

As it was, I only broke a few bones as we slid, muscles straining against the instinct to roll over on her to shed momentum. I managed just to skid on my right side. Spikes of rusty pain drove through each break, right leg cramping, ribs howling.

Concrete. Cold. The hissing roar of the fire as it devoured all the oxygen it could reach. The girl was still feebly trying to struggle free.

It was a clear, cold night, the kind you only get out in the desert. The stars would be bonfires of brilliant ice if not for the glare of Santa Luz's streetlamps and the other, lesser light of the burning warehouse. I lay for a few moments, coughing, eyes streaming, while my leg crunched with pain and the scar hummed with sick delight, a chill touching my spine as the bone set itself with swift jerks. My eyes rolled up in my head and I dimly heard the girl sobbing as she stopped trying to get *away*. She'd be lucky to get out of this needing a few years of therapy and some smoke-inhalation treatment.

Sirens pierced the night, far away but drawing closer. *Here comes the cavalry. Thank God.*

Unfortunately, thanking God wouldn't do much good. *I* was the responsible one here. If that Trader was still alive and the scene started swarming with vulnerable, only-human emergency personnel . . .

Get up, Jill. Get up now.

My weary body obeyed. I made it to my feet, wincing as my right tibia and my humerus both crackled, the bones swiftly restructuring themselves and all the pain of healing compressed into a few seconds rather than weeks. My hand flicked, I had both guns unholstered and ready before the warehouse belched a torrent of red-hot air and the Trader barreled through the hole in the wall, flesh cracking-black and his eyes shining flatly, the sick-sweet smell of seared human pork adding to the perfume of hellbreed contamination.

Traders are scary-quick, not as fast as hellbreed but fast enough. I tracked him, bullets spattering the sidewalk as my right arm jolted under the strain of recoil going all the way up to my shoulders, broken bone pulling my aim off.

My teacher Mikhail insisted I be able to shoot left-handed, too. I caught the Trader with four rounds in the chest and dropped the guns as he reached the top arc of his leap, his scream fueled with the rage of the damned.

I'm sure the fact that half his meat was cooked didn't help his mood.

My hands closed around knifehilts. Knife fighting is my forte, it's close and dirty, which isn't fun when it comes to hellbreed or Traders. You don't want to get too close. But I've always had an edge in pure speed, being female and little. And *nasty,* once Mikhail trained the flinching out of me.

The scar helps too. The hard knot of corruption on the soft inside of my wrist ran with heavy prickling iron as I moved faster than a human being had any right to, meeting the Trader with a bonesnapping crunch.

The idiot wasn't thinking. If he had been, he might have done something other than a stupid kamikaze stunt, throwing himself at a hunter who was armed and ready. As smart and slippery as Traders are, they never think they're going to be held to account.

The knife went in with little resistance, silver laid along the flat part of the blade hissing as it parted flesh tainted by a hellbreed's touch.

The Trader screamed, a high gurgling note of panic. My wrist turned, twisting the blade as the force of his hit threw us both, my right leg threatening to buckle under the momentum. I stamped my left heel, the transfer of force striking sparks between metal-reinforced bootheel and aggregate stones in the concrete.

My other hand came up full of knife, blurred forward like a striking snake as the blade buried itself in his chest, and I pushed him *down,* pinning him as the shine flared in his eyes and roasted stink-sweet filled my mouth and nose.

I wrenched the first knife free and cut his throat. Blood steamed, arterial spray bubbling and frothing as the flat light drained from his eyes. I didn't want to kill him. I wanted to question him and find out what hellbreed he'd made a bargain with.

But you can't have everything. Besides, I could still hear the girl sobbing, the supsucking sound of a child in a nightmare that doesn't go away when she opens her eyes. The thought of what he must have done to her—and what he'd probably *planned* on doing, based on his other victims—drove my hand just as surely as the instinct of combat.

The body began to stink, sphincters loosened by death. I'd almost decapitated him. *Better safe than sorry.* I let out a long shuddering breath, my smoke-roughened lungs protesting with a series of deep hacking coughs. Helltaint drifted up from the corpse, the body contorting in odd ways as contagion spilled through its dying tissues, sucking the life from it. It was an eerie St. Vitus's dance, limbs twisting and jerking as they withered.

If Traders could see what happens after one of them bites it, maybe they'd think twice about making deals with hellbreed.

Or maybe not. *Details, details, Jill. Get moving.*

I turned on my steelshod heel. The knives slipped into their sheaths, and I found my guns, reloaded and holstered them, barely noticing the habitual movements. The warehouse was burning merrily and the girl lay crumpled on the pavement, barely getting in enough breath to sob. She looked pretty bad, and would be terrifically bruised.

But she was alive. The broken bracelets of handcuffs jingled as she tried to scrabble away from my approach. I squatted, ignoring the flare of pain in my right calf, the bone finishing up its healing now that I'd stopped putting so much load on it. My coat, torn, ragged, and now scorched, whispered along the concrete, dragging behind me like a dinosaur's tail.

"Regan." I pitched my voice nice and low, soothing. "Your mom sent me to get you. It's okay."

She cowered, gibbering. I didn't blame her, if I was a civilian I'd probably do the same. So I just stayed where I was, in an easy crouch, listening to the burning as the sirens drew closer.

Goddamn. I think I can count this one a win.

The precinct house on Alameda was still hopping. The graveyard shift hadn't gone home yet and the late drunks were being wheeled in for processing. Montaigne was waiting for me in his office, looking a lot better than usual—no bags under his eyes and a few inches slimmer. Vacation did him some good.

His tie was even still on straight. That meant a relaxing day, for him. Of course, it was still early, and he'd been yanked out of bed to come in and tie off the Regan Smith disappearance/reappearance, and sign the forms for what little remained of the Trader to be cremated. You don't bury them—you never know when a hellbreed will have a need for a nice fresh-rotting zombie skeleton. Why give them one?

"Harvey Steiner," Monty said, leaning back in his chair. A fresh bottle of Tums sat unopened on his desktop, next to his overflowing inbox. "Mild-mannered accountant by day, wacked-out serial killer by night."

"All he needed was a cape and Spandex." I reeked of smoke and foulness, my back ached, and under the buckled leather cuff on my right wrist the scar tingled and prickled like a wire whisk vibrating against the skin. "And all it cost us was one lousy warehouse."

"Plus four insurance claims that need to be filed for the cars you jumped on while chasing him. You're a menace to property, Kismet." Streaks of thinning, graying hair combed across his shining head, Monty raised tired gray eyes to meet mine. "How's the kid?"

I shrugged, leather creaking. Monty's one of the few who don't have much trouble meeting my mismatched gaze. One brown eye, one blue, somehow it just seems to disturb people on a very deep level when I stare them down.

My fingers were at my throat, touching the carved chunk of ruby on its silver chain. I dropped my hand with an effort. "She'll need therapy. But she's alive. Her mom's on the way down to pick her up." *After they finish with the rape kit and the sedation. Poor kid. At least she's still breathing. Quit second-guessing yourself and count it a win, Kismet.*

I *did.* But I didn't think Regan or her mom would appreciate the news that she'd gotten off lightly, all things considered.

The half-open door to Monty's office creaked a little as someone went past. A burst of laughter sounded through the shuffling paperwork, ringing phones, and general murmur of cops doing their work. Homicide was up early, as usual.

Murder doesn't sleep.

Most of the time a hunter interacts with the Homicide division, closely followed by Vice. Murder, sex, and drugs, that's the list of symptoms of hellbreed in your town. Not like humanity ever needs much help to start killing, getting high, and looting.

No, indeedy. But hellbreed do like to help out.

Monty let it rest for a few beats. "How's Saul?"

I don't know, I'm not home enough to answer the phone. It was a pinch in a numb place. "I talked to him a couple days ago. His mom's doing better."

It was half a lie. Once Weres get a particular lymphoma they tend to go downhill quick, bodies burning up from the inside. They call it "the Wasting."

"Good." Monty nodded. His chair squeaked as he shifted, uneasily.

My back still hurt, a lead bar of pain buried in my lumbar muscles. I wanted to go home and scrub the smoke and fear off my skin. I wanted to check the messages and see if Saul had called again. I wanted to hear his voice.

Too bad, Jill. There were other things to do before dawn.

Like whatever Monty was sitting on. "Spit it out, Montaigne." I folded my arms, leaning against the file cabinet. My bullwhip tapped the metal, a soft thumping sound. I had to pick up more ammo soon, drop by Galina's and get a whole run of supplies.

He gave me a look that could have peeled paint and his eyes flicked toward the open door.

Subtle, Monty. I hauled myself upright, padded across thin cheap industrial carpet, and swept the door closed, without even a sarcastic flourish. "That better?"

"I need your help. On a case." He looked down at the drift of paper covering his desk, and I began to feel uneasy.

Normally, he says *There's something I need you to take a look at, Jill.* Like he can't believe he's asking a woman half his size for help.

What the hell. I had nothing else I was doing tonight, other than visiting Galina and patrolling the streets for stray *arkeus* and other hellbreed. There weren't any leads to chase for tonight's Trader—the 'breed who had given him the ability to fling fire was still out there, free as a bird.

It didn't matter. I'd catch up with him, her, or it soon enough. You don't get away with things like that. Not when Jill Kismet's on the job.

I dragged the only unburied chair over to his desk, pushing a stack of files out of the way with my boot. I settled down, resting against the straight wooden back, and fixed my eyes on the piles of paper. "Talk to me."

He opened up a drawer and set a bottle of Jack Daniels down. Amber alcohol glowed under the fluorescents.

Uh-oh. I leaned forward, closed my fingers around the bottle, and twisted the cap off. "A case? One of mine?" *If it is, why haven't you said something before now? It's the rules, Monty. You've done this before.*

"I don't know." He reached down, digging in another drawer as I took a swig. The alcohol burned, and I was reminded that I hadn't eaten yet today.

Come to think of it, I couldn't remember eating yesterday either. Once you get going it's hard to slow down.

And Saul was gone.

"Will you just tell me, Monty? The cloak-and-dagger routine gets old."

"You'd think you'd enjoy that." He didn't quite raise an eyebrow, but it was close.

I sighed, exaggeratedly rolling my eyes. A very teenage movement, which he acknowledged with a sour smile. Neither of us had seen our teens for a decade or two, or three. I doubt Monty even remembered his teen years, and I had no urge to recall mine ever again. "Just get on with it. I have other shit to do tonight." *Or this morning, as the case may be.*

"You're always in such a fucking hurry." He had a file in his hands, a thin dog-eared manila number held shut with a rubber band.

"Hellbreed don't take vacations." *When they do, I'll be the first to celebrate.* I sniffed smoke, still rising from my clothes and skin. *Maybe not with a barbeque, though.* "What's this all about?"

"Marvin Kutchner." He held up the file. "Cop. Ate his Glock about two months ago."

"Has he come back?" In my line of work, that's always a possibility. If you run up against the nightside in Santa Luz—or really, anywhere in my territory, which runs from Ridgefield to the southern edges of Santa Luz; Leon Budge in Viejarosas and I split some of the southern suburbs—you'll see me sooner or later. I will avenge you, if you fall prey to the things that go bump in the night.

And if you come back, I'll lay you to rest. Permanently.

Monty shook his head. "Buried out at Estrada. No sign of him since."

Well, that's a relief. I eyed the folder. "So what's the deal?"

"I want you to look into it."

"A cop suicide? No offense, Monty, but—"

"He was my partner, back in the day." His weak, smoke-colored gaze fixed itself over my shoulder, and his mouth turned down at the corners.

The bottle of Tums on his desk wasn't open, and the whiskey bottle was mostly full. He was laying in for a siege.

I studied him for a long few moments. *What aren't you telling me?* "Is there a suspicion of homicide?"

"Something just don't smell right, Kismet. I don't know. I didn't think Marv was the type, though God knows any cop can be driven to it." He spread his hands, helplessly, like people do when they try to express the inexpressible. "It just don't *smell* right."

Scratch any cop hard enough and you'll find intuition. Most of the time it's an educated guess so reflexive it seems like a hunch, courtesy of working the edges of human behavior for a long time.

A hunter, on the other hand, is normally a full-blown psychic. Messing around with sorcery will do that to you. Po-tay-toe, po-tah-toe. Doesn't matter.

Still . . . *why me, Monty?* "Why not just set IA on it?"

"Them?" He made a dismissive gesture. "Look, Marv was a good cop. Maybe it got to be too much for him, maybe not. He had a wife, she's getting his pension, and if something . . ."

I waited.

"He was my *partner,*" Monty finally said, heavily. As if it explained everything.

Maybe it did. If he was just uneasy, or wanted to know *why,* he was no different from the people who come to me looking for their loved ones. Everyone who disappears is someone's kid, someone's friend, someone's lover. Even if they're not, they deserve someone to care about finding them.

Even if that someone is only me.

Kutchner had pulled the very last disappearing trick anybody ever does. If it didn't look kosher to Monty and he wanted to do right by the widow by having someone *quietly* look at it so the pension wasn't interrupted, it was reasonable. More reasonable than a burning warehouse and a throat-cut Trader.

I leaned forward, holding out my right hand. The leather cuff on my wrist slid a little bit under my coat-sleeve, over the scar. "I won't promise anything. It's not my type of case."

Monty's shoulders sagged as he let me take the file. It could have been relief or a fresh burden. Vacations never last long enough. "Thanks, Kiss. I mean it."

I almost winced. Leather creaked as I made it up to my feet, sighing as my back twinged and settled into aching. The scar burned, a reminder I didn't need, just like the reek of smoke clinging to me. "Don't call me that, okay?" *A few days looking into this, it's the least I owe him.*

Monty wasn't just a liaison. He was also a friend.

Even if he sometimes couldn't look me in the face.

I left with the file tucked under my arm, heading out into the rest of my night. The gray of false dawn was coming up, sky bleaching out along its edges, and I kept my windows down as I drove. The cold air was a penance, but at least it didn't smell like fire.

2

The phone shrilled. I rolled over, blinking hazily. My bed was rucked out of all recognition, blankets tossed everywhere and my clothes in a stinking pile on the floor next to the mattresses. I'd been too tired to shower when I got home midmorning—just shucking off, putting a knife under the pillow, and passing out in the square of sunlight that travels through the skylight every day.

If you're not nocturnal when you start out, being a hunter will make you that way before long. Afternoon is the best, a long slow sleepy time of safe daylight. Dusk will wake you up like gunfire, because darkness is when the nightside comes out to play. Sunlight means safety.

At least most of the time.

I was just going to let the machine take it. But the thought that Saul might be calling when he knew I was probably home brought me up out of deep dreamlessness and set me fumbling for the phone. I hit the talk button and managed to get it in the vicinity of my face. "'Lo?" *Saul? Is that you?*

There was a moment's worth of silence, and I knew just from the sound of breathing that it wasn't my very favorite werecougar. Cold water ran down my spine and I lunged up into full wakefulness a bare second before a low, throaty chuckle echoed in my ear and made the scar on my wrist run with wet heat.

"My darling Kiss," he said. "It has been too long."

I knew he hadn't forgotten me.

It'd be nice if he would, wouldn't it, Jill? My mouth turned dry and slick as desert glass, and the scar thundered under its leather hood. The buckles on the cuffs Saul made for me regularly snapped off or corroded, and I didn't help matters by tearing off the cuff when I needed the full extent of helltainted strength.

I didn't move to sit up in bed. Perry would hear material moving and know he'd gotten to me. Instead, I froze, lying on my belly, one hand under the pillow around the knifehilt and the other clutching the phone to my numb ear.

I'd wondered just how much chain he was going to give me before yanking. I'd left town six months ago in the aftermath of the Sorrows incident, and on my way out I'd paid Perry a little visit. I *knew* he'd been in it up to his eyeballs, thinking he could play both sides of the fence and use the Sorrows to get his wormy little fingers inside my head.

It hadn't worked. I'd spent a lot of time between then and now wondering when he was going to make his next move. The scar didn't twinge much, and it still functioned the same as before, feeding me enough etheric force to make me exponentially more dangerous.

It's not every hunter who has a tainted hellbreed mark. It's saved my life more than once.

And driven me right to the edge of the abyss.

"Perry." I sounded normal. Or about as normal as you can sound, awakened from a deep sleep with a hellbreed on the line. My palms were wet and my nipples, pressed against the mattress since I'd shucked every stitch of smoke-fouled clothing, were hard as chips of rock. I'd tossed most of the pillows off the bed. "Didn't I tell you not to bother me?"

I didn't even have to put any *fuck you* into my voice. Just weariness, as if I was dealing with a spoiled child.

Oh be careful. Be very goddamn careful, Jill. My pulse kicked up as if it was dusk. High, hard, and fast, right in my throat, too.

"Would you like my mark to start spreading, Kiss?" Bland, smooth, and even, as if he was discussing the weather. I could almost see his blue eyes narrowing.

Most of the damned are beautiful. Perry is just blandly mediocre-looking. It's why he's so goddamn scary, and why my left hand started to quiver a little bit.

The woman always has advantage in situation like this, my teacher Mikhail's voice whispered from the vaults of memory.

I hoped he was right. It sure as hell didn't feel like it, sometimes.

"Or perhaps," Perry continued, "you would like it to start rotting and turning black. I believe the proper term is necrosis."

I know what necrosis is, hellspawn. "That would put a little wrinkle in our bargain." I didn't swallow audibly only out of sheer force of will. "And since you're already in dutch by cavorting with the Sorrows not so long ago—"

"Oh, let's not fight. Come see me, Kiss." Silky-smooth, his voice could have been an attractive businessman's baritone except for the rumble behind it. It sounded like freight trains in a deserted switchyard at midnight, rubbing against each other and groaning in pain.

Helletöng. The language of the damned.

The mother tongue of Hell.

"Hold your breath until I show up, Pericles." I peeled the phone away from my ear and hit the talk button again. It disconnected— but not nearly quickly enough to suit me.

I rolled over and stared at the skylight. Late-afternoon sunlight filled the Plexiglas rectangle with gold. I was under the messy blankets, except for my bare foot, with the sheet wrapped around my ankle like a manacle. My toes flexed as sunlight scoured my vision, comfortable safety filling the inside of my skull with white noise. I tuned my mind to a blank, meaningless hum, but my hands were shaking, one of them braced with a knifehilt.

My warehouse resounded with tiny noises. I like to hear every little thing moving in my place, right down to the mice in the walls. Though sorcery is sometimes practically useful—I don't *have* mice in my walls. Creaks as sun-heat made the building expand, the low moan of the wind from the desert, a faraway rumble as a train slid along the tracks, since I live in an industrial district. Nowadays I was liking the solitude more and more.

You knew he wouldn't forget about you. I was cold even under the blankets. The scar, under its shield of leather, ran with moist warmth. It wasn't much to look at, a puckered lip-print as if someone had painted lye on the skin and kissed with a wet mouth. It still functioned the way it always had, feeding me etheric force, hiking my physical strength and just generally making me a lot harder to kill.

I hadn't been in to the Monde Nuit to give Perry payment for that power since Saul and I returned from the Dakotas.

I was all right with that. And technically, he had betrayed the bargain we'd made. I was within my rights never to darken the Monde's doorstep again, never to make another payment no matter how much power I pulled through it.

It's too easy. And it was. Perry wasn't the sort to let a hunter slip through his immaculate fingers. He'd miscalculated badly last time, and I'd outwitted him.

Hellbreed don't like that.

Add to that the fact that he'd done a few things I hadn't suspected he could—like producing hellfire in the blue spectrum—and you had a very unsettling situation developing.

Worry about it later, Jill. For right now you need to get up and start poking around after Monty's dead partner. The sooner you get that looked into, the sooner you can get back to those disappearances on the east side of town. Four women gone, and the whole thing stinks.

The trouble was, I might have to wait until someone else disappeared before I was sure last night's player didn't have anything to do with the situation. But the fire-slinging sonofabitch hadn't bothered going out to the east, he'd concentrated slightly south of downtown, in the warehouses and freight yards near the river. Lots of places to hide where nobody could hear a woman scream.

Regan Smith had been the lucky one. Her mother hadn't been able to look me in the face when she asked me to find her daughter, *or* when I left her outside the curtain to the ER bay her child was behind. Maybe it was my eyes. Maybe it was my long leather coat or the skintight black T-shirt, or the silver tied in my hair.

Maybe it was even the guns. Or the bullwhip.

Or maybe it was her raped, traumatized daughter whimpering even through the sedation. Sometimes people aren't prepared for their loved ones to be brought back hurt or marred. The disappearance itself throws everything off, screws everything up, and life is never normal again even if their loved one comes back.

That was Perry on the phone. A galvanic shudder spilled through me, from top to toes. *He's about to start messing with you again, Jill. It figures he would wait until Saul is out of town.*

I wanted to call Saul, but he would immediately be able to tell something was wrong. He didn't need another burden right now. He already sounded too worried. When he could get me on the phone, that is.

I repressed another shiver. I could still smell smoke, my clothes on the floor sending out invisible waves of stink like Pig-Pen in the old *Peanuts* cartoons.

I should get up, work out, and hit the street.

For a few minutes I lay there, breathing, my eyes full of light. Trying not to follow the inevitable chain of logic.

You know what this means. Perry's thinking about you.

I wished it didn't make me feel so unsteady. He'd al-

most gotten into my head more than once. Almost pushed
me over that edge every hunter lives on.

We commit murder on an almost daily basis. It doesn't
matter if it's hellbreed, Trader, scurf, Middle Way adepts,
what-have-you. It's still killing sentient beings. The fact
that most of these sentient beings are kill-crazy predators
doesn't absolve a hunter of responsibility.

The Church, after all, does not admit us into Heaven,
even if we're buried in hallowed ground.

Sometimes I wonder about that. I wonder more and
more, the longer I do this sort of work.

Getting that close to the edge is necessary. You can't
kill a hellbreed if you hesitate or flinch. But no matter
how close you get to that edge, no matter how you put
your little toesies on it and peer over into the howling
abyss that lies beyond, you cannot go over. It's a razor-
thin line, but you cannot, ever, go over it.

I had been so close.

*Get up, Jill. Work out, and go out and do your job. Let
Perry suck eggs in his little hellbreed hole. When he pops
back up you'll deal with him.*

It sounded good.

I just wished I believed it.

I rolled up out of bed, taking the knife with me, and got
ready to face another night.

3

I'd just given the Impala a tune-up, so my baby purred as I took her up into the suburbs, the red fuzzy dice Galina had given me dangling from the mirror. Kutchner's widow lived in the Cruzada district, nice little houses from the seventies, fenced yards, and neighbors as old as Methuselah—on the right streets. On the wrong streets, the neighbors have bad crack problems that make them *look* like Methuselah.

Only in the 'burbs do you find this combination. No wonder they need sitcoms to dull the pain.

The wrong streets tend to cluster on higher ground, further away from the artery of the river. Closer to the desert. Mrs. Kutchner lived on the edge, high enough up that security bars on the windows were not just a fashion statement. Still, it was an okay neighborhood, and as the sun slid bloody below the rim of the mountains, I slammed the Impala's door and eyed the house, a neat little adobe with a trim, if weedy, yard and a chain-link fence. Out here the grass was yellow; people had better things to spend their money on than astronomical water bills.

I leaned against the car door and examined the place. The right-hand neighbors had kids—someone had to play with the toys scattered around their yard. On the other side, a scraggly greenbelt cut through the neighborhood, edging a ditch that would take runoff in flash-flood season. The fence was higher on that side, and so were the weeds.

The blinds were all pulled behind blank windows and vertical iron security bars. The red-painted door looked like a tight-pursed mouth, and the high arched windows gave the street a perpetually surprised glance. The brick-colored roof tiles were still fresh, not bleached by a few high-grade summer scorches.

Now why does this not look right? I pulled my sunglasses off as the sky turned indigo, pink and orange lingering in the west. The mountains glowed, furnace teeth spearing up to catch high thin cumulus clouds. The original seven-veil dance, performed nightly, hold the applause, just throw cash.

Wind came off the desert, smelling of sand and shimmering heat. Oven-warm, drying the sweat along my forehead and tinkling the charms knotted into my hair with red thread. My silver apprentice-ring rested against my left ring finger. I played with it as I watched the house, hairs rising on my nape.

My smart eye—the blue one, the one that can see below the surface of the world—watered a bit as I focused. A pall lay over Kutchner's house, etheric energy turned thick and bruise-clotted.

There could be a number of reasons for this—grief, or

any strong negative emotion over time. A murder or suicide in the recent past—this was listed as Kutchner's last known address before he ventilated his own skull.

Hellbreed contamination, or even just plain sorcery of the darker variety, will also congest the ether around a place, just like a bruise is congested blood.

Kutchner had been found in a flophouse hotel on the edge of the barrio. Still, brooding about suicide for a while, especially if you're serious enough to actually do it, can cause your house to get a bit stale, etherically speaking.

I dunno. That's an awful lot of static.

Well, no time like the present to stick my nose in and find out.

I crossed the street and opened the squeaking chain-link gate. A narrow strip of concrete unreeled to the steps leading to the entryway, and dried husks of yucca flowers rattled in the breeze. The sound was like clicking small bones together in a wooden cup, and my right hand crept for a gun.

Great, Jill. Show up at the widow's door and scare the crap out of her with a Glock shoved in her face. Monty said he wanted this quiet, you know.

Quiet's one thing, and disregarding your instincts is another. A hunter who ignores instinct is half dead already. The other half comes when you do something stupid, like not drawing when every nerve in your body screams *something's behind Door Number One, sweetheart!*

I drew, keeping the gun low along my side. Leather rustled as I walked up the path, and the dead blossoms rattled, rattled. Like handcuffs. My coat brushed my ankles as I stepped cautiously, the transition to nighttime taking a breath all along the edges of my city. Sometimes I *feel* that deep breath just after dusk, right under my sternum. It's like every instrument in an orchestra tuned to the same key and suddenly giving out the deepest tone it's capable of.

The entryway held pots of cacti, different spiny little things that might have been flowering if they weren't desiccated enough to be used for tinder. The charms in my hair tinkled as they rubbed against each other. Deep shadows at the end of the roofed entryway moved as I stepped forward, cautiously, and my sensitive nose picked out something it was all too familiar with. A ripe, overwhelming smell.

Under my leather cuff, the scar pulsed hotly. It didn't seem to be getting any bigger.

Stop thinking like that, Jill. My entire body flushed hot, then cold.

The wind was coming from behind me, or I would have noticed the smell earlier. The door creaked a little bit as the breeze pushed it.

It was open.

Monty swiped at his forehead. Sweat sheened his face. "Jesus," he said, for the third time.

Usually we only get one *Jesus* out of him per crime scene.

Jacinta Kutchner's corpse hung from a white and blue striped nylon rope looped over an exposed ceiling beam creaking slightly as the house settled for the night. She wore a pale blue housedress and one slipper, and had been dead for a while, if the state of the body was any indication. The air conditioning had been turned off sometime in the recent past, and the house was breathlessly hot and stale.

Not to mention reeking of decay.

I folded my arms, doing my best not to lean against the wall. The forensic techs were hard at work, gathering evidence, photographing, trying to ignore the smell. A few of them had Vicks smeared on their upper lips, it was that bad. A few days in desert heat will dry a body out, but hot moisture in an enclosed house is bad for dead human tissue.

"I don't like this." I kept my voice low. The techs were giving me little sideways looks, except for plump brunette Piper. She was off maternity leave and slimming down again, my very favorite forensic tech and my particular liaison with that department. Not much disturbs her serenity.

Maybe it's having kids that does it. I've never seen Piper even blanch. She's even been known to whistle Disney tunes at scenes.

The mind boggles.

"I don't either." Monty looked miserable. I didn't blame him. One suicide is chance, two coincidence.

I didn't want a third.

"This isn't my type of case," I said again. "There's no smell of anything hinky on this one. Not extra-human hinky, that is."

"What about human hinky?"

You don't want me to tell you anything you don't already know, Montaigne. You just want someone else to say it out loud. I glanced around the living room. "What the hell did she stand on? She's only five-three, recent stretching notwithstanding." It felt horrible, but you don't last long around violent death without evolving some black humor. I ticked them off on my fingers. "Where's her other slipper? Not to mention most women want to look pretty right before they take the plunge. They usually hang themselves in more private places, too."

A fresh wave of stench rolled toward me. There was a large stain on the carpet below the body, and the insect life was having a ball. Not as much as there would be outside, but you'd be surprised how little time it takes for six-legged critters to find a recently deceased piece of meat.

"I thought about that too." His gaze came up, touched my face, skittered away. He palmed a couple of Tums up to his mouth and started chewing. "Goddammit."

Full night had folded around the house, darkness swirling in corners where it wasn't driven away by electric fixtures and portable lights brought in by the crime-scene team. The shadows in the corners had weight, only seen through my blue eye.

Seen from *between,* violent death has its own eddies and currents. She had suffered before passing out of this place and into whatever awaited her.

This isn't one of yours, Jill. Get going, there's other things out there tonight you should be taking care of.

But I made no move to leave beyond shifting my weight from one foot to the other.

"What the hell are you doing here?" Carper said irritably from the entryway, hunching his shoulders. His sharp blue eyes flicked once over the scene, taking everything in.

In his sneakers and tweed jackets, Carp looks more like a college professor than a homicide deet. Behind him, his partner Rosenfeld was conferring with the blue holding down the site log. Rosenfeld's spiky auburn halo threw back what little light made it past the long mirror on the wall.

"Relax, Carp." I let my shoulders drop. "It's not one of mine."

He looked only barely relieved. "Great. What're you *doing*, then?"

"Conferring with Montaigne. If that's all right with you." *Don't get snitty with me, Carp. I'm not in the mood.*

"Hi, Jill." Rosie ambled past her partner, bumping him with her shoulder. Her jaw would have done a prizefighter proud, and her leather jacket creaked a little bit. The Terrible Two of the Homicide department, appearing nightly on the scene. "What's going on?"

It was an excessively casual question. Santa Luz's finest get a little bit nervous around me, though they take bets on where I'll show up next. There's a whole system of verifying hunter sightings left over from Mikhail's time.

It's when they lose track of me for a few weeks that everyone gets jumpy.

Still, very few cops *like* being around me. The mandatory class I put all rookies through takes care of that. My tiger's eye rosary bumped my stomach as I shifted again. "Not much for me here. See you later, Monty."

He couldn't quite bring himself to ask me, but he spread his hands as I passed, brushing close to Carp and almost enjoying when the man stepped away. He used to be able to get a rise out of me. Now Carper and I just go through the motions. It's a comforting routine on both sides.

He rolled his eyes, and I grinned at him. The corner

of his mouth twitched, and he looked away, the twinkle going out of his baby blues as he studied the shape of Jacinta Kutchner hanging, the edge of her robe fluttering a bit. "Goddamn," he said, softly.

I paused at the entryway, next to the blue. He didn't offer me the site log, but he gripped it until paper crackled. If I looked closely I would probably remember his name. "Monty."

"Yeah?" He palmed another couple of Tums. The vacation was wearing off.

What else could I say? He wanted me to look into it, and someone else was dead. *Worst case of suicide I ever saw,* the tagline to an old joke floated through my head. "I'll be in touch."

Then I was out the door, plunging into the night, crossing the street to the Impala. She stuck out like a sore thumb, having no flashing lights, and I noticed something else about the neighborhood.

Jacinta Kutchner's neighbors didn't come out to see what the fuss was. At all.

So much for suburbia.

4

$Gray$ predawn was breaking, again, when the phone rang and my pager went off simultaneously. I left my trench dripping on the rack in the utility room and hobbled through the hall, through the cavern of the sparring space and living room, every muscle I'd pulled singing its own separate note in the orchestra of pain. I'd broken my *left* arm this time, the *arkeus* I'd run across on the east side of town had put up a hell of a fight.

Get it, Jill? A Hell of a fight? Arf arf.

But I'd found out, to my lasting satisfaction, which pile of hell-soaked waste had given the mad accountant his power. It was unmistakable, especially when an *arkeus* pulls a flame-jet six feet long out of its mouth and tries to feed it to you.

The scar provides me with faster healing and damage regeneration, but when it's busy splinting bones and replacing a few quarts of blood, pulled muscles heal more slowly. I didn't want to think about what would happen if it started spreading, or if Perry decided it wasn't such a hot idea to have me drawing on a hellbreed's tainted power if he wasn't getting anything in return—even if it was his own damn fault.

Don't think like that. The phone brayed, the pager buzzed against my hip, and I stopped short of picking up as the answering machine clicked. There were a few moments of silence, then a beep.

"Hey, kitten." A voice I knew as well as my own slid from the speaker, only slightly distorted. "Guess you're out—"

My pager quit buzzing. I was already scrambling for the phone. I scooped it up and pressed the talk button, and the machine clicked over with a feedback squeal. "Sorry about that." Breathless, now, I folded down on the bed. "God, it's good to hear you."

"Hey." Saul sounded tired. "Glad I caught you too, kitten. What's happening in the big bad city?"

A sharp ache welled up in my chest. *I miss you, and Perry called.* "Not much. A couple things Monty wants me to look into. A Trader."

"Bad?" He had a nice voice, to go with all the rest of him.

I shut my eyes, imagining him right next to me. Tall dark-haired Were, looking like a romance-novel Native American except for the gold-green sheen off his eyes in certain light, the rods and cones reflecting differently. "Nothing out of the ordinary. I even got a civilian out alive."

"That's my girl." A warm rumble of approval, carried through a phone line and suddenly threatening to ease every muscle.

"How's your mom?" I swallowed sudden dryness in

my throat. Saul's mother hadn't been too happy to meet the hellbreed-tainted hunter he'd given up his place in the tribe for, but with faultless Were courtesy she'd accepted me into her home as a guest and cooked for me. She'd even introduced me to the extended family and officiated at the firelit ceremony that formalized everything. As far as Saul was concerned, we were formally mated.

As far as his tribe was concerned, we were as good as married, even if I was . . . well, disappointing. But they hadn't said a word, just welcomed me with Were politeness.

I wondered if they regretted it now.

"There's morphine." Saul's tone changed now. Deeper, and just a bit rougher. "It's not bad. My aunts are here. They're singing to her."

Oh, Christ. She must be close to passing. No more needed to be said.

I listened to him breathing for a few moments, knowing he was doing the same thing. "I love you," I whispered. *I can't make it better. If I could I would. I'd hunt down the cancer and put a gun to its head. Slit its throat. Kill it for you.*

"I know that, kitten." A thin vibration came through the phone—he was rumbling, deep down in his chest, a werecougar's response to a mate's distress. "You sure you're okay?"

His mother was dying and he was out there alone, because I couldn't leave the city—nobody was around to take some of the load; the apprentices who had come out last time to handle the overflow while we were honeymooning had gone home and were needed desperately there.

And he was asking if *I* was okay.

I don't deserve you, Saul. The charms in my hair jingled as I played with my pager, unclipping it from my belt. It was habit to take the damn thing with me everywhere, in a padded pocket except when I was hosing blood and stink out of my coat. "Right as rain. Wish I could be there."

"I wish so too. You be careful for me, you hear?" He was already worrying about the next thing, or he wouldn't have told me to be careful. He almost never did that, because it implied I couldn't take care of myself.

Weres are touchy about things like that. "Always am. Do you need me?" *Say the word, Saul. I can't leave now, but I will if you ask me to.*

Should I feel grateful, or more guilty, that he understood and hadn't asked? That he had insisted I stay in Santa Luz, because he knew my responsibility weighed as heavily as his?

"I do, but I'm okay. They need you more." A long pause, neither of us willing to hang up just yet. He broke it first, this time. "I'd better go back in."

"Okay." *Don't hang up. Perry called me, and I'm scared. Come home.* I swallowed the words. "You take care of yourself, furboy."

"You too. Tell everyone hello for me."

"I will." I waited another few moments, then straightened my arm to put the phone down. He hated saying goodbye.

So did I.

I laid the phone in its cradle and watched as the light winked off. Let out a long breath, muscles twitching and sore under my torn, blood-stiff T-shirt. My pants were shredded—the *arkeus* had just missed my femoral artery in its dying desperation, brought to bay and made physical enough to fight at last.

I lifted my pager. The number on it was familiar, and I scooped up the phone and dialed again without giving myself time to think. It rang twice.

"Montaigne," he barked.

"You bellowed?" I even sounded normal, sharp and Johnny-on-the-spot. All hail Jill Kismet, the great pretender.

"We got another disappearance on the east side. And there's something else. Can you come in?"

My entire body ached. I hauled myself up from the bed, looked longingly at the rumpled pillow and tossed blankets. Saul was the domestic half of our partnership, I've never been good at that sort of shit.

The hurt in my heart hadn't gone away. It was still a sharp piercing, like a broken bone in my chest. I made it over to the dresser, wincing as my leg healed fully and the scar flushed under the damp leather cuff. The urge to tear the cuff off and make sure it wasn't spreading suddenly ignited, I pushed it away.

"Jill?" Monty sounded halfway to frantic.

I snapped back into myself and jerked a dresser drawer open, scooping up a black *Frodo Lives!* T-shirt. "I'm on my way."

The message light on the machine was blinking. I ignored it and bolted for the bathroom, another pair of leather pants, and quite possibly a sleepless day.

5

$\mathscr{M}$ichael Spilham." Monty laid the file down on his cluttered desk. "Vanished from a bus stop out near Percoa Park last night. We have a verified sighting at ten-fifteen, when a coworker drove by and saw him waiting for the bus due at ten-twenty-six. The driver on that route doesn't remember him, says she wondered about that because he's a regular. His mother filed a missing-persons when he didn't come home on time; says it's not like him. It might be nothing, but it's in the same area as the other disappearances."

I nodded. Percoa Park. A brief cold wave slid down my spine—we'd found bodies there before. "That's a small window."

"The bus might have been off by five minutes or so. Still, you're right."

If Monty hadn't had something else up his sleeve he would have given me the location over the phone, and I'd already be there searching for clues. The other disappearances on the east side were all the same—people vanish-

ing without a trace, outside, often in very short spaces
of time. Small windows in disappearances are common
enough, but this one smelled fishy to me.

It stank of hell, actually. Or *something* unnatural.
Still. . . . "I dunno. Everything about this fits except the
gender of the victim."

But that meant very little too. Women are just bigger
targets of opportunity most of the time.

"Can you look at it?" He stared down at his desk. The
bottle of whiskey was down by a quarter.

"That's the plan. Want to tell me what's bothering
you?" I hooked my thumbs in my belt, my dangling fingers brushing the bullwhip's oiled curve. The precinct
building quivered, phones ringing and thin predawn wind
boiling against the windows. Monty's office didn't have
any outside portholes. It was more of a luxury than you'd
think—on a summer's day, the air conditioning didn't
have to fight for primacy.

"I got autopsy reports on the widow." His shoulders
dropped, and he cast a longing look at the Jack Daniels.

I picked up the bottle, uncapped it, took a swallow. It
burned on the way down. I used to drink a lot of this stuff,
before Saul happened along. "And?"

"Hyoid crushed and damage to the strap muscles, but
no cervical vertebrae snapped and no rope burns." Monty
dropped down in his chair. "We're waiting for toxicology,
but there was . . . she was . . . there was vaginal bruising.
And semen. We might get DNA."

Oh, Christ. "So we're looking at a murder here, not a
suicide." I said it so he didn't have to.

"Whoever set it up didn't work that hard. There was

nothing for her to stand on to get up there. The rope was tied to the—"

"I saw the scene, Monty." I didn't want to revisit it. As gruesome as hellbreed get—and they get pretty *damn* gruesome—I'm still more upset by things human beings do to each other without needing any extra help. It's in a hellbreed's nature to be vicious, just like a cancer cell or a rabid animal.

I'm still not sure why people do it.

Monty stared at his desk. "Her bedroom was torn apart. Looks like someone was looking for something, or maybe the attack started there. Carp and Rosie are betting on both. The screen in the master bathroom window was torn loose, but it's too small for anyone but a five-year-old to shimmy through."

That was odd, too. I replayed the scene in my head. Something about that bathroom nagged at me. "Who sleeps with their window open in *that* neighborhood? Even with bars on the window." *And why not tear up the rest of the house if they were looking for something?*

"The neighbors aren't worth jackshit." Monty smoothed the fresh manila folder on his desk, the one with Jacinta Kutchner's name on the tab. "Nobody can remember anything out of the usual."

I exhaled sharply. "Monty. This isn't my type of case. There's no inhuman agency at work here. I've got those disappearances to look into and—"

"Jill." He dropped down into his chair and glared at me. "I never asked you for anything like this before. Marv was my partner."

I looked down at the file. Lots of people don't understand that about cops. The partner isn't quite a spouse, but they're the person whose head you think inside of, whose judgment and reactions you trust your life to, the person you spend so much time with you might as well be twins.

It may not be love, but it's close.

It wasn't Monty's tender feelings that made me reach across the desk and tug the file out from under his hand. It was the vision of Jacinta Kutchner's body, gently swinging just the tiniest bit as her empty house breathed around her.

Hyoid crushed. Vaginal bruising. Bedroom ripped to shreds.

"I'll look into it. Can't promise anything." Even though I already had.

Monty almost visibly sagged. His chair creaked, and he dropped his gaze to the top of his desk, drifted with paper. Silence bloomed between us, a new and uncomfortable quiet.

Finally, he shifted and his chair creaked sharply. "Thanks."

"No problem." *What are friends for, Monty? And if you've got one, you might as well use her.* "I'll check in."

"Yeah. Try not to destroy any property, will you?"

For Christ's sake. I was already at the door. "I can't *promise* anything, Monty. See you."

His curse was like a goodbye.

The plastic of the bus shelter's window-walls was scarred and starred with breakage. I examined it minutely. Cigarette butts, an overflowing trashcan, the smell of despair.

Just like waiting for the bus anywhere, really. Dawn

was coming up fast, the sky full of scarves dyed indigo, rose, streaks of gold and soft threads of orange over the furnace in the east. There was a blank brick wall behind the bus shelter, and a drift of paper trash in an alley to the side. Across the street, Percoa Park simmered under a pall of early morning half-vapor, trees breathing in relief as the sun rose.

Michael Spilham. Thirty-four, college dropout, living with his mother and working in a shipping warehouse four blocks away from here. He'd be tired at the end of his shift, overtime wearing down his feet and shoulders. So, he'd probably stand here, leaning against the shelter's support post. A nonsmoker, the file said, so he didn't light up while waiting. He probably just stared down the street, thinking a normal man's thoughts.

I closed my eyes. Took a deep breath. Smelled exhaust, the odor of poverty and footsore wandering, trash and concrete.

A sudden cessation of subaudible buzzing made my eyes fly open. The streetlamp to my left had switched off. I glanced down the street to my right. Edges of broken glass glittered like diamonds as the star we all roll around lifted itself higher over the horizon.

I left the shelter, cautiously. Intuition tingled and prickled down my spine, raised the fine hairs on my nape under the weight of silver-laden hair. My trenchcoat, still damp from hosing, whispered and fluttered. Time for a new coat; hellbreed claws are death on leather.

This lamp was busted, broken glass on the pavement. A star-shape of expended force glittered, bits and pieces arranged along rays of reaction. Intuition turned chilly, raising prickles along the backs of my arms. A faint distinct perfume evaporated as soon as I got a whiff. Corruption, and sweetness like burned candy.

Huh.

I crouched easily, my bootheels digging into the pavement and my leather pants making just the faintest noise as dead cowskin rubbed against itself. My smart eye saw the strings under the surface of the world resonating to a powerful burst of bloodlust and fear.

My dumb eye wasn't so dumb. Streaks and smears along the base of the streetlamp gleamed. Blood dries fairly quick out in the desert, but this close to the misty park it wasn't completely flaking off yet.

Huh again. These were transfer prints. Someone with bloody hands had clasped the bottom of the streetlamp. Now that I was crouched down I could see smears on the filthy sidewalk too, oddly pale—pink instead of red.

Blood shouldn't look like that. Another chill touched my nape, tickling little fingers. "Shit," I breathed, reaching down to touch the smears on the post's concrete base. *"Shit."*

My fingers came away with powdery pink clinging to them. As I lifted my hand, I turned a little so the sunlight hit my skin.

The powder vanished, little puffs of steam rising from my fingertips. "Goddamn shitsucking son of a *bitch*," I whispered. "Motherfucking *hell*."

There's only one thing that dries blood to powder evaporating in the sun. And as much as hunters hate, hunt, and loathe hellbreed, there's only one thing that a hunter fears enough to cross herself and shiver, one thing that sends us looking for backup and polishing whatever weapons make us feel a little safer.

I settled on my haunches, my right hand dropping to the butt of a gun. "Shit," I breathed one final time, before rising slowly to my feet and looking down at the long jagged wet-looking marks on the sidewalk. They pointed toward the mouth of an alley, yawning and shadowed even with the clear light of dawn coming up.

No time like the present, eh Jill?

I headed for the alley as traffic ran like water in the distance. The next bus wasn't due for about ten minutes and the street was deserted. A ruffle of paper twisted in the intersection two blocks away, and I eased a gun out with my right hand and a knife in my left. *Wish I had a flamethrower. Dammit.*

The alley swallowed me with shadows you only get in the morning—knife-edged and clear, like stiff black paper cut into animal shapes. A dumpster loomed in the alley's throat, and I sniffed cautiously, seeking that perfume of burnt sugar and weirdness. *Should have recognized that first-off. Goddammit.* My heart kicked up, high and wild in my throat, a bitter taste in the back of my mouth. Training clamped down on my hindbrain, regulating the cascade of adrenaline through my system. Too much and I'd be a jittery mess, and if this turned ugly . . .

I eased into the dark maw, clicking the hammer back. *They're not going to be in the alley, not with day coming on. But they dragged him back here, you might find something. Pray you don't find something.*

One step. Two. Easing down the side that held a little more light, though the entire alley was shaded. The dumpster was full of garbage, and as a stray breath of breeze touched my cold cheeks, the smell strengthened.

Oh God. Please. I quelled the tremor in my hands by

the simple expedient of putting it out of my mind. Whatever was going to happen was going to happen. Nothing to be done about it now.

I stepped toward the dumpster. It was a big green number, half its heavy plastic lid closed and the other half open, resting against the wall of the alley. At the end of the alley's confined space was a huge rolling door, probably for whoever took out the trash. I scanned the alley again—no, it was a blind hole. No place else to hide.

Don't let me find anything, God. Please. Cut me a break on this one.

Unfortunately, God wasn't in a giving mood today. I saw telltale frosting along the metal edge of the dumpster, a fine powdery substance drifting in complicated whorls. And I heard, straining the preternatural acuity of my senses, a faint rustling.

Yup. God's not in a good mood today, Jillybean. You've got a scurf infestation on your hands.

6

Scurf aren't like Traders or hellbreed. There's no pattern to their movements, no training, no instinctive predator's grace. They're just engines of messy hunger, ravenous and unpredictable.

And contagious.

I emptied two clips into the motherfucker and ended up burying my knife in its side. Brick puffed into dust and the dumpster's side was stove in, garbage spilling out into the alley, body-sized dents in the walls, and blood everywhere. My blood, which just served to drive the thing into a feeding frenzy.

They can smell it. And even though they like it fresh from the vein, so to speak, they'll lick it up from concrete if they have to.

In the end, I drove the skinny naked thing out of the alley, my fingers clamped in its throat and its claws tangling in my ribs. He wasn't fully changed yet, the virus hadn't turned his bones all the way to flexible cartilage or given him the thick slimy coating that makes scurf so slippery. But his eyes were blank pale orbs without iris or pupil—they don't need to *see*—and even though he was newly infected and didn't have the developed instincts for carnage, he was strong and desperate.

When they're newly changed, they're even *more* unpredictable than usual. It snarled and champed, teeth snapping with a sound like heavy billiard balls smacking together; foam splattered rank and foul, burning the skin of my hand and smoking on my leather sleeve. I cried out, miserable loathing beating frantically under my heart, as we tumbled out into the street and a flood of early morning sunlight.

The scurf screeched, damage runnelling its face and its blind pupilless eyes popping, smears of buttery eye-fat glistening down its gaunt cheeks. Thin acrid smoke gushed, pale powdery drifts rising as the thing that used to be Michael Spilham squealed and imploded. The smell was gagging-strong, the reason most hunters don't like cotton candy or caramel. Burnt candy, sweetness, and *bad,* all rolled up in one pretty package.

It screamed again, foam splattering in harsh droplets that sizzled where they landed. It took every ounce of hellbreed strength I had to hold the thing *down,* even as its flesh began to run like plastic clay, stinking and smoking. I held it, *held it,* and heard far-off traffic under its screams, the sound of the wind in the park trees.

Lord, take this soul into Thy embrace. I couldn't help adding my own little touch to the prayer—*and will You do it quickly, please?*

Its throat collapsed into stinking sludge, powder lifting on the wind and sparkling in the sunlight. I coughed, deep and racking, struggling for purchase on the still-moving mass of almost-liquid ooze. *Keep it in the sun, ohGod Jill keep it in the sun, for the love of Christ don't let it go now. . . .*

It squirmed and heaved, almost squirting free. If I lost my grip now it would scurry off into the alley and I'd have another fight on my hands. The longer I fought, the bigger the chance of a bite.

The scurf that had been Michael Spilham collapsed into final true death, and I let out a whispered prayer that was half a sob. *Got off lucky.* It was only then I realized I was bleeding from its claws, the gouges whittling deeper as acid in the powdery slime exhausted itself. The charms in my hair ran with blue sparks and the scar on my wrist throbbed. The dead body subsided, bubbling into powder, and I scraped both palms on the pavement as I backed away hurriedly, staring at the smear. *Lucky, lucky, lucky.*

"OhGod," I whispered, as my left hand grabbed a gun and I cleared leather, pointing it at the stain on the pavement.

That's the trouble with the damn things. Sometimes scurf just don't stay dead.

My heart leapt and shivered inside me. I coughed, tasting blood and adrenaline, stripes of fire along my ribs as acid hissed and bubbled in my flesh. There was another clawstrike on my thigh, and one down my back. Hot blood dripped down my cheek. It had damn near taken out my eye.

Lucky. Jesus Christ I'm lucky. The scar pulsed, pulsed under the cuff. The burning bubbling went away, preternatural healing replacing tissue faster than the acid could burn. Most hunters are walking factories of scar tissue, healing sorcery notwithstanding, I should have been glad I don't need healing spells.

I wasn't. I almost never am.

After a little while I decided the flood of sunlight was enough to take care of the scurf. Besides, I couldn't sit here with a gun out all day, could I? I cautiously hefted myself to my feet, and forced myself nearer the bubbling grease spot.

My tiger's eye rosary bumped against my midriff. The chunk of carved ruby at my throat was warm, humming with power. The scar throbbed. Silver clinked and chimed in my hair. Everything was present and accounted for.

No bites. I'm up to date on my garlic shots anyway, thank God. I stared at the smear for a long time before holstering my left-hand gun. *Scurf. What next?*

Get going, Jill. You've got work to do, and not a lot of time to do it.

Jacinta's killer was going to have to wait. I headed for the alley to collect my other gun and the dropped knives. My knees only trembled a little, but when my pager went off, buzzing silently in its padded pocket, I almost leapt out of my skin.

Micky's on Mayfair Hill is the type of restaurant locals like to keep to themselves. Good food, quiet atmosphere, and pictures of silent and classic film stars on the walls. I'm not used to being in Micky's during daylight, unless it's just before dawn and I'm tired and bloody. Normally I wouldn't go around civilians like that—but Micky's isn't just the best restaurant on the Hill, where the gay night-clubs rollick and roll all night long.

It's also the only restaurant on the Hill run by Weres.

I didn't stop to be seated, just stalked through the tables—very few of them occupied at this hour—and headed for the bar. Two steps down into the dark cavern where it was always dusk glinting off bottles and the jukebox in the corner, and I caught Theron's eye.

The tall lanky dark-haired Were raised an eyebrow and cocked his head. I went behind the bar for once, without breaking stride, and a bleary-eyed businessman with the perfume of something unnatural hanging on him blinked, shifting uneasily on his stool. Micky's is where the nightside comes to drink, and if you don't make trouble you're welcome here.

If you *do* make trouble, well . . . the staff will have you out the door on your ass in seconds flat. Probably minus a few body parts, too. And if I'm around I'll help.

I snagged a bottle of vodka off the rack and headed for the back door. Theron followed, setting his towel down. He waited until I swept the door open and stepped out into the alley, where Amalia, one of the lionesses of the Norte Luz pride, leaned against the wall and made a slight moue of surprise to see me. I'm sure I wasn't in my finest form.

"You going to pay for that?" Theron stopped short when I rounded on him. "Jesus, Jill. What's wrong?"

I twisted the cap free and took down a jolt of colorless liquid courage. "Disappearances on the east side of town. Four women and a man, probably more." I took another slug, wiped my mouth with the back of my hand. The habit of drinking steadied me more than the alcohol would, since I burn it off so quick anyway. "I need every Were in the city running sweeps." I took a deep breath. "We've got scurf."

Amalia paled and straightened. She was golden-blonde, with a cat Were's characteristic dark eyes and wide cheekbones. Feathers knotted into her long honey hair fluttered as she pitched her cigarette into the buttcan with a clean economy of motion. Muscle rippled in her bare arm, the sleeves torn off her Cruxshadows T-shirt. She shot Theron one eloquent look.

"You're sure?" The lean dark Were reached for the vodka. I surrendered it without demur. It was formulaic—I wouldn't be here unless I *was* sure.

I pointed to my leg, where the leather was shredded. Underneath, the angry red of clawswipes was visible, with the trademark jagged curl at the end. "I'm pretty goddamn sure, Theron. I need patrols run in every inch of the city. I'm going home to call Leon right now."

"How many did you tangle with?" Theron passed the vodka over to Amalia, who barely touched it to her mouth to be polite. Most lionesses are teetotalers—when they drink they like to hunt, and not many men can keep up, Were *or* human.

But what a way to go, eh?

"Just one. New one, vanished last night. I found him this morning. Hadn't gotten all chewy and bendy yet, and was probably just a random infection. There was no sign of a nest." *But there has to be one, and he would have found it tomorrow night. Ugh.* My pulse trembled, came back to regular. "Have everyone be on the lookout, and I'll drop by Galina's on my way home. She'll break out the emergency garlic."

Amalia made a mournful face. "I hate that."

"Better than waking up slimy." Theron actually shivered. It was utterly unlike him—but the Weres have been fighting scurf for longer than anyone. There's not a single one of them, even a pup, who doesn't have a scurf scar or two. Of course, they heal faster and better than humans, but still. "The east side of town, you say?"

"Yup. There were disappearances, but nothing out of the ordinary—if you can call anything on the nightside ordinary." My pager buzzed again, but I ignored it. It didn't make me jump this time, thank God. "I'll be digging for the entry point soon. There's *got* to be more disappearances I haven't heard about."

"Okay." Theron's face thinned out, his dark eyes taking on an orange cast in the alley's shadow. One end was blocked off by another dumpster, and there was a row of castoff plastic deckchairs for smoke breaks near the door to the kitchen. That door was ajar, and I smelled the grill, hot oil and bacon frying.

My stomach gurgled. I turned sharply on my heel, heading for the mouth of the alley. "Put the vodka on my tab, furboy. See you soon."

"Get your garlic up to date, Jill. And eat something!" He yelled the last, but I was already gone, gathering myself to leap, one hand thudding onto the dumpster's lid to push me up and over. My boots touched home and I hit the street, up the slope of Mayfair to where I'd parked the Impala. Along the way I stopped right outside the Episcopalian Church—*ALL Welcome,* its sign said, with a rainbow arching over the words to drive the point home—to use a payphone. I dropped spare change in and dialed.

"Montaigne," he snarled.

"It's Jill. Listen, Monty—"

"Where the hell are you?" He sounded about halfway

to frantic. "There's another disappearance on the east side. This time it's a cop."

My skin went cold. "Who?"

"A blue named Winchell. Just walked away from his cruiser. We found it locked on Rosales and Fifteenth. He missed his four A.M. call-in."

I did a few swift mental calculations. That was pretty far away from Percoa, but again in a shabby clutch of industrial buildings and railyards.

Plenty of dark little holes for scurf to live in. If they had a range that big we were looking at serious trouble. "Keep everyone away from the scene. If you have people there pull them *back*. Stay away and set up a cordon."

"How big?" A good lieutenant will never question a hunter. In Monty's case, he'd known Mikhail. And he'd once screamed his lungs out while watching me take down a Trader whose bargain had included a deep, nasty hunger for human flesh—mostly sautéed, with garlic and onions. Monty had a chunk missing from his right buttock, probably the only tender part on him.

After that, there was never a quibble. Most cops are smart enough, after the obligatory orientation, to just do what I tell them. Very few dig their heels in after a brush with the nightside. And word gets passed around, by hook or by crook.

I don't know, Monty. "Forget the cordon. I can't answer for anyone's safety down there. Pull everyone out. If he's still alive, I'll bring him to Mercy General." *If he's still human, that is.*

"Jesus Christ, Jill." He sounded a little pale. "How bad is it?"

You don't want to know, kid. "Nothing I can't handle," I lied. "See you around."

"Jill—"

"*What,* Monty?" The high sharp edge of fear in my voice could be mistaken for irritation. I wasn't known for having the best temper.

Still, he persisted. "The widow. Do you have anything, anything at all?"

What do you expect, miracles? It would do me no good to say it—I was in the business of providing miracles. "Not yet, Monty. Just hang in there."

"Jill—"

"Got to go, Monty. Keep everyone out of the way, will you?" I hung up, dropped in another handful of change. Payphones are expensive these days, but nowhere near as expensive as replacing a cell phone, with as many times as I get shot, dumped in water, knifed, electrocuted, thrown off buildings. Pagers are slightly less expensive, and they're harder to break most of the time.

It rang six times and the answering machine picked up, a passionless recital of the number I'd just dialed. I waited for the beep.

"Leon, it's Jill. We've got scurf. Anyone you can send will be welcome. Call me, I'm dropping by my house tonight to pick up ammo. Yes, I'm up to date on my garlic. Hurry." A terse message, but it got the job done.

I hung up, and the desire to call Saul shook me with its intensity. I pushed it away and headed for my car.

7

I parked behind Winchell's black-and-white on Rosales Avenue. The patrol car was parked neatly at the curb, tires turned out toward the street and doors locked. Its shadow cut knife-sharp toward the sidewalk. It was a little after noon.

Not enough time. Still, that was no reason to be sloppy. I sat for a few moments in the Impala, listening to the engine tick as it cooled, heat shimmering up from the pavement down the road. Dry desert air keeps me from sweating much, and my internal thermostat takes care of the rest. Hunter training is good for that, conserving energy and keeping you from drowning in sweat when you're wearing leather in the desert. With the windows rolled down I could smell sand and the river, baking stone and the effluvia of concrete canyons and human scrabble.

I could also smell the mineral tang of hosewater and a sharp whiff of cordite.

Cordite? What? I inhaled deeply, passing air through

my preternaturally sharp nose. If I took off the leather cuff I could track it better.

Gooseflesh crawled up my back. *Would you like the scar to start spreading, Kiss?*

"He can't do anything." My own voice startled me. Go figure, I was talking to myself again.

But he can, Jill. If he figures out how to up the ante on this, you have no recourse except the bargain. Hellbreed aren't known for sticking to their word.

Then I could kill him. But then I'd go back to being strictly human again, wouldn't I.

Would I? Was it a chance worth taking?

Not yet. So shut up and get to work. I got out of the car, slammed the door, and cast an eye over the street. Deserted in the middle of the day, all it needed was a lone tumbleweed mincing down the pavement to make it a cliché. One block over I heard heavy machinery rumbling and the sound of voices, traffic in the distance, and a low moan from the trainyards stitched under every other noise, something normally only heard at night.

The scar twinged sharply, maybe because I was thinking about it. Maybe because I could still feel the scurf's acid-drenched claws dragging through my flesh. Maybe because somewhere, Perry was thinking about me.

Worry about what you've got in front of you, hunter.

I approached the car, sniffed delicately. No sweet taint of corruption. Nothing except baking automobile paint and the faint fading odor of a man's cheap cologne.

I cast around. There was another shadowed alley not fifteen steps away. I skirted the car and headed for it, my right hand easing a gun out, pulse pounding hard against the back of my throat. Adrenaline boiled copper on my palate. My coat fluttered, tattered by claws and crackling with dried blood.

The alley held nothing. Scraps of meaningless garbage, all the way back. No place for even a scurf to hide, and a locked door leading into a warehouse that didn't move even when I applied a little pressure to it. The whiff of cordite had gone away, too.

Huh.

I slid out of the shade and into the hammerblow of southern sun again. Tested the wind direction and got another fading noseful of gunfire and something else. It was more a pheromone wash than a smell, brittle copper fear and something invisible I'd smelled before.

Death.

I tracked the flaring and fading of the scent as the wind veered, a block down and two over, turning back, zeroing in. I had to backtrack even farther to skirt the side of a falling-down building that might have held offices once.

What's wrong with this picture, Jill?

The structure wasn't up to code, and there was crime-scene tape over the doors. The tape was bleached and fluttering, no longer a bar to passage. The door itself had been broken in and repaired with plywood, also bleached out.

But the padlock through the hasp screwed into the plywood, holding the door shut, was so new it glittered like a diamond under the fierce light.

Huh. I touched the lock tentatively, sensitive fingertips scraping rough new-bought metal. The smell was stronger here.

I thought about it for a little bit. Then I set my heels, wrapped my hellbreed-strong right-hand fingers around the clasp, and wrenched it free of the thin plywood. I could have broken the padlock itself, but why do it the hard way?

I toed the door open and peered into darkness. Spiderwebs fluttered, and I thought of scorpions, the tattoo high up on my right thigh prickling briefly. A concrete-floored hallway vanished into gloom, and I kept my back to the wall as I stepped in and started working my way down.

There was no hint of scurf, but that reek of gunpowder and death called me. A hunter is trained pretty thoroughly not to make assumptions at the scene, it clouds your thinking and can bite you in the ass pretty hard.

Still, this was a disappearance on the same side of town that other people had been going missing in. A chill that had nothing to do with external temperature drifted down my back. I kept the gun low and ready, and my left hand curled around a knifehilt.

Locked doors frowned at me. None of them smelled very interesting, and they all had dust on the doorknobs that gritted under my fingers. The corner took a sharp bend—I covered it and swung around, found the walls and roof soaring away from me as the hall turned into the interior of the building proper. The lower floors had been converted to open space for something, once upon a time.

Seventeen steps in, on a concrete floor littered with slow-rotting cardboard junk, was Officer Winchell, a curly-headed tall young man in blues with a mask of bruising. Nylon rope knotted around his wrists, his arms pulled grotesquely far behind his back as he lay sprawled in the final indignity of death. A lake of congealed blood spread out from him, and the wooden chair he'd probably been tied to was overturned another four steps away, one of its legs sitting right in the still-wet-looking stain.

He'd been shot four times in the chest, close-range. His back was soaked through—hollowpoints can puncture and bleed you dry, sometimes even if you're wearing a vest. Extremely close range, and he'd bled out under the Kevlar intended to keep him alive.

What the hell is going on here? I looked away from the body. Glanced at the hall. Someone had to have locked the door on the outside. Had Winchell let himself in over there, or had he been overpowered and dragged in? His gun was gone.

Four shots to the chest was serious business. The mask of horror that was his face was premortem, but only just. Tied to a chair, untied and shot.

Why do you assume he was tied to the chair, Jill? I examined the chair, then. There was some bloodspatter, and a hank of bloodstained nylon rope still clinging to it.

Blue and white striped nylon rope. I chewed at my lower lip, thinking it over.

Jacinta Kutchner had hung with blue and white striped nylon. Just this kind. The same kind Winchell's hands were bound with.

A cop commits suicide, the widow gets killed and there's this rope at the scene, and now this. This type of rope's as common as a sneeze; they sell it in hardware stores—but to have it here in two out of three murders related to police officers? Something smells here indeed, Jill.

I was wasting daylight even looking at this. A scurf infestation would spread until burned out or contained; this was a stack of human murders with no inhuman agency

I could see behind them. Not my problem, I was already stretched thin enough as it was.

But Jacinta's body swung gently, her house creaking to itself in my memory, and Officer Winchell—I didn't even know his first name—didn't stare at me because his eyes had puffed closed. Someone had beat the hell out of him and shot him.

So we were looking at revenge or money, most probably. You don't get beaten like that just because someone hates your haircut.

Sudden certainty bloomed under my breastbone like a poisonous flower. *It just don't smell right,* Monty had said.

I agreed, one hundred percent.

I straightened, looked down at Winchell's grotesquely puffed face. Noticed all at once how hot it was, and wondered why I'd smelled the cordite first and not the death. Maybe because I've gotten used to the smell of decay.

As used to it as you *can* get, that is.

Daylight's wasting, Jill. Call this in to Homicide and have a word with Piper when you can. Get your ass in gear.

But first, I stood gazing down at Winchell. The lump curdled in my throat. Nobody should have to die like this. Or like Kutchner's widow.

My voice startled me, breaking the eerie quiet over the sound of freight trains and traffic in the distance. "Monty's called me in, Winchell. You tell Jacinta I'm on the job." I paused. "You can let Marv Kutchner know too."

Then I headed out into the daylight to look for a phone.

8

Galina looks like a film star from the thirties. Her sleek dark hair is marcel-waved, and her cat-tilted green eyes, set in a pale face, would have been worth a lot of hope in Garbo's Hollywood. Each All Hallows Eve I want to buy her a flapper's dress and an ostrich feather, but I never get around to it.

Besides, she'd probably take offense. You never can tell, with a Sanctuary. They've got some funny ideas.

She pushed the plunger down and pulled the needle free, tamping a cotton ball down and taping it with deft motions. "You're already up on your garlic, but a little more won't kill you." Her rain-gray skirt whispered as she turned away, laying the tape down.

I leapt to my feet and swung my chickenwing-bent arm. Garlic serum burns like *hell*. "Jesus. Christ. *Hurts*."

Her snort was unsympathetic. The Sanctuary snapped the point off the needle deftly in a pint-sized biohazard container and scooped up the tray. Sunlight veered through the skylights and burnished her kitchen table.

She lived upstairs over her shop, just a regular garden-variety occult store unless you know what you're about. Then you realize you could find just about everything a serious practitioner of sorcery needs—and practically everything a Were or witch might need, as well—in her little store. "Well, if you'd prefer getting all slimy and bloodhungry . . ."

"It might be an improvement." I sighed as the burn settled down, spreading up my arm. "I should stock up on ammo." *I want all the goddamn ammo I can carry if we've got scurf. And a few more hours in the day would be nice.* Monty was probably climbing the walls by now, I'd phoned in the location of the body and not much else.

"Again?" But she didn't demur. "Hang on, I'll fetch it. Will it be on account? I can spot you a few hundred."

"No, I've got it. Business has been good lately." Hunters get backstairs funding, both from the city and county; it's a small price to pay for most municipal or county administrations. We also get federal funding if a paranormal incident is big enough to qualify, or if it crosses state lines.

"Defense spending" isn't only for mundane threats.

Plus, the Church subsidizes training no few apprentices. Even if they do bar us from Heaven, they try to make sure we're funded enough to hold back the tide of Hell. We're usually overworked and just-barely-paid-enough, but that's better than nothing. Resident hunters don't need to worry about rent or their next meal, thank God.

We just have to worry about damnation.

And being psychic has its perks when it comes to investing. Mikhail had done very well for himself. Screw that "not using your powers for personal gain" bit. When you're getting shot, knifed, electrocuted, strangled, dumped in rivers, thrown off buildings, or almost eviscerated protecting the common citizenry, the *least* the world can do is give you a break or two on the stock market.

Of course, living long enough to claim a retirement fund is the problem.

"Are you going to keep the Glocks or switch to something else?" She paused, the sun shining off her lacquered hair.

I have regular Glocks, not the smaller ones most female cops use. My wrists look small, but hellbreed strength means I can handle the recoil better than most men. One of the best days of my life was switching to bigger guns. "I'll stick with the Glocks. But fill me up on hollowpoints and the silver-grain armor-piercing rounds. I want to be nastier than usual."

She nodded, tilted her head as the bell jingled downstairs. "Were," she said shortly, and vanished.

Coming to take me to the dance. I picked up my shredded coat and shrugged into it. The walls quivered slightly, the Sanctuary binding responding to my nervousness and Galina's as well. Inside their little houses Sancs *are* the law; the price they pay is being more vulnerable outside than even a weak untrained psychic. But they usually fix it so they don't have to go outside much—and hunters and Weres, not to mention most hellbreed, will beat the tar out of anyone hassling a Sanctuary. Neutral supply of necessities is the least of the services they provide.

I gauged the fall of sunlight and glanced at the kitchen clock—Elvis in a red jacket, his hips swaying regularly.

The days were long, but still, every hour of sunlight gone heightened the possibility of a nightfight with scurf.

Enough to give any hunter shivers. If I wasn't *already* halfway to twitched-out between tripping over dead cops and getting shot full of garlic.

The scar throbbed. I reached over, fingers trembling, and stripped the leather cuff off my right wrist. Stared down at the band of paler-even-than-my-usual-milk skin.

On our too-short honeymoon I'd left the cuff off, and I'd even gotten a bit of a tan. For all a hunter's sun-worship, I stay out too much at night to be anything but fishbelly. I was back to putting the cuff on when I didn't want to be distracted by the wash of sensory acuity.

Air hit my skin with a thousand sharp needles, suddenly alive again. My nose tingled, picking up the reek of garlic, silver, the dry smell of herbs hung in the large pantry, wet earth from the greenhouse on the roof. Fur and cologne that was a Were downstairs, Galina's perfume, the incense and Power of her shop.

I examined the lip-print. It wasn't any bigger. It was just the same as it had always been, and when I tipped it up into the sunlight uncomfortable, allergic warmth spilled up my arm.

Goddamn you, Perry. Getting into my head again. *Worming* his way in.

My exhaled breath stirred the leaves of small potted herbs growing in the windowsill, under a double drench of light. Air conditioning sent a cool draft across my shoulders. I'd have to change into my first spare and place another order with Jingo out on Cortada Street for another two or three custom jobs.

They don't sew ammo-loops into regular leather

trenches, you know. And I don't have time anymore for sewing, if I ever did.

I was shaking. My fingers almost blurred. It had been so *close* last time, and the time before that. Perry had brought me right to the line, made me look over, and I still didn't know how I had stepped away from the edge.

Yes you do. Get moving, Jill. I slapped the cuff on and buckled it as footsteps sounded on the stairs. *"Jill!"* Someone shouting, and I knew the voice.

I met Theron halfway. "What's up?"

"Barrio's emptying out." He wasn't even out of breath, though his dark hair was disarranged and his eyes were lambent, sheened with orange. An excited Were is like an excited hellbreed, the eyes get all glowy. "One of the 'cougars ran across spoor on the east side, right near where you said. They're tracking now."

My heart settled into a high fast thumping and I pushed a strand of dark hair, weighted down with a silver wheel-charm double-knotted with red thread, out of my face. It clinked against more charms. "Great. Let's roll. Galina, that ammo, please?"

"Be careful." She was at the bottom of the stairs, the pendant at her throat winking with its own light as the air conditioning kicked off again. Her hands were full of cartridges stacked on a red cloisonné tray.

She's pretty much the only person who tells me that. Anyone else knows it's useless. Then there's Saul, who would never tell me that because it implies I couldn't take care of myself. Except he had last time . . . because he was worried, and tired, and watching his mother die by inches.

More unpleasant thoughts, arriving right on schedule.

"I can't be careful, Galina. It's not in the job description. Is the sunsword still black?" It was a good weapon in a dark hole, but it had been drained past recovery a while ago.

When it had been shoved through Navoshtay Niv Arkady's chest by a half-crazed hellbreed female crouched on a burning car. Just another day in the life of a hunter.

I wish shit like that wasn't so routine.

"No, it's silver now, but nowhere near fully charged. You want it?" She looked almost pathetically hopeful, but her eyes didn't stop at me. Instead, her gaze touched my face, flinched away, and found Theron, who leaned against the wall between us, running his long fingers through his hair.

I stowed the ammo and made sure the guns were easy in their holsters, ran my fingers over the knifehilts. "Not unless I'm sure it won't snuff out and leave me in the dark. Come on, Theron. I'll drive." *If you can peel yourself away.*

"Give me a second, Jill." Quiet and courteous, not like the unpredictable smartass I knew. Still, everyone minds their manners at Galina's.

Even Perry.

Stop thinking about that. "Fine." I headed for the front of the shop, brushing past the Sanctuary. The scar throbbed wetly. I couldn't resist one bad-tempered little goose. "Stay inside, Galina. We'd hate to lose you."

I didn't miss her muttered reply, which contained at least one term highly unsuitable for a lady's use. We all mind our manners at Galina's—but sometimes it's fun hearing her cuss like the rest of us.

Outside, it was a solid ninety in the shade. I stamped

across the street toward my Impala and stopped, suddenly, right in the middle of the ribbon of concrete, heat waves shimmering up on either end of the block.

The sensation of being *watched* spilled gooseflesh down my back. You don't live long as a hunter by ignoring that feeling. I turned a full three-sixty in the middle of the road, scanning the buildings, roofs, the sidewalks, contemplating all the angles.

Who would be watching me? And in the middle of the day, no less, when the sun's power is at its highest.

I concentrated, still as a cat watching a mousehole. *Come on. Stick your nose out, whoever you are. Come and get me.*

The wind quieted, ripples dying in the cauldron of the day. Inside the scurfhole, wherever it was, it would be hot too. They would be piled in on top of each other in a lump of contagious slime, dozing through the danger of daylight. Shedding heat while they breathed sickness on each other.

I need more flash grenades. Three just isn't going to do it. It was one of those random thoughts that floats across your mind right before all hell breaks loose.

Something punched me hard in the chest. I staggered, the wind knocked out of me, and folded down as the hammerblows continued. It didn't hurt until I tried to roll over and pain crested in a fierce wave, driving iron spikes into muscle and bone. Little twisting jitters of sparkling agony slammed through me, each one so individual I could name it.

The world went dark, heaved, turned over, and rammed me back into myself with a shock like lightning striking. Only it wasn't lightning. It was the scar on my wrist exploding with furious power as my punctured heart struggled to beat, bullets tearing through my body, shattering, spilling, blood steaming on the road and chips of concrete flicking up.

Someone was *shooting* me. Doing a handy job of it, too.

More pain, a river of it, a new brand of pain. By *brand* I mean shape and type, and burning hurting *godpleasemakeitstop*—

Half-choked screaming. The walls of Galina's shop tolling deep notes of distress. The coughing roar of a Were having a fit, and it sounded like Saul—but he was somewhere else, wasn't he?

Saul? My lips tried to shape the word, a bubble of something hot broke on them, ran down my chin. Alone and unprotected in the middle of acres of burning road, except I was being dragged by one arm, shoulder popping out of joint with a short *thop!* that would have been funny if it wasn't mine. The scar burned, working inward toward the bone, burrowing in with sick delight. My heart exploded again, body convulsing as weightlessness swallowed me whole.

The scar had actually shocked me, just like a defibrillator. Sparks crackled from the charms lacing my hair.

"Don't you *dare,* Jill!" Galina screamed. The sound was a bright ribbon through dark water closing over my head as I thrashed, moaning sounds spilling from my lips along with the bright red. "*Don't you dare die on me!*"

Scratching, scrabbling sounds. I opened my eyes and gasped as another lightning-shock, this one different from the first, slammed through me. The flayed, exploded meat of my heart was a live coal buried in my chest, systems struggling to deal with the sudden trauma and loss of blood pressure.

WHAM! This time it was Galina, the power had her distinctive flavor of incense and growing green things. Slamming into my heart, *making* it beat through the damage as cells regrew, each one a scream of pain.

I coughed, choked, and yelled, striking out, dislocated arm flopping uselessly. The blow was deflected, and my chest was an egg of red-hot pain. Tearing, horrible, agonizing heat coalesced, snapped into a lump in the upper left quadrant of my ribs; the scar chortled to itself as electricity popped, and I arched, mouth full of blood and eyes bulging, a scream locked behind the clotted stone in my throat.

Heartbeat. I had a heartbeat again.

"—*fucking* dare die on me, Jill Kismet, I've seen two hunters go in my time and I won't lose you, now *breathe!*" Galina's voice was deep and irresistible, she leaned on my chest, thumping me a good one, then clamping my nose shut and blowing into my mouth, trying to inflate my lungs but doing a good job of drowning me in my own claret.

I spat blood, a good chunk of it geysering out through nose and lips both. Galina let out a yelp, choked midway by the volume, and I stopped myself from instinctively striking out again. The walls thundered, wavering like seaweed. If I hit a Sanc in her own house, it would get pretty damn uncomfortable pretty goddamn quickly, and I was uncomfy enough already.

The trouble with almost dying is that it makes you weak as shock sets in and the body struggles to function. I curled over on my side, spitting to clear my mouth of blood and lungfluid, the deep drilling ache in my chest intensifying with each labored pulse. My dislocated shoulder throbbed, a bass note drowned out by a whole orchestra of nasty sweating pain. I twitched, several times, nerves firing without any real reason except *holy shit, we're still here? Still working?*

"Good girl," Galina whispered. "That's my good girl." Patting my back as I retched, coughing and choking to clear passageways violated by lead and fluid.

The ridiculous little bell she had on the shop door tinkled. "Gone." It was Theron's voice. "Tell me she's okay."

"Just fine." The Sanctuary, wonder of wonders, sounded *nervous.* "Or as fine as you can get when you've lost all your blood."

I haven't lost all of it, dammit. It still hurts, there must be some left. But I felt weaker and more unsteady than I liked. Agony receded, becoming just garden-variety pain.

That I could deal with.

Get up, milaya. Mikhail's voice, memory sloshing inside my skull. *Or I will hit you again.*

He never said anything he didn't mean. I struggled to get *up,* to fight.

"Relax, killer. Take it easy." Hands on my aching shoulders, so familiar. A deep rumbling sound—a Were, purring to ease another's distress.

Saul? No, he's miles away. What?

Lassitude poured over me, a sucking swamp of lethargy so huge it threatened to close my eyes and drag me down. "Whafuck?" I slurred, my tongue too thick, not working properly.

"Someone just tried to kill you, Kismet." Theron, uncharacteristically serious. No wonder he sounded like Saul. "An assault rifle from a rooftop halfway down the street. You know anyone who drives a blue Buick?"

It was so ludicrous I could only repeat myself. "Wha*fuck?*"

"Just lie still for a moment." Galina's skirt swished. The walls calmed down, settling into regular lath, plaster, and paint instead of shimmering curtains of energy ready to enforce a Sanctuary's will on physical and psychic space. "I'm going to get the first-aid kit."

Best of luck to you. I don't think I need a Band-Aid. "Arm," I whispered, through another mouthful of blood. *Stop bleeding, Jill. Goddammit.* "My arm."

"Sorry about that." The Were crouched over me, a bulk radiating safety. He didn't smell exactly like Saul, but it was comforting nonetheless. "Had to get you out of the middle of the street, dragged you too hard."

It's not the first time that's popped out of the socket. At least I'm still alive. "Thanks." My voice was a thin thread. I passed out briefly, a stripe of warmth across my face reminding me that daylight was slipping away, and someone had just tried to kill me.

In the middle of the day, with an assault rifle, no sorcery or claws or teeth. Just like a human would kill.

Why?

9

I shifted, let the clutch off, and the Impala responded, leaping forward. Theron grabbed for the dash. Dried blood crackled in my hair, and I rammed the car into third gear like it was going out of style, goosed it, shifted up to fourth and put the pedal to the floor.

"Jesus!" Theron yelled over the rush of wind.

Men. They never like my driving. Of course, nobody likes my driving. I've never been in a single accident—basic precognition takes care of that—and the cops all know my car well enough to leave me alone when I'm bending the laws of physics and traffic to get somewhere.

They don't like to think about why I hurry. Or what I might be hurrying to get to.

Rubber screamed as we took a corner like it was on rails, and I thought about who would want to kill me. A blue Buick and regular ammo—not even silver.

Not even silver. Anyone coming after a hellbreed-tainted hunter is going to have silver ammo. It wouldn't kill me but it would at least mean someone knew what

*they were doing, knew it would take me longer to heal
and hurt like a motherfuck. Or is that a red herring?* I
stood on the brake as the intersection ahead of me ran
with traffic, the red light looming, juggled probability
and precognition, felt the little tingle along my nerves
that meant *okay GO NOW* and stamped on the accelerator
again.

The Impala zoomed through the light just as it turned
green, skidding around a red Caprice as I jerked the wheel
and shot us through traffic like a greased pinball.

Who would try to kill me right on Galina's doorstep,
too? Someone who had a bone to pick with both the Sanc
and me? Someone who wanted to make a statement, or
who knew I'd still be alive afterward?

Or just someone who knew I could be found at her
place every few days? Which was just about anyone on
the nightside and quite a few regular folks.

We roared onto the east side a few minutes earlier than
I'd thought. My traffic karma was still holding. Theron
worked his fingers free of the dash while I unclipped my
seatbelt. More blood crackled, drying on my skin, and I
felt a little pale.

"You okay?" Theron's knuckles cracked as he
stretched.

"Never better," I lied. "Getting shot just pisses me off,
furboy. Now I'm aching to take it out on a whole nest of
scurf."

"You'd better calm down." He confined himself to that
mild statement, and the glance I shot at him splashed right
off the concern on his lean dark face.

I didn't dignify the obvious with a reply. Angry is the
last thing you want to be in a nest. Anger is good fuel,

yes—but it clouds judgment, and a hunter can't afford that. *Not thinking straight* is one step away from *getting your ass blown off.*

And I'd already had that today, thank you very much.

Another thought occurred to me, terrible enough to make my hackles go up again.

I got shot in the heart. I felt it. Worst piece of lead I've ever caught—and the scar just sewed me up and zapped me, Galina zaps me, and I'm fine.

Well, maybe not fine. But still alive. That's what counts.

But if I'd still been meeting Perry every month at the Monde to pay for using the scar, what would he have made me do? How could I have paid for that much power thundering through my still all-too-human flesh?

It doesn't matter, Jill. It's a non-issue. Worry about who's trying to kill you now, for Christ's sake.

Put that way, the question of Perry began to take on different dimensions. But he would have sent someone with silver, wouldn't he?

Wouldn't he? If hurting me more was the point, yeah. But not if just half-killing me is the point. Perry wouldn't send a human, either—he'd send a Trader. Stop thinking about him, Jill.

Percoa Park lay under a motionless flood of hard bright light, the trees looking dusty and grass scuffed to yellow wherever the sprinklers didn't reach. A baseball diamond simmered kitty-corner, and the streetlamps over the bus shelter Michael Spilham had spent his last human moments on earth standing in were just visible.

The park thrummed. I caught flickers of motion between the trees, and Theron's face eased a bit. The Were's stride lengthened, and I glimpsed the predator in him. It's easy to forget, sometimes, that they're built for hunting. They do it, just like they do most things, far better than humans. He raised his head, his dark hair suddenly more alive, curling a bit longer, and sniffed the air.

My nose was sensitive even with the cuff on. Fur. Musk. The smell of healthy animals, sandy dust, and tinder-dry bark. An outside smell. A good smell, one that means safety. Weres have been allied with hunters ever since the beginning, working back-to-back. Even through the Middle Ages, and that was a right fuck of a time to be a Were *or* a hunter, between the Inquisition, the open mouths to Hell, and the general state of chaos.

Weres provide muscle and speed when it comes to hunting rogue Weres, backup when facing down Traders, and general support, since human hunters are spread so thin. Hunters keep things smoothed over with the police, function as leaders who don't have to work by consensus during crisis times, and take on hellbreed—one of the few things Weres can't do as well as a human.

It takes a hunter to kill a hellbreed. Or a Sorrow.

The thought of the Sorrows tasted like bitter ash before I turned it aside.

"Good turnout," was all Theron said, before loping down a slight hill toward a stand of cottonwoods. I followed, my coat flapping, suddenly aware I was covered in dried blood again, my shirt shredded and my leather pants two steps away from the rag bag.

At least my weapons were still okay, and my rosary. Shoot me all you want, but if you shoot one of my knives, my blessed charms, or God forbid my guns, I'm going to get *pissed*.

The scar brought me back, or I'd've bought it. Not even Gulina could get me back after that much lead poisoning. The sudden certainty was chilling.

Had Perry felt it, etheric force thundering through the scar to keep my body alive? Was he up during the day, sitting in the quiet of the Monde Nuit, staring at the television screens in his office? Maybe fondling the flechettes, stained with black hellbreed ichor, though they were always pristine each time he told me to open up the flat rosewood case.

I shivered. My coat flapped and I touched my guns, the knifehilts, the other little surprises strapped to leather and taped down to cut the clanking. Silver chimed in my hair since I didn't have to be quiet, and the rosary bumped against my belly.

Quit thinking about it, Jill. You almost-die every week. Just get over it.

Maddeningly, it didn't seem quite *right*. I was too busy to tease out why just yet.

The small clearing was full of Weres, and lambent eyes turned to me as soon as I brushed past an anonymous trashwood bush and into full view. They were too polite to ask what the hell had happened, and sadly it's more common than not to see me when I've just been through the wringer.

Hunting is a messy business.

"Trackers are on it," a lean tall woman said. Lioness from the look of her, she had the characteristic broad face and sleek arms, muscle moving supple under honey skin. "Not too far from here, zeroing in on a couple blocks."

"We're burning daylight." A slim young male, barely past puberty if you could believe his skinny build, with the prominent nose of a bird Were. Brown feathers were tied into his shag of a haircut, and he made a graceful, contained movement expressing impatience and controlled enthusiasm all in one.

"Patience, Rubio." Theron's entire face wrinkled into a snarl of a grin, smoothed out.

"It's not a virtue," the lioness added. "It's a survival tactic."

That caused a ripple of laughter, and the kid laughed too. It wasn't the type of nervous laughter you get in an autopsy room, but its intent was the same. To bleed off a little steam, make the waiting palatable.

I set my back against the bole of a cottonwood and closed my eyes. My heart was thumping a little harder than I liked. A rebuilt heart, shattered by a bullet less than half an hour ago. Good thing I was a domestic model, maybe they had a hard time getting import parts for a ticker.

Get it, Jill? Arf arf. You're a regular comic. Should go on the circuit.

Now think about something useful. What the hell is going on here? A blue Buick, Theron had said, speeding away down Macano Street. Nothing but shell casings left on the roof, some of them jingling in my coat pocket. And a smell. Male, Theron had said, human, and sweating. But a professional, to pump me full of lead and get the hell out of there.

Or very lucky.

Why? If I knew the why I'd know the who, wouldn't I.

Pure lead bullets and a professional hit. My life was certainly never boring.

The air pressure changed and my eyes snapped open.

Every Were in the clearing was standing poised and looking in the same direction, the same way a flock of birds will wheel with tremendous in-flight precision. As if by prearranged signal they broke, some running, others merely loping, Theron glancing over his shoulder at me.

No muss, no fuss. The trackers had found something, and communicated in that way Weres sometimes have, through instinct, pheromones, or just sheer air.

No more time for thinking. The hunt was underway.

10

Running with Weres is like hunting on full-moon nights, when everything goes just slightly sideways and it can either be dead quiet . . . or a sliptilting screamfest from beginning to end, not even stopping at dawn. There's the same breathless expectation, the same pulse in the air, hitting the back of the throat like copper-tinged wine.

I know almost every hollow and corner of my city, and it's that knowledge that lets me keep up. Even hellbreed speed has a hard time when it comes to Weres in full asshaul mode. They run like quicksilver, not like the hellbreed's habit of blinking through space too fast for mortal eyes.

Pounding feet, exhilaration, the heat of the day shimmering off pavement, alleys and fire escapes flashing past, we swept through the industrial district in a tide of half-seen shapes. Most hunts are run at night, when there's less chance of normals out on the street.

When there's a scurf infestation, the Weres run by day. They use that little *don't look here* trick they're so fond of, the same trick animals use for camouflage. It's more of a blending-in, really, but it makes the eye slide right over them.

Me? I rely on sheer outrageousness. People don't *want* to see violations of the laws of physics. They don't want to see anything un-ordinary. Their brains will convince them their eyes aren't telling the truth. It's part of what makes eyewitness testimony so tricksy. Given enough time, people will talk themselves out of seeing just about anything—if they're lucky enough to survive seeing it, that is.

And if they're lucky enough not to crack under the strain.

So we ran, me skipping and skidding, not as graceful as the Weres but just as fast, until they coalesced around me and there was a pause, my ribs heaving, silver shifting and chiming in my hair as I took a deep breath and peered off the roof of a dilapidated trucker's depot right on the river's edge.

"Goddammit," I breathed. I'd've suspected someone's nose was off, but hunting scurf is a Were specialty. "Near the *water?*"

"Funny." Theron crouched in the shade of an old HVAC unit. "They usually hate water. And the place is up on stilts, for Chrissake. Hard to keep warm."

"Not in summer." My coat flapped as I shrugged. "It'll be a regular tinderbox in there."

"I hate getting sweaty." He actually delivered the line with a straight face, too, damn him. "Whenever you're ready, Jill."

I don't think you can ever be ready for this, Theron. "Let's not burn any more sunshine." My fingers tingled, aching for a gun, and my mouth turned dry and slick again.

11

*I*t wasn't just a nest. It was a full-blown nightmare.

Coughing howls, barks, growls and the exploding sweetsick smell everywhere, sinking into hair and clothes and even the boards of the decrepit building. No time for thought, only motion, because I'd popped the hatch on the roof and dropped straight down into a pile of scurf, Weres suddenly swarming through the boarded-up windows and kicked-in doors, more tearing off the HVAC vents on the roof and boards from the windows, letting in sword-shafts of sunlight as the scurf began screaming their keening glassine cries.

Theron landed lightly, half-changed, the cat in him overcoming the man as he dropped. They are creatures of power and grace, and no matter where on the continuum between human and animal they are they still express the best of either. His claws sprang free, the cat rising to the fore like smoke, and he unzipped the scurf leaping for me in one graceful motion. I spattered bullets through it, missing him by a miracle of reflex, and clocked a scurf on

the head with the butt of my pistol. Another Were leapt
with a spitting snarl, colliding with the scurf and knocking it away.

Most fights, a hunter takes point and the Weres watch
her back. Facing down a rogue Were or scurf reverses
that—a hunter is there to coordinate, to provide a leader
who doesn't have to function by consensus, and to clean
up any problems with the authorities afterward.

In the middle of a fight with scurf—especially full-
blown scurf with cartilaginous bones, powdery-slime acid
coating, and active viral agents in their saliva and coating,
even in their exhalation and pheromone wash—you want
Weres. Because they do not hesitate, and they are largely
immune to the viral agents, their systems peculiarly anti-
thetical to scurf infection.

It mostly falls to a hunter to give the *coup de grâce,*
and keep out of the way otherwise. It's only a little harder
than it sounds.

The smell coated everything. Cloying burnt sugar and
illness, like the breath of a dying child given a lollipop.
And there were so many of them—fifty at least, drifts of
them jammed into corners, wedged between boxes, waking to find Death moving among them with fangs and fur,
claws and lambent eyes.

That was the first wrongness. There should not have
been so many. People go missing all the time, it's true, it's
a fucking epidemic, but a nest this big should have made
a *huge* pattern of disturbance.

The second wrongness was how old they were. Scurf
get more bendy and vicious the longer they survive, and
these were full-blown, two weeks to a month old, the scurf
equivalent of Methuselahs. Their skin glowed with pallid

moonsickness, and their bodies had become humanoid instead of human—potbellied, loose flaps and wattles under hyperdistending jaws, skinny arms far too long and attenuated to be as strong as they are, spindly legs that bend in ways no human's would, and new tadpole legs beginning from the muscle mass of what had been the glutes and also to a lesser degree from the groin, sexual difference only showing itself in the savagery and thrust of a scurf's attack.

Those that used to be male go for your throat. The used-to-be-female go for the chest or the gut, impatient to get at the entrails.

Battle of the sexes, right there. If it wasn't so deadly, it might even be funny.

I jammed the muzzle against a hairless skull as the scurf screeched, its cry like a rabbitscream, and pulled the trigger. No time to think—Weres were pouring into the building's wide-open inner space, reinforcing their brothers and sisters.

The sense of wrongness grew as I killed another wounded scurf, poisonous fluid spattering, acid hissing on my sleeves and against my pants. My boots slipped and slid in powdery slime, and I choked on hot candied fumes as the warning crested, running down my back in rivers of sharp metal insect feet.

I jerked around to see a slice of floor opening, darkness at its mouth as more scurf boiled out from the trapdoor and leapt for me, and I fell back, firing, as the Weres wheeled and poured past me, a tide of glowing eyes, feathers, and fur. The noise was incredible, and I was just beginning to think that maybe we had a handle on this one when the world turned over, the scar clotting with iron prickles on my wrist and burrowing into the bone.

Another hole stove itself into the wall, sunlight streaming as a body hurtled through. A male hellbreed with a glaring white stripe in his black hair hit me so hard my teeth snapped together, I twisted in midair and the knife was in my hand, a natural movement, I rammed it forward and it hissed as it touched Hell-tainted flesh. Wood snapped as we shot sideways, the 'breed's teeth champing scant millimeters from my cheek and the *smell,* the sweet corruption of its breath and the sick candy of scurf mixing to bring up everything my stomach had ever thought of digesting in a painless mess, but I couldn't throw up—I was too goddamn busy.

Wood splintered and crackled as I was rammed through it, splinters popping up. Hellbreed hate Weres, and the feathered and furred return the favor. But while a Were is built to handle scurf, it takes something different to deal with a hellbreed's stuttering, awesome speed, not to mention the corruption that fills them.

Yeah, for scurf you need Weres. But for hellbreed, nothing but a hunter will do.

The problem was, I had just been tossed into a natural enclosure, wooden boxes stacked up on three sides, the hellbreed coming in fast—and scurf on every side, hissing as they bared their teeth and scented me.

Thin blades of fire ran up my leg and I made it upright, reflex moving my entire body with jerky, fantastic speed. The knife was still buried in the skunk-haired hellbreed's chest, and my free hand came up with another one, the gun still in my left hand speaking as the 'breed jerked and twisted in midair, coming down on me, claws out, and the oddly narcotized flood of hot blood as scurf teeth clamped in my calf and the hellbreed collided with me, flinging me back even as it bled runnels of dying foulness. The corner of something clipped my head hard enough to break a human neck, and consciousness left me all in a rush. I didn't even have time to worry about what would happen when the scurf swarmed my unconscious body.

". . . jill . . ."

Drifting. Patches of glaring white. The smell of blood and roasting sugar.

Whafuck?

". . . hold her head . . ." A deep thrumming, like a Were in distress. Sounds came in shutterflashes—cries, moans, the high yip of hurt animal. No nails-on-slate squealing of scurf, though. That was good.

. . . bit me. It bit me. I've got a bite. I tasted blood and foulness, then something heaved off me and I could breathe again.

Pain broke over me. It was red and smoking, the flesh of my calf boiling as the viral agents worked their way up. The scar ran with sick hot delight, burrowing into skin bubbling with heat, and the agony became immense, compressed, a point of hurtfulness in the gloom of twilight consciousness.

I hate this part. Coherent thought snagged, turned into a soup of confused reaction as etheric force slammed through me again, spiraling out through broken bones, fusing them together, rebuilding tissue. The low deep hum of the Weres gathered around me helped, taking the edge off the pain, smoothing sonic jelly over my flesh as the scar fought with heaving infection running up my leg. The garlic should have been helping too, but I couldn't feel it.

I was *bitten*.

I moved. Silver chimed, hitting the pavement—my hair, flung around as I tried to leap up and failed. I blinked, finding I had eyelids after all. Consciousness returned along with sound and color, rushing into the cup of my brain. I wasn't ready for it—who is?

But the pain receded a little bit, and that meant I could function. And if I *could* function, I *had* to.

My lips refused to obey me, but I made a garbled sound anyway.

"Jill." Theron, as close to frantic as I'd ever heard him. "Stop it. Calm down. We're trying to help."

I'm not moving. It was a lie as soon as I thought it, and I pulled the punch even before strong fingers twisted on my wrist, pushing the momentum of the blow aside. The rumbling didn't die down.

How bad was I hurt? It was hot, heat like oil against the skin, a nova of pain exploding as my entire leg cramped. *This is ridiculous. Can I go home now?*

The cramping eased slightly. I went limp.

"Something is not right," Theron said grimly.

No shit, you think? I couldn't say it, my mouth refused to work. Even for a hunter, dying twice in one day is a little too much. *I'm tired. So tired.*

"Where's Dustcircle?" A female Were, the voice hushed under a thrumming purr.

"He's on the Rez. His mother has the Wasting." Theron braced me, his hands on my shoulders oddly familiar for a stranger's touch. It felt like Saul holding me, the purr he used when I was really hurt but the danger was past resonating in my bones.

"We should call him."

No. I opened my eyes. "N-n-n—" My mouth *still* refused to work.

Even if the body is patched up after something like that, the psyche shivers and jolts like a junkie doing cold turkey. The human animal isn't built to take this type of damage and live, and it can shake certain floor-deep bits of your mental furniture around and around until you're no longer sure who you *are.*

"Easy there, hunter. Relax." A sharp edge under Theron's tone, he was worried. "Just give yourself a second, Jill. Lay back, or I'll sit on you."

I didn't think he *would,* but my muscles were limp as wet noodles, the skin over them throbbing as if I had the mother of all sunburns. I could have gotten up to fight, but it would have taken gunfire and some screaming. The entire conscious surface of my brain retreated from the glare of sunlight, seeking a deep dark hole to hide itself in, to wrap itself in velvet unconsciousness until it got over dying *twice* in less than two hours.

The bite on my calf lost its pulsing heat, the feeling of infection retreating along a map of veins.

"Someone's trying to kill her," Theron was saying. "Maybe more than one someone."

This is news? I wanted to say, but darkness closed over me, my brain finally having enough and shutting off. The party was over.

12

I came to on my couch, a huge orange naugahyde monster that was actually pretty respectable once Saul got around to slipcovering it with some cream linen he'd found on sale. The warehouse creaked and settled, singing its usual greet-the-dawn production number.

Darkness was kind, but I had to open my eyes. As soon as I did, Theron's face loomed over me, and I smelled bacon, Were, and a hot griddle.

"Just stay where you are." His eyes glowed orange in dimness. Gray dawn edged up through the skylights and the lights in the kitchen were on, sharp yellow blocks throwing shadows into the living room. A single lamp burned at the far end of the couch. "I thought I heard you. It's five A.M., nobody else has died, we're running sweeps. Your ass stays on that couch, Jill. Clear?"

I blinked. My lips were cracked and dry, I licked them before I could speak. "How many—" *How many did we lose?*

"Two down. The scurf swarmed your body; we had a

hell of a time with it." He nodded shortly, turned on his heel, and stalked toward the kitchen. "Saul called," he said over his shoulder.

Oh, Christ. "What did you tell him?" It was hard work to pitch the words loud enough, my throat was dry as desert glass. I felt feverish, my body fighting off the viral infection. But I was conscious and talking, and if Theron hadn't killed me I wasn't in any danger of getting chewy and bendy.

Or at least, so I hoped.

"What did you want me to do, lie? He'd skin me." Dishes clattered, steam hissed. "We're supposed to look after you, hunter."

Blankets slid aside as I gingerly levered myself up. I felt like I'd been drawn and quartered, then sewn back together all wrong. *Jesus. What the hell is going on?* "He doesn't need to be worrying about me, Theron. I can take care of myself—".

"You got bit, Jill. You're fighting off the infection, but it was close. How many times have you almost-died recently?" It wasn't like him to interrupt me. An egg cracked, and the sizzling was bacon, I was sure of it. "What the hell's going on?"

Scurf. And people trying to murder me as if I was a normal human being instead of a hunter. "I wish I knew." Guilt pricked under my skin—two Weres, probably with families, dead because I hadn't been fast enough to kill a hellbreed popping up in the middle of a scurf hole. I would have asked Theron who, but it would be rude— they don't speak much of the dead, and they especially don't often name them.

I could have asked Saul. If he'd been there, what might have happened?

Theron made a short sound of almost-annoyance. "Well, start at the beginning. What's been going on?"

Where do I begin? "There was a Trader that burned down a warehouse. An *arkeus* I killed the other night— last night? Or something. The scurf, those disappearances have only been going on for a week or so." *And Perry called. And Monty.* My brain refused to work just right. *What was a hellbreed doing there?*

"Anything else?"

"A friend asked me to look into something." Dried blood crackled on my clothes. I held up my hands, tendons standing out under pale skin, the cuff dyed with blood and noisome fluid on my right wrist.

"Like what?"

"Some murders without a nightside connection. So far all I have are three bodies and nothing else." There was a small pile of silver charms on the coffee table, tangled in red thread. They'd probably fallen out when the hellbreed hit me, or gotten torn off in the heat of battle. I *did* feel like handfuls of my hair had been ripped out. I almost never get my hair cut. Saul sometimes trims it for me, but I was probably rocking the punk look right about now. The back left of my skull was tender, and I could feel the scab there when my face moved. My neck ached, a vicious dull pain.

Goddamn. Sonofabitch hit me hard enough to knock me out of my hair. That's a first. I almost wished I hadn't killed him, though you can't second-guess things like that in the heat of battle.

What the hell was a 'breed doing there during the day? And in a scurf hole?

"I didn't know you did murders without a nightside connection."

"*All* the murders I personally commit have nightside connections, Theron. Don't burn my bacon, Saul bought those pans." I tried to lunge up to my feet, sank down on the couch with an internal curse, holding my head. Dehydration pounded in my brain like a padded hammer rolled in glue and ground glass.

"Why he cooks on copper bottoms I will *never* understand, not when there's perfectly good stainless steel around. There's orange juice on the table, Jill. Drink the whole thing, it'll help with the headache."

"How do you know I have a headache?"

"You're usually much nastier than this. Not up to your usual speed right now."

I half-groaned, spotted the glass pitcher Saul usually made ice tea in. There was a clean glass set right next to it, which told me Theron had washed dishes. "Fuck you, Were."

"Nice try, but doesn't have your usual snap. Drink something, will you?"

I poured myself a huge dollop of orange juice, couldn't resist. "Where's the bourbon?"

He was having none of it. "Do the non-nightside murders have anything to do with someone using plain lead to kill you?"

"I don't know, Theron. The bigger mystery is a fucking hellbreed in the middle of a scurf nest." *Not to mention the nest was in a place where no scurf would build it, and . . . Jesus.* It made my head hurt to think about it.

No assumptions, milaya. *Never assume.* Mikhail's voice, the injunction repeated so many times it was worn into memory like a groove on a record. *Shortest way to get ass blown off sideways.*

"So more than one person is trying to kill you."

"Christ, I'd hope so. If this is only *one* enemy I'm going to turn in my hunter's union card." The banter came naturally, punctuated by the sounds of cooking; it was so much like home I could have cried.

"You guys have a union?" The sizzling ended, and he came out of the kitchen with two plates. Fragrant steam rose. I'd never had any of *his* cooking before, but Weres— especially Were males—are very domestic. It was likely to be good.

Missing Saul rose like a hand clamped around my throat. I took a long draft of orange juice, acid stinging my chapped lips and dry tongue. It took a physical effort to stop before I drank myself sick on it, but I put the glass down only three-quarters empty. "Of course not. Did you make any coffee? How long have I been out?"

He set a plate down in front of me. "I'll go turn the coffeepot on, and you've been out about fourteen hours. Missed a whole night of fun and games, cleaning up scurf stragglers and all."

Shit. "Anyone call? Other than Saul, that is?"

"Your pager buzzed once or twice. Otherwise, quiet as a mouse."

I spotted said pager on the table, scooped it up, and blinked through the layer of blurring closing over my eyes. The plate held scrambled eggs, crispy bacon, and a mountain of grits holding up a pat of butter. It looked *good.* "Thanks."

"I'm running backup on you until this is over." His lean dark face didn't change, but his eyes flashed orange before settling back into their ordinary darkness. "Saul's request. So don't argue."

"What exactly did you tell him?" Monty had paged me twice, Carp once, and the last number sent a cold finger tracing down my spine.

Goddammit.

The Were shrugged. "I told him you were fine, and sleeping, and that we have scurf. Told him you were playing everything by the book and there was no need to worry, but I'd keep an eye on you. He asked me to not just keep one eye but both on you, since you have—and I quote—a habit of getting yourself beaten to a pulp. He calls it your particular brand of charm."

"I do love my work," I muttered, and set the pager down, exchanging it for the plate. Everything else could wait. I was *hungry.* "Did you mention coffee, or not?"

"I did. I *didn't* tell Saul someone tried to assassinate you." One shoulder lifted, dropped, Theron's particularly ambiguous shrug added to a raised eyebrow. "If he finds out, we'll both be in dutch. So you'd better get cracking."

I couldn't answer, I had a mouth full of grits. But I glared at him, and Theron snorted, set his plate down, and went to turn the coffeepot on.

Damn Weres.

My eyes snagged on the pager again. But first things first.

I peeled up the remains of my trouser leg and looked at my calf. There was an angry red chunk taken out of the muscle, already scabbed-over. It *looked* nasty, but the flesh around it wasn't inflamed. There was no telltale blue network of viral spreading around its edges. It was just a bit of missing meat, about the size of a mouth, and I couldn't tell which shape the final scar would take. It was healing far slower than anything else, and the scab on my head was still throbbing as I chewed.

I pushed the shredded leather down, smoothed it over my leg. Let out a heavy, only half-relieved sigh. Took another bite, ignoring the way it turned to ashes in my mouth. The orange juice started going down easier once I had some food in me.

Why would Perry be calling me now? *Especially* now, with someone trying to kill me and scurf in town? It was too neat a coincidence not to be suspicious, coming from him.

And with a hellbreed bursting in on a bunch of scurf. A skunk-haired 'breed who didn't look familiar. Well, I didn't know *every* hellbreed in town. That would be impossible.

But still.

I weighed the idea of going into the Monde Nuit to ask Perry a few questions—preferably up close, personally, with a few silver-loaded bullets—and shivered. Took a huge bite of bacon, chewed mechanically, and sighed as the coffeemaker started to gurgle and Theron came out. He didn't make his bacon like Saul did, but it was still crispy and good, and he'd added cheese to the eggs.

"There's more when you're finished with that plate," he said, settling himself on the couch and picking up his own plate. "Want to tell me what's really going on?"

"If I knew, I would. Whoever's bringing in scurf probably wants to kill Weres as well as me."

"Things have been awful quiet lately. I should have

known that would change." He stretched out his long legs and got down to the serious business of eating. "Eat up, Kismet. When are you gonna slow down and start eating properly?"

"Why waste time on that when I could be killing hell-breed?" I shoveled in another mouthful of grits. I *also* waited for him to get the last word in, as usual, but he didn't.

Jesus. Miracles do *happen.*

13

$\mathcal{M}$onty was out of his office. I left a message on his voicemail and dialed Carp's cell, popping the last bit of buttered toast in my mouth as I dropped down to sit on my bed, taking a deep inhale of the mixed smell of hunter, leather, and Were that reminded me again of Saul. My hair dripped. I'd taken a few minutes to reattach all the loose charms, braiding some in with red thread, tying others close to the scalp, and shaking my head to hear the reassuring jingle.

It rang twice. "Carper," he snarled, the sound of open car windows roaring behind him.

"It's Jill. You bellowed?"

A full five seconds of silence, and the wind-noise cut down. He must have rolled up his window. "I need to see you. Somewhere private."

Well, miracles never cease. "I'm a married woman, Carp. What's up?"

"No shit, Kismet. It's serious, and I *need* to see you.

Now." Did he actually sound *nervous?* It wasn't like him at all.

I juggled everything in my head, sighed. "Is it a case?"

"It's the Kutchner case."

My heart gave a bounce, my innards quivered, and I let out a short sound that might have been a curse if I hadn't swallowed the last half of it with my mostly chewed toast. *Now this is really too much, Carp. Goddammit.* "Where?"

"You know Picaro's, on Fourth?"

It was downtown, a little hole in the wall bar. I was going to have to wear my replacement trenchcoat. "I can be there in half an hour. Care to drop me a clue?"

"Not without seeing you. Try to be inconspicuous."

I'm a hunter, Carp. I could be standing right next to you and you wouldn't know, if I wanted it that way. "I'm bringing a friend."

"Come alone."

You know, I would if people weren't trying cut me in half with machine-gun fire or sic scurf on me. A shiver of reaction cooled along my skin, the scar a hard quiescent knot. "Can't. Don't worry, it's one of my people."

"Fine." Bad-tempered as usual, he hung up, but not before I heard the click of a lighter and a sharp inhale.

I hope he's not driving, smoking, and *juggling a cell phone.* I laid the phone back in its charger. "What the *hell* is going on?"

The empty air of my bedroom gave no answers. I heard Theron humming as he did dishes, rattling and clinking and sounding so much like Saul tears rose in my throat again.

Jesus. How was it possible to miss someone this much?

I touched the soiled leather of the cuff. He'd left mc three, each custom-made with snapping buckles, fitting close to the wrist. This was the last one. I wondered if he'd thought he was going to be home sooner.

Two Weres were dead. Someone had tried to kill me, or kill them. A whole mess of old, contagious scurf—*and* a hellbreed. Which was like seeing a snake in a beehive— something you don't expect at all.

What did it *mean?*

I don't know. But I'm damn well going to find out.

To get into Picaro's, you have to go down two flights of stairs from a plain door on the blank side of a skyscraper set in a hill. The main part of the bar doubles as a res- taurant, a dim little hole with frayed carpet, sticky-tabled red vinyl booths, and stained-glass lamps hanging every- where.

Picaro's main claim to fame is their two-dollar drink specials, and large cheap breakfasts you can nurse a hang- over on. Of course, they're nothing compared to a Were's cooking, but you take what you can get.

I was actually even contemplating a second breakfast as I slid into the booth opposite Carper, my replacement trench creaking as it folded. There were deep shadows under the deet's blue eyes, and he'd taken off his tweed jacket. An actual *tweed* jacket, for Christ's sake. He looked like an English professor in mufti, except for the shoulder holster and the flat oily stare of a cop who's seen too much. He was also scruffy, sandy stubble standing out on his chin and the flat planes of his cheeks. Carp's face is built like a skewed skyscraper, all angles that should work together but don't. He's handsome in the untraditional way of a character actor.

Theron dropped into the booth right next to me, and Carp opened his big mouth.

"Jesus. Are you dating *another* one of those fur rugs?"

I know you like ruffling Saul's fur, but this is different. I winced, and opened my mouth to reply. The Were beat me to it.

Theron gave him a wide, toothy, sunny smile. "Maybe she just likes a little more than skinboys can give, Officer."

For Christ's sake. Save me from males and their pissing contests. "It's *Detective,* Theron. And you're looking at my temporary backup, Carp. Which means he's deputized, and technically fellow law enforcement. So quit yanking his chain and tell me what's on your tiny little mind. Sunlight's wasting." *And I have other business to handle. Like finding out who's trying to kill me, and why. If I knew one, I'd know the other.*

Carp cupped his coffee in both palms, studying Theron. His gaze flicked to me, and he let out a loose, gusty sigh. The waitress came back, stepping into our armed truce with a bored "whaddalya have?"

I asked for orange juice and two orders of bacon, extra-crispy. Theron politely declined.

The place was deserted except for the bar, where a blue haze of cigarette smoke whirled slowly. A few anonymous male shapes sat in the cloudbank, and the waitress became a ghost among them as she headed for the kitchen.

I touched the fork laid at my place—cheap metal, poorly stamped. "So why don't you want anyone seeing you with me? Afraid people might start to talk?" I meant it as light banter, but Carp's face immediately set itself hard like he'd sucked on a lemon.

He reached under the table. Theron stiffened, an infinitely small movement, and I wanted to roll my eyes. Carp's hand came up holding nothing but his badge, which he flipped open and set on the table between us.

"I'm Internal Affairs." He said it baldly, like it was a bad taste in his mouth. Maybe it was. "I had a hell of a time getting away this morning, but I had to talk to you. What were you doing at the Kutchner widow's place, Jill?"

I studied him for a few moments. *Internal Affairs? No wonder you're paranoid.* Still, Carp was a good cop with a finely-tuned sense of the weird; he knew when to call me in and get out of my way.

He *also* taunted Saul mercilessly and came off as a cracker asshole sometimes. Nobody's perfect.

"Marv was Monty's partner back in the day, and the suicide didn't look right. So Monty asked me to poke." I rubbed the fork's surface, wishing it was a knifehilt. But Carp was already jumpy. "I have to say, it's looking less and less like suicide and more like someone's hiding something."

"Only a few million dollars and thirty dead people at last count." Carp leaned back against creaking vinyl. "Kutchner was dirty, Kismet. As dirty as they come."

Huh? I replayed the three sentences inside my head. Yes, Carper had just said what I thought he'd said. "But Monty—"

He dropped another bomb. "Montaigne's under review. I don't like it any more than you do. Do you think he's involved?"

Monty? Hell, no. "Why would he ask me to take a look at it?" I picked up the fork, tapped it on the tabletop. "Would there be any reason for someone to try to kill me because I'm poking around in this?"

Theron shifted uneasily, staring off into the distance. He looked bored.

Carp shrugged. "Let me put it this way, I wish I was wearing some fucking Kevlar assplugs. This is *big*, Kiss."

The waitress returned with a stack of pancakes and eggs for Carp, filled his coffee cup, and plunked down my orange juice. "Be a sec on the bacon," she announced to the air over my head, before shuffling off.

Yeah, thanks. I got that. "Are you going to take it from the top, or are you going to be all cryptic? This isn't the only iron I have in the fire."

"Actually, I was going to ask you to help me." He stared at his plate like it contained a pile of snot. I got the idea maybe Carp had lost his appetite. "Since you're already involved, might as well."

I so do not have time for this. But I heard the creak of a nylon rope rubbing against a ceiling beam, and saw a mask of bruising on a dead man's terrified face. "What are we dealing with? Use small words, and speed it up."

He stuck his fork into the pile of eggs, worked it back and forth. "You remember a barrio case, about three years ago? Two illegal immigrants found in a cheap-ass room, kidneys gone, blood on the walls?"

A quick fishing trip through Memory Lane produced

zilch. "Nope. Unless something my-style hinky was involved, I don't."

"I remember," Theron said quietly. "The *Herald* did a long series on organ thievery. An all-time high nationwide, they said. Whole underground economy."

Cold fingers walked up my spine again. The last huge paranormal incident in the city had touched on black-market organ trade, but only briefly. By the time I'd unraveled it, everyone was already dead, the organs were sold—and I'd almost become a host for a Chaldean Elder God.

I still have nightmares from that. Just like the hundreds of other cases I have nightmares about. At least if I'm dreaming about it I know it's over and done with. "Sullivan and the Badger were on that, weren't they?"

"They got yanked. Sullivan thinks someone high-up is involved, since there were more deaths than could be accounted for even with whatever happened with those hooker murders you were chasing." Carp had turned milk-pale. Those homicide sites had probably figured in a few of his nightmares too. "But still, they were pulled off it and the files were put in a deep freeze. We think whoever's profiting mostly strips wetbacks of their kidneys, because they're a transient population."

I nodded. Illegal immigrants are victims in more ways than one. Coming to look for the American dream, they usually end up raped one way or another. If they're lucky, they get more of a wage than they would back home while it happens.

If they're *un*lucky, they become just another statistic. Or not even that.

I blew out a long frustrated breath. "Okay. So what does this have to do with—"

"I think there's cops finding illegals for stripping, and cleaning up after it happens, a real body farm. It's a safe bet the cash is laundered, but I don't know how. I don't think Marv Kutchner ate his Glock. He was in too deep and making too much money. That shitty little suburban house was small potatoes. He had plans to retire to a nice tropical paradise."

"Who doesn't?" I was only half sarcastic. And another question arrived, flirting at the corner of my consciousness. *I never found out who they were selling the organs to. I assumed it was out of town, since I didn't find anything here afterward and—*

There I was, caught *assuming*. There was always a market for organs. I hadn't thought the Sorrows would foul their own nest, but I'd been kept running around after other cases, chasing my tail. By the time I'd caught wind of their operation they were winding down. They could very well have been supplying brokers inside the city; the distribution network for organs was probably even better-funded than the one for drugs. Where there's a will—and a profit—there's always a way to get a product to someone who needs it.

If they can pay.

The waitress came and plunked down my bacon, or some charred sticks that resembled something that might have been bacon in the distant past. "Anything else?"

"No thanks," Theron said promptly, and we waited until she disappeared into the smoke-filled bar.

I wondered if she smoked—I didn't think she'd need to, breathing that fug all day. *So this could have been going on for longer. Or it could be the tail-end of the Sorrows' operation. Too many variables.* "So if it wasn't suicide, why did Kutchner die?"

"Jacinta Kutchner was an accountant. Her office was tossed as well as her bedroom. We think she had a set of cooked and uncooked books, either in the office or in the safe in her closet. Yesterday a blue bit it—"

"Officer Winchell," I supplied helpfully. "Was he implicated too?"

A vintage Carper shrug, his shoulder holster peeping out. He didn't look surprised at my supplying the name. "Only up to his eyeballs. Would it surprise you to know Winchell and Kutchner's grieving widow were having an affair?"

Huh. That puts a new shine on things. I picked up a slice of charcoaled bacon. "You do such fine police work, Carp. What do you need me for?"

"The trail dead-ends with Marv's retirement fund disappearing. All half-a-million of it. I think the widow was about to blow the whistle on the whole dirty deal, or she double-crossed someone and hid the money. Maybe she even loved her husband, I don't know. But without her and without the books—and without Marv and Winchell—we have exactly what we started out with. Dead wetbacks and a whole lot of nothing."

And here I was getting all bent out of shape over victims. The thought was too bitter to let out of my mouth. "That doesn't tell me what you want."

"I want to know how far up this goes." He blinked at his food as if he couldn't believe he'd ordered it, took a long draft of coffee. "I have to tell you, Kiss, I'm willing to break a few laws to do it. And you're one of us, but you don't have a lot of the same . . . limits . . . that I do."

"Someone tried to kill me the other day." *Jesus. Was that only yesterday?* "They didn't use silver-coated ammo. Which leads me to believe someone knows Monty's called me in and feels just a wee bit threatened."

"You think?" Carp went pale. He was sweating. If it was concern for me it was awful cute. "Marv and Winchell weren't the only ones to end up dead over this. Six months ago Pedro Ayala over in Vice stumbled across something, gave me a call, and turned up dead less than four hours later before I could meet him. It's filed as a random gang-related shooting, since Ay did the gang beat. He was tight with a few of the old-school 51s, their territory's a chunk in the barrio near the Plaza. He used to run with the old-sters before he turned all law-abiding. I can't get any of them to talk to me about him."

I vaguely remembered Ayala from rookie orientation—slim, dark, and intense. They blur together inside my head sometimes. All those cops, each and every one of them passing through my hands before they're allowed out on the streets.

You'd think I'd feel better about that. "Jesus."

"Yeah. They won't talk to me or to Bernie—his partner—but it doesn't seem possible that one of them pulled the trigger on him. He was out of *la vida* since he was sixteen, but he once or twice brought in some of the 51s as material witnesses during a turf war."

I let out a low whistle. That was a not-inconsiderable achievement. "Did they walk afterward?"

"When the killing stopped. Ay was a good cop. He didn't deserve lungs full of lead. The coroner said it probably took him ten minutes to suffocate on his own blood."

I could relate. *Jesus.* I poked at the bacon some more, nibbled at a bit of it, set it down. "You want me to go into the barrio and poke around the 51s."

Theron made another restless movement. But he held his peace, which was more than I would have expected.

Carp held my gaze, did not look away. "I'm asking for a hot chunk of lead if I go down there. Monty's already called you in, Jill."

He was serious. The trouble was, *I* was asking for more than one hot chunk of lead if I went into the barrio. The Weres run herd out there and keep everything under control. I *know* the streets and alleys—there's not a slice of my city I don't know by now—but going into the depths of Santa Luz's *other* dark half isn't something to be done lightly if your skin is my color.

I can't spend more time on this. There's scurf, goddammit. And the widow and Winchell weren't victims in the usual sense.

But still. The rope made a small sound inside my head, a human being reduced to a clock pendulum, and I knew I couldn't let this rest. Something else was bothering me about the whole goddamn deal, but damned if I could lay a finger on it.

I hate that feeling. It usually means something is about to take a big bite out of my ass in a very unpleasant way. "All right. Hand over the paper."

His hand slid under the table and came up with a manila file, rubber-banded closed. It was dauntingly thick. "This is what I've got so far. A collection of fucking dead ends. If you can make something of it . . ."

"Dead ends don't mean the same thing to me that they do to you." I pushed the bacon across the table, took the file, and laid a ten down to cover a bit of breakfast. "Keep your head down, Carp. I would hate to lose you just when I've gotten you toilet trained."

His reply was unrepeatable. I slid out of the booth, following Theron's graceful motion. I tipped Carp a salute, he shot me the finger, and we parted, friends as usual.

As soon as we got up the stairs and stepped outside, the Were took in a deep breath, rolling it around his mouth like champagne. "No news," he announced, needlessly. "Maybe that was the main nest, maybe we got them all."

I'm not so sure. They were too old. "I'd feel better if we *knew* instead of guessing." I slid my shades on; the sun was a hammerblow even this early in the morning. "And I'd feel a lot better if we could have ID'd some of the scurf as our missing people." *Good fucking luck doing that, scurf all look the same.* "Or if I could have asked that skunk-haired 'breed some questions."

"*I'd* feel a lot better if you hadn't just volunteered to go down in the barrio." He fixed me with a sidelong stare. "I suppose this is something else I'm not supposed to tell Saul about?"

"I never told you not to tell him anything." I set off for my Impala, parked in a convenient alley some two blocks away. It was going to be another desert scorcher of a day. "I go where I have to, Theron."

"This sounds like a human affair." His tone was carefully neutral.

"So are scurf, if you look at it the right way." Sarcasm dripped from each word. "Don't ride me, Were. I know what I'm doing."

"Easy, hunter. I'm just pointing it out." He didn't crowd me like Saul would have. He didn't smell like Saul, not really. He was just similar enough, his bulk just familiar enough, to remind me of what I was missing.

"Thanks." *You don't have to come along.* But that would be a direct insult, since Theron had appointed himself my backup. It would imply I didn't have any faith in his capacity to defend himself.

Weres are funny about things like that.

He apparently decided he'd pushed me far enough. "When are you going in?"

Well, if I wait for nightfall it will only get more dangerous. But sunlight's best for hunting scurf. "If they find anything while doing sweeps you'll know, right?"

"Of course." He didn't sound offended that I'd asked. "Do you think they're connected?"

A hot breeze came off the river, ruffled my hair. Carp hadn't said anything about me looking torn-up and exhausted. Dim light and some breakfast must have done me some good, though I'd never win any prizes in the looks department. "What?"

"The scurf, and this."

Jesus in a sidecar, I hope not. "I don't know. I'm not assuming they are. There's no visible connection." But he knew as well as I did that I wasn't ruling it out, either.

He digested this. "Something's off. They were too old, and too many of them."

Just what I'd been thinking. "I know. But a hellbreed, busting in on a scurf nest . . ." *There's one small note off here, and it's throwing the entire orchestra out of whack.* "If this gets much deeper I'm going to have to do something drastic."

"Huh." He visibly restrained himself from making a smartass comment. "Like what?"

"Like something unsafe."

"More unsafe than the barrio?"

Visiting Perry makes the barrio look like a cakewalk, Were. "Much, Theron. Now shut up, I need to think."

"*I'll* say you do."

I let it go. A Were sometimes needs the last word. It makes them feel better.

14

Santa Luz's barrio isn't a shantytown, though it has a forest of shacks on the edge between "suburb" and "desert" where even the Weres go in pairs when they have to run through. There is the Plaza Centro, which used to be a railroad station but is now a *mercado* with a giant mezzanine, the center of the barrio's seethe. There are bodegas on every corner, and Catholic or Pentecostal churches sprinkled throughout, sometimes even in abandoned storefronts.

The rest of the barrio is quiet, watchful streets. Violence occurs pretty rarely in most of its sprawl, but it's always a breath away. The feeling is like a storm hanging overhead, ready to toss thunderbolts at the slightest provocation. A crackling edge of expectation blurs the air, and your entire skin turns into a sensitive canvas, ready to catch any breath, any faint tingle that might warn you a half-second before a bullet punches through your meat.

The 51s run in the south part of the barrio, in a wedge-shaped territory with its thin end pointing at the Plaza

Centro and the wider, trailing hind end spreading almost halfway through the closest slice of shackville—what bigots in my fair city mostly call Cholo Central or, in slightly more politically correct terms, "that goddamn sinkhole."

I surveyed the pockmarked sloping street. Ranchero music blared from the bodega on the corner, *cholos* lounged on every front porch. Two driveways down, a vintage orange Nova was up on blocks with someone's head under the hood, two men in flannel shirts with only the top button buttoned offering advice while clutching cold bottles of Corona. *Frijoles* and sweat, beer and cumin, chili sauce and hot burning wax from novenas all mixed together, with the tang of poverty underneath—a bald edge of desperation, marijuana fumes, and old food.

Theron slammed his door. Down here he looked normal—the darker tone of his skin and the strangeness of his bone structure became *mestizo* instead of just-plain-brown-person. "You sure you want to do this?"

I shrugged. "I go where I have to. Why don't you put that nose of yours to good use and find me a 51?"

"This whole street is theirs, hunter. But we're going to see Ramon."

"Head honcho?" I didn't ask how he knew all this he was a Were; this was his part of town. Most Weres in Santa Luz live either on the fringe of the barrio or in a narrow corridor between it and Mayfair Hill where the houses have been in the same families, packs, and prides for generations.

"Lieutenant. He'll give you a safe-conduct if you act nice and polite. Let me do the talking."

"I wouldn't have it any other way." I slid my shades on, silver chiming in my hair. The sensation of eyes on

me was palpable, my hackles rising and the scar prickling with dense wet heat. Almost-living heat, like a flower
opening under sunlight.

It's not growing. Don't even think about that.

Instead, I thought about the black-market trade in organs. I would have to meet up with Sullivan and the Badger if I had time, and if I could do it without endangering
them. I thought about why a hellbreed would burst in on
a scurf nest in the middle of a fight, and the thing that
occurred to me was so plain and simple I stopped in my
tracks for a good five seconds.

"Jill?" Theron looked over his shoulder. Morning sunlight touched off a furnace of highlights in his dark hair.
"Everything copacetic?"

"Scurf don't attack hellbreed. Their ichor doesn't
carry any hemoglobin or the right proteins for the viral
agents."

He didn't think my revelation was worth the name.
"No shit."

I suddenly wished for Saul. He would have understood the way my thoughts were wending. "Which means
someone might have laid the scurf like bait in a trap. A
nightsider who's not only able to handle them, but who
knows I'd go after them with Weres."

"Yeah?" Theron folded his arms. *Time's a-wasting,* his
body language said.

"So someone is probably *profiting* from the scurf.
Nobody would want to kill me in the middle of a scurf
hole just because I'm annoying. Someone is making some
money, and there *could* be a connection to this other case.
Profit's a strong incentive. And what makes scurf so dangerous?"

"They're contagious," he said, flatly. But his head tilted a little, listening instead of dismissing.

"*And* cannibalistic. What better way to get rid of bodies?" I hated to assume these two cases were linked, but it wasn't out of the ballpark. And part of not assuming, as every hunter is trained to realize, is also not ruling out the possible. "Murder attempts from nightsiders and normals when I'm working a nightside *and* a normal case means they could very well be connected."

"It's a lot of assuming." Theron scratched at his temple, thinking. His dark eyes had gone distant.

"If a better idea comes along, I'll latch onto it." I fell into step beside him as he set off again, heading for a ratty adobe house sandwiched between a gas station and a ramshackle tenement taking up most of a block. Its sliver of lawn was weedy but neat, and the sidewalk in front of the chain-link gate had been freshly swept and sprinkled with Florida water, if the ghost of orange perfume in the air was any indication.

Interesting. But of course, down in the barrio you find all sorts of . . . interesting . . . things.

Theron opened the gate for me, and the feeling of being watched intensified. My hands itched to touch a gun butt, but I carefully kept them loose and easy. I know I look odd—wandering around in a black ankle-length leather trenchcoat in the middle of a Southwestern summery simmer isn't the best way to appear harmless. Plus there was the silver in my long dark curling hair, throwing back darts of light. And the pale cast to my skin wasn't guaranteed to blend me in either.

The porch creaked under my boots and Theron's weight. He opened the screen door and knocked, and

I heard stealthy little sounds inside the house, my ears pricking. All human.

The thought that I had my back to the street touched my nape with gooseflesh. It was *too* quiet, eerie-quiet, under the ranchero blast from up the street. The kind of deep silence right before a gunshot and screaming.

The door opened, and a young *cholo* with a fedora, a white dress shirt, red suspenders, and a pair of natty sharp-creased chinos eyed us. He had a face that could have come off a codex, it wouldn't have looked out-of-place under a quetzal-feather headdress. Dark eyes met mine, flicked down my body, and dismissed me, moving over to Theron. "Eh, *gato, que ondo?*"

"*Que ondo,* homes." Theron actually grinned, showing a lot of teeth. "Ramon in?"

"Who's *la puta?*"

"This is *la señora bruja grande de Santa Luz, cabron.* Watch your mouth. Is Ramon in, or do I get to go to the cantina?"

"*Bruja grande?*" The boy snorted. He peered at my face again, I slid my shades a touch down my nose and gave him the double-barrel impact of my mismatched stare.

The reaction was gratifying. Sudden chemical fear glazed his smell of healthy young man, and he forked the evil eye at me. "*Madre de Dios,*" he muttered, and looked hurriedly away, at Theron.

"Ramon," the Were said, quietly, irresistibly. "It's business."

The *cholo* backed away from the door. "*Mi casa, su casa, gato.*" But the sweat breaking out on his forehead said different.

Don't worry, kid, I'm harmless. At least, to you. I

didn't say it, just followed Theron over the threshold and into the quiet cool of a real adobe. The floor was tile, and my steelshod heels clicked on it.

"Iron," the kid said, in the entryway's gloom. My eyes adjusted to see his swift gesture, index fingers out, thumbs up, a short stabbing motion.

"Come *on*." Theron gave short shrift to the notion, probably guessing there was no way in hell I'd hand my weapons over to this kid. "You know the iron mean less than nothing. Who the hell are you, anyway?"

"Paco. Ramon's *mi tio*."

"Then go fetch him, Paquito. I don't like waiting." Theron still hadn't put his teeth away. He also seemed to get a few inches taller, his shoulders broadening, and a slight crackle told me he was puffing up for my benefit.

Gangs are all about face, really. Paco was in that dangerous stage where he was still a young *wannabe* and not a full-fledged *is*. Which meant if Theron made this a pissing match, the boy might feel compelled to throw him some sauce.

The prospect was amusing, but I didn't have time to fuck around. Sunlight was wasting and someone was planning on trying to kill me again, I could just *feel* it.

Theron stepped forward, looming over Paco, still showing his teeth. The boy flinched, covered it up well, and retreated up two swift steps before turning on his heel and hurrying into the adobe's gloom.

"I take it these are friends of yours." My fingers relaxed, and I controlled a sharp flare of irritation. My heart rate had picked up, walloping along harder than it should. Theron shut the door with a click and leaned against the wall, all hipshot Were grace.

"We like to know who's doing what out here. You okay?"

"Peachy." Adrenaline coated my tongue with copper. I was all twitched-up. Dying a couple of times a day will do that to you, redline your responses even to garden-variety aggressiveness. As hard as hunters are trained to deliver maximum violence in minimum time, we're also trained to clamp down on the chemical soup of the body's dumb meat responding inappropriately.

The scab on the back of my head had come away in two graceless chunks in the shower, blood clots large enough to give even me pause. I still felt them peeling free of my scalp, bits of dead tissue clinging to my fingernails under the hot water.

Focus, Jill. Now's not the time to go postal. Save it for later. Save it for hellbreed or scurf. Relax. I took in a deep cool breath, aware of the prickle of reaction-sweat along the curve of my lower back, calming my heartbeat with an effort.

Mercifully, Theron let it go. I slid my shades back up my nose. The dimness gave me no trouble, even through dark lenses my vision was acute enough to pick out the clean tiles, the pattern in the plaster on the wall, and the way Theron tilted his head slightly, testing the air.

I smelled Ramon before I saw him. The cologne was musky, mixing with the smell of healthy male and dominance every charismatic man exhales. I also smelled metal and cordite, and my palms itched for a gun.

Settle down, Jill. He's only human, after all. He couldn't even break you out in a sweat.

The voice of reason didn't help. I calmed myself with

an effort. The scar prickled, sensitive to the tightening of my aura.

Cholos run to two types: beanpole and brick shithouse. Ramon was the latter, wide and chunky, the 51 colors showing on his do-rag and knotted around his left biceps. He had a broad cheerful face and eyes as cold as left-over coffee. He also had a cannon of a .45 stuck in his waistband and looked about ready to blow his own balls off with pure *machismo*. "Eh." He greeted Theron with a lazy salute. His gaze barely flicked over me, lingered on my breasts under my T-shirt, completely dismissed the guns and knives, and returned to the Were. "Paquito's a fuckin' idiot. You wanna beer, *ese?*"

"Love one. This is Kismet. *Bruja grande.*" Theron was making it, in essence, impossible for Ramon to dismiss me.

The gangbanger eyed me. I eyed him right back through the shades. My heart rate settled down. The body sometimes likes to pitch a fit, thinking it can stave off death or injury by working itself up into the redline *after* the fact.

Still, you can't blame the body. It's wiser than the idiot pushing it through the valley of danger.

Ramon said nothing. He was still deciding. I tilted the shades down a bit and gave him my second-best level glare.

He took it well, only paling and stepping back once. The scar prickled under its cuff, responding to the sudden fog of blood-colored fear tainting the air.

It's not getting bigger, Jill. Goddamn it.

Theron laid an easy hand on my shoulder. "She'd probably like a beer too."

Ramon said something under his breath, probably

a prayer. When I didn't disappear or scream in pain, he shrugged. "C'mon back, then. Whatchu here for?"

That was my cue to open my mouth. "Pedro Ayala." I left it open-ended.

Ramon took another half-step back, his gaze sharpening and his hand making an abortive movement for the .45, stopping in midair and dropping to his side. "What for? He dead."

I didn't relax, but I was glad he hadn't put his hand near the gun. "Whoever killed him is fucking with me and mine." I didn't mean it to come out quite so baldly. "You're not the only people who take care of your own."

Gangbangers, if they're smart, understand loyalty. This one didn't look like an idiot, and he was capable of thinking twice. Both good signs, but you never can tell.

Ramon studied me for another few moments, no sign of warming in his cold-coffee stare. "Pedro was one of yours?"

He was a cop. That makes him one of mine. "He was. I'm after whoever unloaded on him, *señor*." I let it hang for five long seconds. "I would *also* like a beer."

The gangbanger's eyes didn't get any warmer, but his shoulders dropped. He eyed me from top to bottom again, then shifted his inspection to Theron, who spread his hands and shrugged in the particular way Weres have— not volunteering an opinion, but giving polite consent to listen to whatever the questioner wants to say next.

My fingers stopped itching for a gun, and the scar quit prickling as his fear stopped drenching the close air of the foyer.

Ramon visibly decided it might not hurt to be sociable. "C'mon into the kitchen, *bruja*. I tell you about Ay."

15

*I*t was a productive half-hour.

I ended up with a bandana in the 51 colors, a short lesson in how to wear it and where in the barrio *not* to go when I had it on, and a full rundown on Pedro Ayala—the scene of his death, and who rumor said saw him gunned down and where to find *them*. Ramon promised to make a few calls so I was greeted with courtesy and not a hail of bullets if I went from door to door in 51 territory asking about a murdered cop.

It was more than I'd hoped for. The beer didn't hurt, either.

Even my Impala wasn't stripped at the curb, which showed someone was watching when we trooped into Ramon's house. It was a good thing, too.

There were three *cholos* in flannel despite the heat, watching the car. They looked amused when I went around to the driver's side instead of Theron. Women's lib hasn't penetrated much into the *barrio*. Still, none of the *vatos* hanging around would dare dishonor or disregard their *abuelita*. If they had one.

I almost thought we would get out of there without a fight.

"Eh *gato*," one of them called. "Who's *mamacita puta?*" A long stream of gutter Spanish followed, asking in effect how much I cost for a few acts that might have been funny if the *cholo* in question could have gotten it up at all.

Yes, I hate men catcalling at me. It doesn't precisely *bother* me—I quit walking the flesh gallery of Lucado Street a long time ago—but I dislike it so intensely my hands itch for a gun each time.

"Does everyone in the barrio know you're a Were?" I said over the car's roof, controlling both the urge to drop down into the driver's seat and the persistent itching for a weapon in my hands. A thin scrim of sweat filmed my forehead, prickled along my lower back.

Control, Jill. It's just a mouthy little boy. Don't go off the deep end.

"Not everyone." Theron showed his teeth again. He was just as on edge as I was. "But they know how to see us down here. *Gringos* are stupid."

Gee, thanks. Sour humor took the edge off my temper. "Yeah." I heard the footsteps behind me and didn't tense, but my hand did move a bare half-inch, ready to draw and fire if necessary.

They're civilians, Jill. You can give them a few free shots and you'll still come out ahead.

But even civilians can get a lucky headshot in. And I had no desire to die again today. I turned on my heel and heard Theron take in a long sharp breath, as if bracing himself.

For a moment I was almost angry. But then, I couldn't blame him if he was nervous. I was pretty goddamn nervous myself, and hunters are meant to be unpredictable.

The kid standing on the sidewalk couldn't have been more than fourteen, but his dark eyes were empty as a vacant lot, an emptiness I haven't seen on many non-nightsiders. Acne pocked his lean face, and I couldn't tell how long his hair was, since it was slicked down and trapped in a hairnet knotted on his dewy brown forehead. He wore a shining-white wifebeater over a torso all scrawny muscle, and I knew he was carrying just from the way he moved.

He stopped, considering me, and a chill rippled along the edge of my skin. The scar prickled.

Even among normal humans with no scent of the nightside, there are killers.

This one stood easy and hipshot, his dead eyes flicking down my body once, not with a regular man's ticking-off of breasts, ass, and desirability. No, this young man looked like he was evaluating my ability to interfere with him, and coming to an answer that had nothing to do with my gender.

Score one for a surprise in the barrio, Jill. I eyed him, and my hand eased a little closer to a gun.

He didn't move. Didn't even shift his weight, but a line of tension unreeled between us.

His voice had broken, thank God. Because if he'd had a reedy little whine with a Spanglish accent, I'm not sure I wouldn't have smiled from the sheer lunacy of the juxtaposition. And *that* might have gone badly.

"You lookin' for Ay, *señora?*" A light tenor, not piping. He hooked his thumbs in the pockets of his well-pressed chinos and his mouth turned into a thin line.

Say what? Word travels fast down here. "Pedro Ayala's dead, *señor.*" I kept my tone respectful enough and throttled the uneasy smile once again. It died hard, my lips wanting to twitch. "I'm looking to serve whoever did him in."

A spark of interest died a quick smothered death under his ruler-straight eyebrows. "Why you wanna do that?"

I took a firmer hold on my temper. *Easy, Jill. He's just a kid.* "Why do you want to know?"

His thin shoulders went back and his chin lifted. The sun gilded his thin arms and a chest that stood a good chance of being sunken, and the sullen fury passing over his face was shocking in its intensity—and just as shocking when the emotion fled and he was back to flatline.

Of all things, he unhooked his right hand and offered it to me. "Gilberto Rosario Gonzalez-Ayala." The words were a monotone. "Ay was *mi hermano.*"

Brother, huh? My nose itched and the heat, while not enough to make me sweat, was still oppressive. My entire back prickled with vulnerability. "They tell me he was shot in the lungs and drowned, *señor.*" I kept the words just as flat as his. "Whoever did him is doing others just as bad. Worse, even. I'm going to stop it." I slowly clasped his hand, careful not to squeeze too hard. Hellbreed-strong fingers can make for a goddamn uncomfortable handshake.

He was under no such compunction, bearing down with surprising strength. His entire arm tensed. "Then you better watch your back, *chiquita.*"

That's enough. I doubled the pressure and watched his eyes widen as something creaked in his hand. It sounded like a bone. I tilted my head down, looking over the rim of the shades, and let my lips curl up in a wide, bright, sunny, and utterly false smile. "Thanks for the warning." A deliberate pause. *"Señor."*

It might have been a misstep, but I don't like threats *or* veiled warnings. You get them every day in this line of work, and pretty soon the gloss gets worn off. Yawn.

Now those dead dark eyes had lit up, and the change made him boyish. Under the acne and the hairnet, that is. "Ain't no warning. It's fact."

I let him take his hand back. *Get into a pissing contest with a hunter, gangboy? Not the best way to stay breathing.* "I'm sure of that, Gilberto." One thing about living in Santa Luz for a long time, my accent was dead-on. *"Gracias."*

His thin face wrinkled up into a smile that might have actually been handsome if not for the boils of acne. He would scar badly, this boy, and with those dead eyes . . .

"Call me Gil, *chiquita.*" Thin brown fingers flicked, he lit himself a cigarette. "You do who did for Ay, you come down to *nuestra casa* here. I give you beer."

Thanks, kid. Like you're old enough to drink. "I'll keep it in mind." Making friends and influencing people among all walks of life, that's your friendly neighborhood hunter.

"Jill?" Theron, his tone halfway between *what the hell are you doing* and *can we go now please.*

"Let's roll." I dropped down into the driver's seat and slammed the door. A faint breath of cherry tobacco lingered in the car—Saul smoked Charvils. Right now I was half wishing for one myself. "Where next, *gato?*"

"Christ, don't you start too." He closed his door with fussy precision. "Go west, we'll cut across on Antilles. Isn't that where he got shot?"

"Antilles and Tabasco, the 3100 block. Good idea to check it out, at least. Put your seat belt on." I buckled myself in and twisted the key in the ignition, the engine roused with a sweet purr that turned a few heads. Sunlight skipped heat off the road, the buildings all leaning tired and sweaty under the assault. I seconded that emotion— one beer was not *nearly* enough, the way things were going. *Go ahead, Theron. Say something. I dare you.*

He responded with all the valor of discretion. "Well, that's not 51-friendly, over there. Put that bandana away."

We crossed out of 51 territory in ten minutes, and I had a mounting sense of unease, precognition not specific enough to really mean anything. About twelve blocks later I realized the popping, pinging sounds were someone shooting at my *car.* By then a lucky shot had taken out a tire and the entire contraption—tons of metal—was jigging and jiving like a hellbreed jacked full of silver.

Oh no. No. Skidding, skipping, a flapping noise as the tire gave up the ghost and I struggled against the sudden drag on the steering wheel, time slowing down as if dipped in cold molasses. The engine leapt, straining against inertia, and things got *very interesting.*

I steered into the skid, mashing the accelerator to the floor to get us out of the firezone if possible, and heard Theron's coughing roar as the car bucked once more and lifted, physics taking her revenge in a big way. The silvery crinkle of glass shattering married to the crunch of metal folding in ways it didn't want to. The world blanked out, down was up and up was down, for a long moment. I was picked up, shaken, tossed a few different ways at once, and thrown into that blank spot between normal life and disaster for an endless moment of disorienting darkness—and roared out on the other side in an explosion of too-bright color and sharp pain.

The edged reek of spilled gasoline burst in my sensitive nose. I blinked something wet and warm out of my eyes.

At least I'm right-side-up. Or am I?

It took me a second to figure out which way gravity was dragging, the blood in my eyes streaking in fat globules down my cheeks. *Must be a head wound, they're messy. Bleed a lot.*

More pinging and popping sounds, my body moving instinctively, seeking what cover it could, *that's gas I smell, move, Jill, get the fuck out of here, Theron, where's Theron?*

Broken glass littered the seats. The Were was gone. I tore myself free of the seat belt and squirmed around the gearshift, its head ripped free of the shaft. The red fuzzy dice Galina had given me had disappeared and the car had rolled, coming to rest right-side-up. *Goddamn. I'm still alive. Again. Go figure.*

I braced my shoulders against the seat and kicked. The jolt slammed my shoulders deeper into glass-strewn upholstery. No dice—the entire car was crumpled, I couldn't bust the door open.

The passenger-side window had been rolled down and

was now an irregular hole. Stink of flammable fluid rose gagging-thick. *Get out of here, Jill. All it takes is a spark.*

I wormed my way toward the window. The pings and whines of bullets still smacked the side of the car. More glass broke. It was a regular fusillade. *Jesus wept. What NOW?*

The choice was to stay where I was and possibly roast if the car went up, or get shot as I wriggled out the window. I froze, half a precious second trickling away through molasses as the body, idiot meat that it is, expressed in the strongest possible terms that it didn't want to get shot again, thank you.

MOVE!

My arms shot out, fingers closing around the edges of the hole, jagged metal slicing deep. I didn't care, hauling myself free, a high keening sound I realized was my own voice, yelling filthy obscenities I probably would have blushed at a few years ago—before I was a hunter.

Now I know how toothpaste feels when it's pushed free of the tube. It's a good thing I'm skinny. I worked my way free while the crackling sounds receded from the forefront of my consciousness. Black smoke belched and the unholy reek of vinyl burning scoured hot water from my eyes. My coat got stuck, was sliced, I wriggled free and fell on concrete, fetching my head a stunning blow. Rolling, trained reflex bringing me up to my feet just as my baby, my beautiful Impala I'd bought from a junkyard and nursed to apple-pie order, exploded.

The shockwave flung me flat, leather scraping the pitted surface of the road and my head snapping back, bouncing as I hit again. I scrambled away from the car, already going in the direction the blast had pushed me.

I picked myself up. My ears were bleeding, thin trickles of evaporating coolness down my neck.

Goddamn. My car.

The rest of the world returned in a rush of diluted noise. A woman was screaming in Spanish, high-pitched babble. Kids were yelling. *Oh God did I hit someone? Hope not. Cover, find cover*—I rolled, heading for the far side of the street, my back wrenching in a quick burst of red pain.

They were still shooting at me, but the bulk of the burning car shielded me from view. It was a small mercy, and as soon as the smoke thinned a little they would have a clear field of fire.

There were acres of cracked sunstruck pavement and no cover. Then Theron landed gracefully, his fingers tented on the concrete as bullets spattered. He grabbed me, shifting his weight, and I *pushed* with the long muscles in my legs, uncoiling in a leap as awkward as it was effective. My back wrenched again, and the scar woke, prickling and roiling as I *pulled* blindly on etheric force, a completely nonphysical movement that nevertheless echoed in the physical world, adding lift.

The alley opened up like a gift, swallowed us whole, shadows sharp in the flood of sunshine. *"Car!"* I gasped, and Theron's hand closed on the collar of my coat. He hauled me back as I tried to reverse direction and take off.

"Goddammit *they're still shooting!*" he yelled as I lunged again for the mouth of the alley. More bullets pinged against adobe and brick, puffs of dust turning gold. Black smoke belched up—my car was absolutely totaled, a twisted wreck at the end of three loops of black rubber smeared on patched, cracked pavement.

My baby. Gone in a heartbeat.

Theron yanked at me again, so hard my head bobbled. "Jesus *Christ!*"

I seconded that emotion. "They blew up my *car!*"

"Woman, you're lucky they didn't fill you full of lead again. This is getting ridiculous." His hair was wildly mussed, two spots of high color standing out on his cheeks.

"They blew up my *car!*" I sounded like they'd pissed in my Cheerios. Blood dripped salt-warm and stinging in my eyes. "Goddammit, you fucking Were, *do something useful!*"

"What am I supposed to do?" He dragged me further into the alley, swearing under his breath. "Jesus Christ. Who wants you dead this bad, Jill?"

"How the hell should I know? It's someone different every fucking week." I had to suck in breath, burning muscles starved for oxygen and complaining.

Shadows moved at the mouth of the alley. Theron pulled me behind a dumpster and shoved me down. We both crouched there, my ribs flickering with deep hard breaths and the hot explosive reek of garbage climbing down my throat. "Where are we?"

"Shush." He waved a hand and cocked his head, a cat's inquiring movement. His eyes glowed orange, swords of sunlight piercing the high blank wall of a ratty old tenement across the alley. There were still screams and spatters of gunfire and a low harsh tearing sound—my car, burning.

Oh, my God, I swear I am going to kill *whoever is*

responsible for this. I softened my breathing, drawing silence over myself. More movement at the mouth of the alley. A fire-escape jagged up on our side further back, but it looked rickety and rusted; both of us were probably too heavy for it. It's the price you pay for heavier muscle and bone—less vulnerability, but more mass in the ass.

Still, if they come through we'll either have to kill or flee. There's no third option, we can't vanish here. And it's the middle of the goddamn day.

Quick liquid streams of Spanish, tossed back and forth. I listened hard. *"Acqui?"* someone asked.

"Nada, ese. Caray."

More voices. Men's voices, and the piping of boys. Their heartbeats were so high and fast I heard them even though the cuff half-blinded the scar. I *smelled* them—sweat, cordite, beer, and grease, along with the deep brunet scent of dark-haired men.

Theron's hand tightened on my shoulder. My hand had curled around a gun butt.

My car. Goddammit.

Then it came, at the tail end of a string of expletives. "You better tell *el pendejo gordo.* He said you had to see the body."

My skin chilled. *Think, Jill. Think.*

Someone asking for kill verification was someone serious about murdering me. And *el pendejo* has two meanings.

One is *fool,* or *stupid idiot.* A looser translation is *sonofabitch.*

Not very PC, you know. Because the other meaning, in Santa Luz, is *cop.*

16

The blue Chevy Caprice smelled of sourness. It was clean enough, despite the bottle of bourbon shoved under the passenger's seat and the funk of burned and mashed cigars. It was hot, but the heat was bleeding away as the sun retreated and shade fell over the parking lot.

He parks out here because it's the only time he gets alone. The insight was unwelcome. I lay in the back seat, still and quiet as a stone. Of course I was pretty much in plain sight, except for the thin thread of sorcery running through my aura. Complete invisibility is expensive, energetically speaking. It's much easier, and cheaper, to simply avert the gaze. To hook onto that quality of the repeatable in the physical world that lulls most people into sleepwalking.

It makes them good prey. Even cops, who notice more than most.

Dappled shade from a tall anemic pine tree clinging to life at the edge of the lot fell over the car, yet another reason for him to park here.

I waited.

Shift change swirled through the lot, snatches of conversation, car doors slamming, engines rousing. My quarry opened the driver's door and dropped in, pushing his battered briefcase carefully over into the passenger's side. I waited until he buckled his seatbelt and sighed, reaching over for the bottle tucked under the folded newspaper in the passenger-side footwell.

I curled up into a sitting position, glad for the liquid shadows. I clapped a hand over Montaigne's mouth and poked the gun into his ribs. "Drive. Take your usual route home."

I was sorry about the gun. But I had to make sure. *Completely* sure.

His eyes got really, really wide. But he didn't question me—just twisted the key to grind the starter, got the Caprice running, and pulled forward through an empty spot, taking a right and sliding through pools of orange as the lamps in the lot tried ineffectually to light the gathering dusk. Once I was sure he wasn't going to yell, I eased my hand away from his stubble.

Monty kept quiet, but sweat dewed the back of his neck. His tie was loosened and his jacket rumpled. He was still chewing a mouthful of Tums, a chalky undernote to his tang of heavy maleness, not at all clean and musky like a Were's smell.

We hit Balanciaga Avenue from the lot, and he began to work his way toward the residential section. He still didn't ask any questions.

I decided it was time. "Someone's been trying to kill me, Monty. Someone not on the nightside, someone who doesn't know you need special bullets and a lot of luck to take me down. A real execution-style hit uptown, and then just today a whole bunch of gangbangers took exception to me and started talking about cops wanting kill verification on my sweet little behind." I kept the gun steady. "You want to tell me why you wanted me to look into Marv's death so much?"

"Jesus." He was still sweating, and it smelled sour. "Put that thing away, Jill."

I wish I could, Monty. "Not a chance, not yet." I paused as his eyes flicked up to the rearview mirror, then cut longingly over at the passenger side. "Bourbon in the *car,* Montaigne? What the hell is going on with you?" Leather creaked now as I shifted my weight, he was keeping nicely to the speed limit.

Drinking in the front seat on the way home from work is a Very Bad Sign.

Score one for him, he sounded dry and academic. "It's the stress of putting up with you, goddammit. Your car was reported firebombed in the fucking barrio. They're whispering you're dead. Everyone's nervous."

"Well, as far as the Santa Luz PD is concerned, I'm going to *stay* dead. You're not going to tell anyone you saw me. But before I go deep and silent to flush this one out, Monty, you're going to level with me." I took a deep breath. "You knew Kutchner was dirty."

More sweat beaded up on Monty's neck. He leaned forward—slowly, slowly—and flipped a switch. Hot wind blasted into the interior—the engine hadn't been on long enough for the air conditioning to do much. "It didn't feel right. I just suspected *something,* I didn't know what. Goddammit, he was my *partner.*"

You must have done a lot more than suspected, Mon-

taigne. What, you think I'm stupid? "His widow's dead
and so is Winchell. And so is Pedro Ayala. How many
other cops are dead, Monty? Was I supposed to end up
one of them?"

"Ayala? What the fuck?" Monty sounded baffled. But
he was sweating.

But it was hot as hell in the car. What precisely did *I*
suspect?

Not much. Except who else would know where I was
likely to be, if not my primary contact on the force?

And the whole betting pool, who would be tracking
hunter sightings. I didn't bother hiding from the police;
they were my allies.

Or at least, most of them were. It looked like not all of
them felt the same way. "Ayala over in Vice. Got himself
taken down a bit ago, shot on gang territory—but it wasn't
a gang hit, it was because he uncovered something." I slid
the gun into its holster, he wasn't going to do anything
silly now. "Listen to me, Monty. You need to keep your
head down and stay away from all of this. I don't want you
catching any flak. Who did you tell?"

"Tell?"

"That you'd called me in on the Kutchner case. Who
did you tell? Anyone?"

He took a hard right on Seventeenth, still driving like
a prissy old maid. "Not a fucking soul, Kismet. Jesus, you
think I'm stupid?" His eyes flicked up to mine in the rearview, returned to the road. Traffic was light. "How big is
this?"

"You've got some suspicions, don't you. You did from
the start. God*dam*mit, Monty, you should have told me.

I don't like to go into something like this with my ass hanging out."

He looked just the same—an aging fat man, with haunted eyes and a stained tie. "So Marv was dirty? How dirty?"

When I didn't answer, he stared at the road. After a few tense seconds he slammed his palm on the steering wheel and let out a string of curses, finishing with, "And I didn't have a fucking clue, Jill. I woulda told you, for fuck's sweet fucking sake!"

Christ. Monty had never held back on me before, I didn't think he had it in him. Still, I had to be sure. If there's one thing I hate, it's someone supposedly on my side sitting on the information I need to pursue a case. I still hadn't forgiven Father Gui over at Sacred Grace for that episode with the wendigo and the firestrike spear, and I wasn't sure I ever would.

I wasn't sure I *should,* either.

"I know. But something here stinks." *Who would guess you'd ask me to look into the Kutchner suicide? Or was it showing up at the widow's house that did it, I wonder? Jesus, twenty people must have seen me there.* I stared thoughtfully through the windshield as cold air spilled through the vents. The car rapidly became more comfortable, but didn't smell any better. "You can go ahead and smoke if you want to."

"Gee, thanks." But he pulled a Swisher Sweet from his breast pocket and champed, lighting it while he steered with one hand. I glanced away from the flash of the lighter, a star in the darkness. Orange streetlight bounced off the road's hard paleness. He rolled his window down a little and exhaled oddly scented smoke.

I suddenly, completely, missed Saul like there was a hole in my chest. Again. It was like missing a hand, or a leg. I'd grown so used to working with him, having his quiet presence clear up any mess in my head.

"So you think I should leave this alone?" Monty sounded uncharacteristically uncertain.

No shit, Batman. "Let me put it this way. I don't want to avenge you too. I like you breathing."

"That bad?"

I let the silence answer him.

"How dirty was he?" He braked, we were fast approaching a stop sign at Tewberry and Twenty-Eighth. I coiled myself for action.

"Don't worry about that, Monty. Worry about keeping out of this. Don't go anywhere alone. Be careful. And for God's sake don't tell anyone I'm still alive."

"That's going to be rough. What if someone else shows up missing on the east side?"

That's more likely than you can possibly know. I wish we knew we'd gotten all the scurf. "Don't worry about me doing my job. You just keep yourself out of trouble." The car rolled to a stop, I hit the door, and was gone before he could even curse at me. I watched his taillights vanish from the roof of a convenient apartment building and hoped like hell he wouldn't do anything silly.

Theron was waiting in the darkened doorway of a bakery, doing the little Were camouflage trick. If my blue eye hadn't been able to look under the surface of the world, I would have had to depend on the thin thread of *wrong* touching my nerves, and really *looked* to see him. I also would have had a gun out while I did it.

Theron's eyes fired orange in the gloom, like and unlike the streetlamps. "Is he clean?"

"Squeaky." *Or if he isn't, I haven't given him anything to go on other than I'm alive—and if word gets out I'm still breathing, I'll know where it came from.* "He suspected something was wrong, that's all. Intuition still happens."

The Were shrugged. My back prickled—other Weres were still out running sweeps, but they hadn't found any trace of scurf.

Yet.

And I'd lost a full day.

It was enough to turn anyone into a pessimist.

"What next?" He moved restlessly.

"You stop by Galina's and pick up some ammo for me, drop by the barrio and squeeze your gang friends for the word on why a cop would want me dead, and I'm going home to change clothes."

Predictably, he decided to argue. "Like I'm going to let you out of my sight."

This isn't negotiable. I need a few minutes to myself and some hard thinking. "Everyone thinks I'm dead, Theron. There aren't many cops who know the amount of damage I can really take, or what it would take to kill me. Nobody is going to be looking for me just yet. Besides, the longer you wait to go talk to your friends in the barrio, the more chance they'll 'forget' something." *If you were Saul we wouldn't be having this conversation; you'd be doing what I told you. Goddammit.* I rolled my shoulders in their sockets, a habitual movement easing muscle strain.

"I don't like it. I promised Saul I'd look out for you."

"I'm just going *home,* Theron. I promise not to talk to strangers and to look both ways before crossing the street." I stepped out of the doorway, smoke taunting my nose. It drifted up from my coat, the smell of burning vinyl, cooked leather, and gasoline.

What a reek. I'm never going to be able to wash it out.

The Were shrugged. "You'd better," he muttered darkly, before easing out of the shadows himself and taking a few steps in the opposite direction. Then he gathered himself and blurred, running with fluid finicky feline grace.

I strangled the urge to get the last word in. It would take me about a half-hour to get home, longer if I had to wait for a cab. I might as well use my own share of preternatural speed.

What I hadn't said hung in the air. Hunters depend on the police, they are our eyes and ears. What we do is law enforcement, in its strictest sense. And as Carp had pointed out, we didn't have some of the restrictions ordinary cops had. No hunter was ever hauled into court.

When you couldn't depend on your backup, where did that leave you? *Fucked* was the only term that applied. And until I knew more about who was trying to do me in, I couldn't even answer my pager. If someone else went missing or a new case popped up . . .

Then you'd better finish this quickly, Jill. Start thinking about how you're going to do just that.

17

I hate having guests. Especially uninvited guests.

And most definitely, especially, uninvited guests who barely wait until I'm through the door before they try to kill me.

Word of advice: If you are looking to catch a hunter by surprise, *don't* do it in her house, for Chrissake. Any place a hunter sleeps is likely to be well-defended, and if it's easy to break in you should be wondering how hard it's going to be to escape. A hunter does not sleep somewhere without knowing every crack and creak in the walls— which includes knowing when some sloppy-ass hellbreed has slithered through a window and is breathing heavily behind your door.

So I was ready when I stepped through and dropped down into a crouch. The dirty-blond 'breed hesitated, flew over my head and smacked himself a good one on the jamb. Wood splintered and I drove upward with the knife, the silver laid along the blade hissing with bluespark flame as it met Hell-tainted flesh.

The 'breed twisted on himself in midair with that gut-loosening spooky agility they all have. The hardest thing to get used to is how they *move,* in ways human joints can't and human muscles never would. I spun a full one-eighty, bootsole scraping the linoleum just inside the door, and went down flat on my back in the entry hall.

Come to Mama, you stupid fuck. The bleeding 'breed didn't disappoint, dropping down with claws outstretched, face twisted into a grinning mask of hate. Maybe he thought I was vulnerable, since I was on the floor.

I spend half my fighting life on the floor. Judo's not just fun, it's a lifesaver. Once you ground a 'breed or, say, a Possessor, their advantage in speed is gone and their edge in strength is halved if you know anything about leverage. But I had no intention of wriggling around with this jerkwad.

No, I shot him four times, punching through the shell of hellbreed skin, and flicked a boot up to catch his wounded belly, deflecting his leap by a few critical degrees so he sailed over me and splatted, screaming like a banshee, onto the hardwood floor.

I was on my feet again in a trice, knife dropped chiming to the floor, kicked away so the 'breed couldn't reach it, and my fingers closing around the bullwhip's handle. A quick jerk, a flick of my wrist, and braided leather snapped through the air, the tiny sharp bits of silvery metal tied on the end of the whip breaking the sound barrier and scoring hellbreed flesh.

This is why hunters use whips. It gives us reach we otherwise wouldn't have. I was already pulling the trigger, firing twice more, the reports booming and echoing through my silent house. I was only a half-inch off on the

right shoulder, but my first shot took him right through
the ball-joint of the left. That took some of the pep out of
my unwanted visitor—but not all of it.

The whip flickered again, like a snake's tongue
weighted with razorblades. It tore across the 'breed's face,
and by now I'm sure both of us had figured out I wanted
him taken alive.

I wanted answers.

He still put up a fight, but when I broke his left arm
in three places and got him down on the floor, the silver-
loaded blade of another knife to his throat, the squealing
from him took on an animal sound I was more than familiar with.

I didn't recognize this chalk-skinned scarecrow of a
'breed. He was definitely male, catslit blue eyes glowing
even in the wash of electric light. *Fucker left my lights on.
How stupid can you be?* "Do I have to cut your throat?"
I whispered in his ear, knowing he would feel the brush
of my breath through the matted fringe of blond hair. He
was bleeding thin black ichor, a wash of the stinking stuff
all over my dusty wooden floor.

Once the hard shell is broken, the bad in a hellbreed
leaks out. Once that shell is breached with silver, an allergic reaction sets in too. The blade ran with blue sparks,
reacting to the brackish foulness of Hell the scarecrow
exhaled. He wore a black silk button-down and designer
jeans, but his battered, horn-callused feet were bare, the
toes too flexible to be human and graced with curling yellow nails.

He went still. I bore down with all my hellbreed-given
strength. The scar pulsed, sensing something akin to its
corruption. He whined, right at the back of the throat, and

went limp, the subvocal groaning of Helletöng rattling in my ears.

"I don't speak anything but human, asshole." I kept the whisper down, my breath heaving. My head hurt, a pounding stuffed between my temples. *Hell of a day. Stay focused, Jill.* "You going to settle down?"

He writhed a little, testing, but subsided. I was braced and exerting leverage on the broken arm, grinding both shattered shoulders into the floor. He was losing a lot of ichor. *Don't you dare fucking die before I find out who sent you.*

A long string of obscenities, made all the more ugly by the tenor sweetness of his voice. The damned are always beautiful, or the seeming they wear to fool the world is. I've never seen an ugly 'breed—except for Perry, and he wasn't truly ugly.

Did Perry send you? "Who sent you?" I ground down again, was rewarded by a hiss of pain. My arm tightened, and the silver-loaded knife pressed lacerated skin.

The hissing yowl of his pain was matched only by the sound of sizzling. It ended on a high almost-canine yip when I let up a bit.

"I've got all night to make you talk." My throat was full of something too hot and acid to be anger or hatred. The smell was eyewatering, terrific, colossal, burning into my brain. I ignored it, braced my knee, and tensed. "And I enjoy my work, hellspawn."

"*Shen,*" he whispered. "*Shenan—*"

Oh holy shit. But there was no time, he heaved up and my grasp slipped in a scrim of foul oil. I set my teeth and my knees and yanked, twisting; an easy, fluid motion and a jet of sour black arterial spray. His cry ended on a gurgle, and his rebellion died almost before it had begun.

Cold night air poured through the open door, cleaner than anything inside. I coughed, rackingly, my eyes burning as I struggled free of the rapidly rotting thing on the floor. A young, hungry blond 'breed, maybe thinking to prove something.

But. *Shen. Shenan.*

There was only one thing that could mean.

Shenandoah. Or, if you had your accent on right, *Shen An Dua.*

In other words, seriously fucking bad news. If Perry was the unquestioned leader of the hellbreed in Santa Luz, keeping that position through murder and subterfuge, Shen was the queen, or an *éminence grise.* She was the biggest contender for replacing Perry if he ever got unlucky or soft—and *that* thought, friends and neighbors, was enough to break out any hunter in a cold sweat.

Gender means less than nothing when it comes to 'breed, but all in all I'd rather deal with a male. Female hellbreed just *seem* deadlier.

I coughed so hard I retched. The stink was amazing. It had been a day of varied and wonderful stenches, that was for goddamn sure. Theron was due to come back and find this mess lying around. If there's anything I hate more than cooking, it's cleaning up hellbreed mess from my own goddamn floor.

I toed the door closed, wishing I wasn't silhouetted in the rectangle of golden electric light. Locked it, and stood for a moment. Fine tremors began in the center of my bones, the body coming down from a sudden adrenaline ramp-up and successive shocks. I shook so hard my coat creaked, responding to my weight shifts. An internal earthquake, and me without any seismic bracing.

Jill, you're not thinking straight. You could have handled him, gotten more information. You're beginning to blur under the pressure, who wouldn't? You have got to get some rest.

Yeah. Great idea. Unfortunately, like all great ideas, this one had a fatal flaw. There was no rest to be had.

Not if one of the most powerful hellbreed in the city— and one that had a reason to bear me a grudge—was sending 'breed to kill me in my own house. But why would she send a callow idiot like this, one who didn't know the first thing about hunters?

One who hesitated before attacking me?

It didn't make any *sense*.

I gathered my dropped weapons with shaking hands, tacked out across the broad expanse of floor for the kitchen. A sudden shrill sound yanked me halfway out of my skin, guns clearing leather with both hands and fastened on the disturbance—that is, in the direction of my bedroom.

The phone was ringing. I tried not to feel like an idiot as I reholstered my guns.

It never rains but it pours. Black humor tilted under the surface of the words. I made it to the kitchen, letting the phone ring, the noise sawing across my nerves. A cupboard squeaked when I opened it, and I lifted down the bottle of Jim Beam as carefully as if it was a Fabergé egg. *Jesus. Jesus Christ.*

The habit of drinking helps more than you'd think with something like this.

The ringing stopped. The answering machine clicked

on. The same few seconds of silence as always, then a hiss of inhaled breath, static blurring over the line as he started to speak.

"Kiss." Carp sounded ragged. "Goddammit, Kismet, answer your fuckin' phone. Pick up if you're there."

Sorry, honey. No can do. I uncapped the bottle, took a healthy draft. It burned all the way down, but the heat helped to steady me. My metabolism burns off alcohol like nobody's business, but it's still . . . comforting.

"Things are gettin fuckin' ridiculous," he continued, the words spilling over each other. "Jesus. There's a lead. If you're there, if you get this message, there's this place downtown on First and Alohambra. It's a club, the Kat Klub. I got a line on someone who knows something, she works there. A waitress named Irene. I'm goin' in."

My heart did its best to strangle me by climbing up into my throat. I slammed the bottle on the counter, sloshing the amber liquid inside, and bolted for the bedroom.

"Carp!" I yelled, pointlessly. *"Goddamit!"* As if he could hear me. But he hung up before I could scoop the handset out of its cradle.

"Shit!" I yelled, and almost hurled the damn thing across the room. "Oh, fuck. Fuckitall, no."

I barely paused to grab a dose of ammunition, wriggle into a fresh T-shirt and leather pants—the ones I wore smelled of hellbreed, gas, and burning vinyl, as did my coat—and to take another long jolt off the bottle before hitting the door at a run.

Please, God, don't let me be too late.

18

First and Alohambra is a ritzy northern part of downtown. Despite spending most of my time in alleys and on rooftops, I also know where to find gentrification if I need it—upscale eateries, boutiques, art galleries, and the smell of money. A fair amount of the nightside has its fingers in high-cash trades; the rich can pay for pleasures that might not be strictly earthly.

I like to think it doesn't matter, that I pursue every criminal equally. God knows I try to care a bit more for the poor, since they get shafted most often. What's that old song? *It's the rich what gets the pleasure, and the poor what gets the blame.*

Truer words never spoken. No matter how hard I try to even the score, basic inequality looms over human life from cradle to grave.

Getting more pessimistic all the time, Jill. Why is that?

I crouched on the rooftop, watching the front of the Kat Klub, a long-time fixture of downtown Santa Luz.

Its current incarnation dates back to the Jazz Age. The

normals think it's just a restaurant with a cabaret dinner show that turns into a nightclub at about midnight, shutting down just before dawn in merry defiance of the liquor laws. It's a venerable institution, housed in the bottom of the granite bulk of the Piers Tower, one of the oldest skyscrapers in Santa Luz. Mikhail told me once that the property had been a mission long ago—before the town got big enough to attract hellbreed.

One thing is for sure, there is no sacredness left in those walls.

The heat of the day had run out like the heat of the Beam in my belly. I crouched, and considered.

If I went in my usual way, guns blazing, there would go my advantage in being thought dead. On the other hand, if Carp was in there he needed all the help he could get. And hellbreed would know better than to think a burning car would do *me* in.

The thought that any hellbreed would know that one punk scarecrow wouldn't be enough to do me in, either, was not particularly comforting. Something about this was stinking even worse than the mess left on my floor. *That* was going to be a pain in the ass to remove.

Why are you dilly-dallying, Jill? If Carp steps inside that place, you'll have to do more than bleed to get him out.

I weighed every possible alternative. Cold hard logic said to just keep watch, see what happened, and return once I'd developed some other leads—with the benefit of whatever cops involved in this thinking I was dead, so I didn't have to worry about more bullets flying my way from *that* quarter, at least. It was the way I was trained to think, a straightforward totting up of averages and percentages, the greater good balanced against personal cost.

Screw that. Carper's in there.

You don't get to be a hunter without knowing when to buck the odds.

I rose to my feet slowly, breathing. *Just like burning a hellbreed hole, Jill. Go fast and deadly, you don't have Saul with you this time. You did it on your own before he showed up.* My fingers crept to the leather cuff over the scar; I undid the buckles and peeled it away.

Cold air mouthed my skin with hundreds of vicious little wet lips. I let out a soft breath, every muscle tightening as the welter of sensation spilled through nerve endings already pulled taut with worry and stress.

It's gotten stronger. Hasn't it? Oh, God.

The cold machine inside my head jotting down percentages replied that if it had, that was good; it would give me an edge I sorely needed. I would worry about the cost later. Story of my life. I was mortgaging myself by inches—the most dangerous way to do it.

Well, I never did like doing things by halves. Go for the quick tear, Jill.

The rooftop quivered slightly, the world flexing around me. I was pulling on etheric force, the scar moaning and thundering against my wrist. Too much power for me to really control, it wasn't obeying my will. A piece of my own flesh, turning traitor. My aura sparkled in the ether, a sea-urchin of light.

I leapt out into free air, physics *bending* and the pavement smoking under a sudden application of strain. I hit the street like a ton of bricks, bleeding off some of the etheric force boiling through me and leaving behind a star-shaped pattern of cracks; streaked through a gap in late-night traffic toward the door—a massive, iron-bound oaken monstrosity, guarded by two bouncers just this side of gorilla with flat-shining Trader eyes behind smoked sunglasses and the taint of Hell swirling in their once-human auras.

A waitress named Irene. But first, we get Carper, and we make a statement.

The only question was whether or not to shoot the bouncers. I was already going too fast; I hit the door with megaton force, sharp-spiked edges of my aura fluorescing into the visible as blue sparks crackled off every piece of silver jewelry I carried. Oak splintered, iron buckled, and my boots thudded home, I rode the door down like a surfboard, my knees bent when it hit the parquet inside; I was already leaping, a compact ball of bloodlust and action, my coat snapping like a flag in a high breeze.

The restaurant was down a short hall behind swinging soundproofed doors. A skinny hat-check girl with the brackish aura of a Trader bared her teeth, cowering back into the plush darkness of her booth. Three more bouncers converged on me, I shot two, pistol-whipped the third, and plunged down the hall. I hit the swinging doors so hard they both broke against the walls and was suddenly in an oasis of silk palms, hanging fake greenery, and the quiet tinkling sound of a fountain made of whipped glass and creamy spun metal.

Glass eyes regarded me, shining in the soft light. There were at least a hundred stuffed cats, maybe more, draped in the greenery, their fur brushed and glossy and their fangs exposed. From little calico housecats to sleek stuffed panthers, even four or five (I shivered to see them) cougars arranged artistically on branches with bark too rough and shiny to be real.

The place was stuffed with hellbreed and Traders. Linen-draped tables in nooks shrouded by false plants clustered around a wide glassy dance floor, currently hosting a set of contortionists in spangled costumes— three unbreasted girls and two stick-thin boys, tall and stretched-out, all with blank dusted eyes and empty loose mouths—writhing around each other. They didn't even pause when I shot the maître d'.

Murmured conversation stopped. The maître d' collapsed, half his head blown away and the sudden sharp stink of hellbreed death exploding with the oatmeal of his brain.

I eyed them all, they watched me. The scar thundered and prickled, running with sharp diamond insect feet against my skin. "Huh." My voice was unnaturally loud in the stillness. "Must have forgotten my reservation."

Forks hung, paused in midair. The fountain plashed, sequins on the contortionists' costumes scratched, and the sounds of clinking and cooking came from the open kitchen, set along the back wall. Later on in the night it would convert to a bar, and ranked bottles of liquor glowed mellow behind a counter where hellbreed bellied up, the old-fashioned equipment of a soda fountain gleaming as it dispensed booze—and other liquids and powders.

I scanned the whole room once. Everything was frozen in place except the contortionists, twisted into pretzels. One of them distended her jaw with a crack, and made a low groaning sound as her spine extended into a hoop.

Great. "A waitress." I kept my tone conversational.

"Named Irene." One thumb clicked back the hammer on a gun, the *snick* very loud. *"Now."*

A clattering crash, my eyes flicked toward the sound. A black-haired Trader, as thin and beautiful as the rest of them, had dropped her tray. The short black skirt on her French-maid uniform made a starched sound as she backed up under my gaze, blundering into a knot of hellbreed and Traders who scattered in a flash of uniforms—harlequins, maids, one female in a super-retro Batgirl costume—*what the hell,* I thought, and promptly dismissed it.

I took two steps forward before a table full of Traders erupted into motion and things got *seriously interesting*— but not before I got a flash of hellbreed and Traders parting to show a slumped body on a table, blood bright red and human decorating the linen, and Carp's blue eyes wide open with terror and glazed with either death or unconsciousness.

Four shots, whip cracking across a Trader's face and snapping back, I *kicked;* my steel-toed boot caught the snarling hellbreed just under the chin with a sound like thin glass wrapped in bread dough when you drop a hammer on it. Clearing a hellbreed hole is messy, even with heavy-duty sorcery and silverjacket lead. Thin black ichor coated the floor, not yet ankle-deep but we were going to get there.

I landed on the table, heels slamming down bare inches from Carp's head on either side. Stood over him, gun in one hand, whip in the other. Spared a quick glance down—his eyes had half-closed, and his mouth wet-flickered, closing, opened again.

He's alive. Thank God. Now to get him out of here.

The world froze between one moment and the next, every hellbreed and Trader in the place dropping to the ground like they'd all been caught with cyanide Kool-Aid. The doors from the kitchen swung open, a wave of coldness pouring through the room, and the tinkling of the fountain began to seriously get on my fucking nerves.

Dainty, delicate, and dolled up in a red kimono, Shen An Dua stepped between the doors. They swung shut behind her and framed her with blank industrial steel; it was a good look for her. Catslit yolk-yellow eyes cradled in slight epicanthic folds swept the room, waist-length blue-black hair with the body of well-oiled straw was pulled into some sort of elaborate confection atop her well-modeled head. *Probably matches the fountain,* I thought with an internal snigger, and the scar on my wrist gave such a burst of burning pain my fingers almost clenched.

Great. Just great. Her aura was the deep sonorous bruising of a full hellbreed, the taint of Hell warping the strings of the physical world. Plucking, like little flabby fingers, the harpstrings of this place of flesh.

I pointed the gun, let it settle naturally so the bullet would follow its own path of consequence right between her eyes. Decided that the best defense, so to speak, would be a good offense.

Hey, it's my usual method. Along with ripping Band-Aids off in one quick jerk and throwing myself off buildings after hellbreed, you could even call it my job.

"All right, bitch." I bit off the end of the sentence. "Irene. The waitress. Bring her out, and maybe I won't burn this whole pile of bad taste to the ground."

Shen placed her small hands together and bowed from

the waist, a slight inclination of her upper body. "Kismet. You honor our humble business with your presence."

"Can the so-solly routine, Shen. Bring out the fucking waitress, or I start wasting paying customers *and* staff. Your call."

The tip of a tongue, far too pink and far too glistening-wet to be human, crept out and touched her candy-apple lips. "What is the nature of her sin, avenging one?"

Perry asks me that occasionally. It's some kind of formula in their weird twisted society, I suppose. Not that I cared enough to ask. "You just let me worry about that, hellspawn." My pulse eased, settling into a hard rhythm, slower than the energy demand of combat but a helluva lot higher than just lounging on my couch. "Hand her over for questioning. And while you're at it, sit yourself down and prepare to answer a few questions yourself."

Her smile broadened. Her teeth were white bone behind bleeding lips, and her cheeks plumped up adorably. The kimono swished slightly as she settled—maybe on her heels, maybe not. I didn't know what was under the long skirts she habitually wore, and experience has taught me not to even guess. "I do not think you understand the situation, hunter."

Oh, you did not *just start this game with me.* I didn't lose my temper. Instead, I squeezed the trigger. The report smashed all the air in the room, silver in my hair alive with blue sparks, their crackling suddenly a counterpoint to the dishes crashing in the kitchen.

"Huh. Will you look at that." I sounded damn near gleeful, a laugh riding the razor edge my voice had become. "A thousand apologies, most honorable Shen An

Dua. I must have become irritated. Do you want to see what'll happen if you make me *angry?*"

Black strings of hair fell in her face. I'd shot whatever architecture underpinned her elaborate coiffure—a trick no less amazing because it was only half-intentional. It had occurred to me at the very last moment that maybe just killing her would be a tactical error in here.

But oh, it would be so satisfying.

That was a bad thought to have, because it was treading right on the edge.

I didn't care as much as I should right now. Getting killed a few times will do that to you.

Carper made a thin moaning sound. I didn't want to think about what had probably happened to him before I quit dithering and busted down the door. Instead, I shook the whip a little, its flechettes jingling. The circle of hellbreed and Traders around the table, like darkness pressing against a sphere of candlelight, shivered at the tinkling sweet sound.

The situation quivered on the edge of violence. If I was going to really get into it here, I would have Carp to protect. It would handicap me.

Deal with it, Jill.

Shen's fingers flicked. I tensed, but a blood-haired female—the mop was really amazing, crimson hair to her nipped-in waist, a sequined maroon sheath just like Mae West's hugging dead-white curves—was pushed forward out of the crowd. She had a pale, hard little face with the rotten bloom of hellish beauty on it like scurf powder on blood, and her eyes were dark and liquid under the flat shine of a Trader.

"This is the one you seek." Shen hissed.

Great. Now I had to figure out how to get us all out of here.

"Now we're all going to be civilized, aren't we?" The whip moved, tick-tock, just like a clock pendulum, before it coiled almost of its own accord and was stowed in its proper place. My free hand now touched a gun butt, but I didn't draw just yet. "I'm taking the waitress and this—" My heel gently prodded Carp's temple, he made a thin moaning sound of a man caught in a nightmare, "with me." My gun eased away from Shen, the assembled hellbreed flinched under its one-eyed stare. Then it came back to the mistress of the Kat Klub, settled on her forehead. *If I kill her, the rest of them will swarm me. She knows it. Think fast, wabbit.* "Anybody have any *problems* with that?"

Dead silence. The kitchen had quieted too, maybe finally noticing something was amiss out here in the dining room.

Shen made another quick movement, her dainty hands fluttering. I almost pulled the trigger—but no, the assembled damned pulled away, crawling or skipping, pressing back as if I had the plague.

Leaving a nice clear corridor between the mistress of the Kat Klub and yours truly.

Great. Wonderful. Jill, this is going to hurt.

"You and your master will pay for this." Fat, oily strings of black hair writhed over Shen An Dua's face, tangling together like live things. She didn't look half so pretty now, her eyes alive with running egg-soft flame and her upper lip lifting like a cat smelling something awful.

My master? Mikhail's dead. "My teacher's in Valhalla." Nothing in the words but flat finality. If Shen thought mentioning Misha would yank my chain enough to get me to make a mistake, she was either stupid—or holding something in reserve. And whatever else Shen An Dua is, she's not stupid. "You can't touch him, bitch."

"His is not the hand that holds your leash, hunter." Her razorpearl teeth showed in a snarl, all the more chilling because of the full-cheeked sweetness of her face. The kimono's skirt rustled, shapes bulging underneath it. "Tell the master of the Monde *he will pay for this*."

It was so out of left field I almost couldn't connect the words together. *Perry? Oh good God. Please.* "If you think I'm here for him, you're wrong. Perry has no hold on me." *Other than the fact that I'd rather deal with him than you any day of the week, since he has a vested interest in keeping me alive so he can fuck with me.* I hopped down from the table, the gun tracking smoothly. The waitress flinched, cowering, I eyed her. "Pick him up, Trader."

"You will not—" Shen began, and my heartrate eased, smoothing out, as I lifted my head and regarded her again. They could all hear my pulse, and the sudden calm washing over me was as ominous as a thunderstorm.

Talk your way out of this one, Kismet. "This is one of mine, hellspawn. You don't get to eat him tonight."

There are six pounds of center-trigger pull on a Glock and I was at about four and a half. The world had turned into a collection of edges too sharp to be real, all my senses working overtime and amped up into the red.

Shen's face contorted once, smoothed out, crumpled again. The bruise of her aura tightened like a fist. I watched, waiting. If Shen was more than normally upset at Perry or needed to regain some face in front of her minions and clients, this would get ugly really quickly.

"You are only one, hunter. And we are legion." The black strings of her hair rubbed against each other, squealing as she subvocalized. Helletöng rumbled through the floor, vibrating against my bootsoles.

"That does not particularly bother me." I sounded like it didn't, too. "I've killed more in a night than you have in this dining room, Shen." I paused. "You, Trader. I told you to pick him up."

The Trader squeaked as if she'd been pinched and moved to obey. I kept both guns on Shen. *I might get out of this alive. All hail the poker-faced hunter and her ability to talk smack.*

Shen took two long strides forward, the fabric of her kimono's lower half moving in odd ways, silk groaning and stretching. "You will not leave this place alive," she promised, and the helltainted on every side moved closer. A rising growl slid through them, Helletöng rubbing at the walls.

Oh, so that's the way we're going to do this? My free hand was suddenly full of Glock. "Outside, Irene. And *gently.* If he dies, you're fucking next." I waited until I heard her start moving, Carp's shapeless groan as he lay cradled in her stick-thin, dead-white arms, her purple satin gloves now stained with blood. This I took in through my peripheral vision, my heartrate cool and steady, both guns still locked on the mistress of the Kat Klub. "Is that the way you want to play it, Shen?"

Nothing human lived under the skirt of that antique kimono. The scar prickled, a mass of hot needles burrowing into my wrist, and the world got very still again, clarity settling over each edge and curve. The contortionists were still writhing on the stage, joints crackling and sequins scraping.

"Take her," she whispered. But none of the assembled 'breed or Traders moved.

Apparently, right at this moment, even fear of Shen An Dua couldn't make them swarm me. It was an indirect compliment.

I showed my teeth. My entire body relaxed into the flow of the moment, the absolute chilling certainty of violence taking all indecision out of the equation. "Bring it," I whispered. My forearms tensed, cords of muscle standing out as I edged toward that last pound and a half of pressure on the triggers.

A new voice cut across the warp and weft of the interior, slicing cleanly even if it was loaded with Texas so thick the drawl dripped over the sides. "Jesus fuckin' Christ. What the hell's this?"

I almost twitched. Relief threatened to unloose my knees, and the situation tipped from *ohmyGod I am not going to survive this* to *Thank God someone else is going to die with me.*

Shen's head turned, a slow movement like a servomotor with oiled bearings. I kept both guns trained on her. I'd once seen her unzip a Trader's guts and lift a double handful of wet intestine to her plump little candy-apple-red mouth.

Things like that will make a hunter cautious. Add to that the fact that I'd wanted to question the Trader about a certain stable of high-priced underage sex slaves, and Shen's calm inscrutable smile as strings of human gut hung from her mouth, and you had bad blood between us. I knew she'd been in it up to her eyeballs, but I hadn't been able to make any of it stick. I couldn't *prove* it to my own satisfaction.

I could prove little of what I suspected when it came to her. Which meant I couldn't kill her with a clear conscience. Or even just a reasonably clear conscience, which, some days, is all you're going to get in this line of work.

"Hi, Leon," I said. "Nice to see you."

"You've got crappy taste in restaurants, darlin'," Leon Budge drawled. "Why don't we go somewheres civilized where I can get me a got-damn drink?"

Shen surged forward again, and there was a familiar, ratcheting sound. Leon had worked the bolt action on his rifle. "Oh, now, sweetie-pie, don't do that. Me and Rosita here, we gets nervous when a slope-eyed gal like you gets twitchy."

Jesus, Leon, how much of a racist cliché can you be? I took two steps, sidling away from the table. Helletöng crested, the sound of skin slipping as drowned fingers rubbed together, chrome flies buzzing in chlorine-laced bottles—the scar sent a wet thrill up my arm, hearing its language spoken.

Two more steps. I took a quick glance, made certain I was out of Leon's field of fire.

He stood in a battered leather trenchcoat, plain dun instead of black, his hair a crow's nest of untidy brown waves, copper charms threaded on black heavy-duty waxed thread and clinking slightly as a breeze ruffled his hair. The wreck of the swinging doors smoked around him, and he held the rifle like it wasn't capable of blowing a 'breed in half with the modifications he'd put on it.

Chubby cherub's face, wide shoulders, a body kept in

shape by a hunter's constant training but still managing to give the impression of pudginess. Leon looked like a newscaster trapped in goth-boy drag, an impression helped along by the eyeliner scoring rings around each hazel eye and the clinking mass of amulets around his neck on cords, thongs, and thin copper chains. Four plain silver rings on his left hand ran with blue sparks, echoing the silver in my hair. One of them was the apprentice-ring his teacher had given him.

Leon was smiling under a scruff of dark stubble, white teeth peeping out. "Should I put 'er down, Kiss?"

Don't call me that, dammit. "If she moves." I turned my back on Shen An Dua and her assembled footlickers and customers, guns sliding into their holsters. "Or hell, even if you don't like her hairstyle."

"It's somethin'." The cheerful, thoughtful tone never wavered, and he didn't blink. The bandoliers crossing his chest held small silver-coated throwing knives, each one sharp enough to take a finger off.

Or pop right into a 'breed's eye and pierce the brain with blessed metal.

"Well, the barber was an amateur." I shrugged, my knees threatening to buckle with each straight, strutting step.

Rule of dealing with murderous hellspawn: try not to look weak. It gets them all excited.

"You have earned my hatred," Shen was back to whispering. "Hell and Earth both witness my vow, hunter. *You will pay for this.*"

Yeah, one way or another. Sure. "You already said that, most honorable Shen An Dua. Don't be boring." I would have pantomimed a yawn if my hands weren't quivering with the urge to take the guns out again, turn around, and put this murderous hellspawn down like the parasite she was.

Leon's gaze flicked to mine for a fraction of a second. It was a purely professional look, gauging what I was likely to do next. I sounded cool and calm, but something in my cheek twitched like a needle was plucking at the flesh. The glance was also a communication, one I heard as clearly as verbal speech—*are you gonna throw down, darlin'?*

If I did, he was willing to back me. But Leon knew just as surely as I did it would be a terrible mistake. These hellbreed and Traders weren't surprised anymore, and they'd had plenty of time to think about how to take the two of us apart. Shen could threaten all she wanted now and still retain some semblance of face, but if we killed her it wouldn't be a free-for-all that would allow us to divvy them up and pick them off. No, if we insulted her, *then* killed her, whoever wanted to step into her shoes would have to kill us to prove they were worthy of taking Shen's place.

Well, Jill, you fucked this up six ways to Sunday. Cool night air poured down the hall, touching Leon's hair. He backed up, covering me with the rifle as I retreated from what had certainly been a bad idea in the first place.

We made it through the hall, past the crumpled bodies of the bouncers. The hat-check girl was nowhere in sight. Sirens wailed in the distance, and I was suddenly struck by an entirely new feeling.

I was used to the sound being a relief, as in *the cavalry's on its way.* Now I felt the way any criminal feels— like the sirens were baying hounds and I was the fox.

The crowd out front had vanished. Most of them were likely to be Traders and hellbreed, probably thanking their lucky stars they hadn't been inside.

"Fucking *hell*." I restrained the urge to kick something.

The blood-haired Trader was gone.

So was Carp.

19

Leon drove, of all things, a big blue Chevy half-ton. The interior smelled of grease and jostled as the engine labored.

"This thing needs a tune-up," I told him. "What the hell are you doing here? Not that I'm not happy to see you."

"Where the fuck's your car, darlin'? And I'm here because you called, and because someone's been trappin' scurf in my neck of the woods. I wouldn't mind, since we got enough and to spare, but trappin' 'em means they have somethin' planned, and that I don't like. I tracked 'em over the city limits. We got ourselves a genuine grade-A problem goin' on here."

"My car blew up. What do you mean, *trapping* scurf?" I clung to the oh-shit strap while he took a corner, working the gears like they were going out of style. Beer cans rolled around my ankles and a metal footlocker containing ammo and various other odds and ends rattled, sliding forward to smack my boots.

Then Leon did something I hated. He closed his eyes. *Oh shit.*

I came back from Hell with a gift or a curse, depending on which way you look at it. My blue eye can see *between* and *below* the surface of the world. It is that ability to go *between* that sets me apart from other hunters—that and my bargain with Perry. Most of us just come back from Hell with some interesting instincts, a grasp of sorcery, and the ability to see through the masks hellbreed like to wear.

But some of us return with more.

Leon came back a tracker. You name it, he can follow it. All it requires, he says, is the right mindset.

And a healthy amount of Pabst Blue Ribbon to dull his sensitivity the rest of the time. If Budge wasn't half-drunk, things were very bad indeed. The only good thing about it was he needed a bathroom about as often as a female hunter does.

Beer does that to you when you've got a human metabolism. Me, I can't drink enough of the damn stuff to even get a buzz.

I didn't ask who we were following. Leon had seen Carp, unmistakably human and bleeding in the middle of a hellbreed haunt, and had further seen me unwilling to leave without him. Some things are just understood.

Leon floored it, and the pickup began to shimmy in interesting ways. "Movin' fast, and agin the wind."

Not like wind matters to Traders or hellbreed, Leon. I hung on for dear life as he slammed us through traffic, missing a semi by bare inches and almost dinging the paint job on a showroom-bright black SUV that blared its horn and dropped back. Leon's eyelids flickered like he was dreaming.

"What do you mean, *trapping scurf?*" I repeated. That was bad, bad news on all fronts.

"I mean catching the little bastards and shipping them out of town, both by rail and by water. I didn't think it was possible—who the hell would *want* 'em, huh? Hang on."

Hang on?

Leon twisted the wheel, hard. We cut across two lanes of traffic, he floored it, and I started to feel a little green. It wasn't the speed, it was the fact that he had his eyes shut tight.

Even when you're used to Leon, it's creepy.

"You might want to slow down. I'm having some problems up here."

"What kinda problems?"

Where do I start? "There's a case. Some dirty cops. They've already tried to kill me."

"Holy *shit*." That snapped his eyes open for almost fifteen seconds, but it wasn't comforting at all. His dark gaze was filmed as if by cataracts, shapes like windblown clouds rolling over the eyeballs. Wind roared through the half-open window; I didn't have a hand to spare to roll it up. I was busy hanging on.

For some reason, nobody ever says a goddamn thing about the way Leon drives.

He closed his eyes again, stamping on the accelerator, and I was seriously considering commending my soul to God yet again that night when he jagged over, zipped into an alley neat as you please, stood on the brakes, and bailed out like his pants were on fire.

I followed, sliding across the seat and hopping out his

side. He'd taken the keys with him, so I swept the door closed and pounded after him. He was only capable of human speed, but human speed is pretty damn fast when you're a hunter.

He plunged through an alley, up a fire escape, zigzagged across a low rooftop and came to an abrupt halt, staring across the street. I skidded to a stop right next to him, gave the street a once-over, and looked up at the granite Jesus glowering at downtown.

"Holy shit. She brought him to the hospital?" I didn't mean for it to come out as a question. *Well, I told her that if he died she was next. I suppose it's logical.*

"That's one almighty-big statue there," was all Leon said. He blinked a couple times, his shoulders coming down and the colorless fume of urgency swirling away from him.

"That's Sisters of Mercy. Used to be Catholic. I thought you were in there once, when Mikhail and you—" I bit off the end of the sentence, swallowed it, and looked for a way down. "Well, let's go on in, then. I need that Trader and I need that cop, too."

"He's a cop?" Meaning, *I thought you said they was tryin' to kill you.*

"He's one of mine, Leon. Move your ass." I paused. "It's good to see you."

And it was, too. Some things only another hunter will understand, and moreover, sometimes you don't want to be questioned. It didn't matter to Leon what the hell was going on, if I was in it, he was going to be in it too. Up to the eyeballs, if necessary, and without counting the cost or thinking twice about it.

And while we were at it we would find out who was shipping scurf around, for God's sake.

I hopped up to the ledge, but Leon's fingers curled around my arm. Only another hunter—or Saul—would be able to do that without me instinctively twitching away. "Jill."

The street below looked quiet. I took a second look, to make sure. "What?"

"You doin' all right, darlin'?" Quiet, with absolutely no Texas bluster.

The street swam with light as if underwater, wavering, and snapped into focus when I made an almost-physical effort to clean up my mental floor. "No. I'm not." The truth burned my tongue, but you can't lie to another hunter.

You just *can't*.

His hand fell away. "Well sheeee-*yit*."

"I heartily concur. Now come on." I leapt out into space, pulling etheric force through the scar at the last moment, and slammed down on the pavement, smoke flashing in the air as the sudden violation of a law of physics rippled around me.

Jesus, Jill, what would have happened if the scar failed? You'd be lying on the pavement bleeding, now.

I told myself not to borrow trouble and stalked for the entrance to the ER. Leon would find his own way down.

Of all the wonders the world has to offer, a Trader hovering by the bedside of a foul-mouthed homicide detective is surely one of the most uncommon. Carp was beaten up, bruised, and had bled all over Kingdom Come from a couple shallow head wounds and a more serious one on his right thigh that looked like a huge dogbite.

I kept one eye on the Trader while I examined Carp. A phlegmatic Filipina nurse swabbed the hole in his leg. He was shocky but not too bad, and I was worried about being seen here.

Leon crowded into the curtained cubicle, eyeing the Trader in her evening gown and blood-colored hair just exactly as he would eye a critter crawling on his boot before he crushed it.

"You stupid son of a bitch." I kept my tone calm, low, quiet. "Carp, I should peel your skin off in strips. You *idiot*."

"Mom . . ." He shivered, mumbling. The nurse— *Concepcion,* I remembered her name with another one of those wrenching mental efforts—merely glanced at me. They see a lot of me at Mercy, and they've long since stopped caring what I do or look like as long as I don't shoot anyone.

Sometimes they get disappointed, but they're used to that in the ER.

"Kismet?" His tone was too dreamy, and I glanced at Connie.

She shrugged, brushing me aside with one soft shoulder as she handed his wallet and badge over. Her shoes squeaked on the linoleum. "Shock. Head wounds are messy. And this thing. Looks clean, but the edges are ragged. *Madre,* you bring in some interesting things, no?"

"No other wounds?" Raw disbelief married to unwilling hope inside my chest. I hate those pairings. They usually end up badly. The edges of the leg wound weren't discolored, and held no trademark candy-sweet corruption. He wasn't poisoned, thank God.

"They only wanted to play with him before Shen came down." Irene tilted her head, a tendril of that fantastical hair brushing her flour-pale cheek. "I tried to—"

Leon made a restless movement, as if he couldn't believe she was stupid enough to open her mouth. "Speak when you're spoken to, Trader."

"How soon can I get him out of here?" I gave Connie the full benefit of my mismatched stare.

She paled, but gamely rolled her eyes. "*Señora,* this needs stitching. And he's in shock—"

"We can fix that. Get some sutures."

"I am no doctor—"

"*Now,* Connie." I said it very softly. *I am not going to wait around here for someone to come to finish him off.* "Get some fucking sutures and get him ready to travel."

"Galina's?" Leon made another restless twitch, and I glanced at him.

"Of course." *There's no place else in the city I can be sure he's safe, not after tangling with Shen like that. Jesus. I shot her* hair. *She'll really be after me now, and I have to question this Trader.*

Hard.

The nagging sense of something not-quite-right returned, but I didn't have the leisure to ferret it out.

The Trader chose that moment to pipe up again. "I brought him here, I was worried—"

I barely saw Leon clear leather, his Smith & Wesson suddenly pointed at her forehead. The knife in his other hand pressed its flat, silver-loaded blade against one milky shoulder, and the Trader shuddered. A slight sizzle;

the silver ran with blue sparks. Under the smell of Lysol and human pain endemic in emergency rooms, the sweet-pork foulness of burning Hell-tainted flesh cut sharp, a serrated edge.

Concepcion gasped.

"Shut the fuck up," Leon said, conversationally. "You one small step from being sent to face Judgment, Trader. Got that?"

No flush crept up through Irene's sick pallor, but a greenish tinge bloomed along her cheeks. Her jaw worked, her gaze shivering back and forth between Leon and me, but otherwise not a muscle flickered. She nodded, and my fingers eased off the gun butt. My gun remained in its holster.

Why would a Trader help Carp? There must be an advantage in it for her. Of course, not having me kill her is an advantage. Am I really that scary?

When he peeled the knife away, an angry line of blisters boiled through her skin. They weren't reddened either, but tainted with green like the pale underside of a poison-bearing frog.

I wondered if she would bleed green, and didn't want to find out. What had she bargained for, to end up like this?

Not your problem, Jill.

I could sense no sorcery hanging on her, and she didn't appear to have much in the way of invulnerability or superstrength. Of course, I hadn't tried to kill her yet, so that didn't mean much. "Sutures, Connie. And move it along, I'm on a schedule here."

"Si, señora." Concepcion didn't waste further time arguing, just brushed past me and pushed the curtain aside.

"Jill?" Carp sounded even more dreamy and disconnected. It was a bad sign.

"Right here." I did something that surprised me—I picked up his hand where it lay discarded against the remains of his slacks. Whatever had made the hole in his leg had chewed right through his clothes; thank God it hadn't hit the femoral artery.

His fingers were limp, cold and clammy. I squeezed them. "What were you doing there, Carper?"

"Waitress. The waitress." His eyes rolled up into his head and he shivered. "Teeth. They all had teeth."

No shit, Carp. They all do. My pager went off, the slight soundless buzz against my hip a reminder of how vulnerable I was. I fished it out of its padded pocket with my free hand and glanced at the number.

It was familiar. Someone paging me from my own house, most probably Theron. He was likely to be climbing the walls by now.

Concepcion reappeared with handfuls of medical supplies. "I should not do this, *señora*. He needs to be admitted."

"He'll be admitted all right, Connie. Suture him up and give us a few cc's of adrenaline in case he goes under, and something for the pain."

"There are more *policia* here," she whispered, shoving the crackling plastic into my hands. Sterile packaging, each tool in its own little pouch. "They are asking if any of their kind has been admitted. Go."

"Oh, *Christ*." Would this ever end? "All right. We'll go out the back. Don't worry, I'm not going to let your patient die."

She shrugged. "Tonight I have many patients, not just one."

"And you can't remember this particular one, right?" I handed over a fifty-dollar bill—hey, she had kids to feed, I knew that much—and nodded to Leon, shoving the packets in assorted pockets of my trenchcoat. "Help him. I'll watch the Trader." A few moments' work had a tourniquet above the hole in Carp's leg. He wasn't bleeding badly but moving wasn't going to be a fun experience for him. Leon got him up off the bed, and I heard raised voices toward the Admissions section of the ER.

The Trader stared at me, her lips parted. All of her had a matte finish except her lips and the dark holes of her eyes. In dim light, or nightclub shine and flicker, she was probably a sight to behold. Here under the fluorescent wash, she just looked tubercular, but with a green undertone instead of consumptive flush.

"Get moving." I pointed. "You're still alive because you brought him here. Don't make me reconsider."

20

"*W*here have you *been?*" Galina got that much out before she saw Carp, who was pale as death and hanging onto Leon like a shipwrecked man clinging to drifting wood. His injured leg wouldn't work quite right. She moved forward to help him without missing a beat. "Goddammit, Jill, you just missed Theron."

Dammit. I made another one of those gut-wrenching physical efforts, trying to prioritize. There were too many things to do. "Is he okay?"

"He said something about your house infected with hellbreed—oh, my goodness. Hello, Leon. Get him in here, lay him on the table. Open up that cupboard on the left—"

I started unpacking medical supplies from my pockets. "Infected with hellbreed?"

"He barely got out in time. Says there's at least six there. And they've found more scurf—" Galina's eyes widened as she took in the Trader, but she didn't mention it, just helped Leon get Carp onto a table in the small room off the main showroom of her store. The table, an old butcher-block number matching the one upstairs in her kitchen, had legs carved with the winged serpent of the Sancs and a system of straps that could hold down a pain-maddened hunter or a dangerous, untreated victim of a Possessor. The old thick leather straps also sheathed thin flexible silver wires, blessed and knotted specifically to constrain harm and evil. Coupled with a Sanc's traditional protections in the house walls, this was an excellent place for stopgap exorcisms, interrogating reticent Traders, or engaging in a little trauma surgery when a hunter's life gets interesting.

Though not as interesting as it is right this second. "Scurf? Where?"

"Near the river. The 3700 block of Cherry, he says you'll know when and if you get there. Good God, what happened to this guy? Who is he?"

"Homicide detective. Name's Carper. Keep him here, and keep him alive for me. This Trader stays here too, I need her in one piece and available. You." I pointed at Irene, who jumped as if pinched. "You come with me into the other room, I've got a few questions. Leon, we're going scurf hunting in a few minutes. Stock up on ammo and whatever else we need."

Some days it's nice being the resident hunter. It means some decisions are just not consensus. Leon nodded and sidled against the wall. Galina hunched over Carp and kept working to patch him up.

"The ammo is in that cabinet there. Take what you need," Galina said as I left the room.

The Trader followed me out into the darkened front room, the walls humming and alive with Sanctuary shielding. Crystal balls in the glassed-in case under the counter sparked, swirling softly with golden light. The stock rustled, books and materials all alive in their own specific ways in a store that has the advantage of being completely useful—unlike a few other occult shops I've had the bad luck to try to supply myself from.

Sometimes I wonder what hunters do without Sancs in their territories. Santa Luz is lucky to have Galina.

"All right. Start talking." I rested one hand on my bull-whip, the other on a gun butt. If it made her nervous, she didn't show it.

Much. Her eyes were wide. The dim light was kind to her, making her bloody hair a river of softness and her shell-like hips curves of delight. The stain on her lips made her look just-kissed. She must have been pretty in her own way, while human. "I'm allowed to talk now?"

"Don't get cute. Carper had a lead in the organ-theft case, and it was you. You have exactly thirty seconds to tell me what you know, everything you know, leaving nothing out, or we learn if you bleed green too." I didn't even have to snarl, the flat matter-of-factness in my tone was more chilling than ranting and raving would be.

I was too tired to rant and rave. The successive shocks were beginning to wear on me.

Get over it, Jill. Focus.

"Organ theft." Did she sound relieved? She nodded, and a curl fell forward, sweetly and fetchingly, into her face. A shadow of hardness in her eyes told me the attractiveness was only skin-deep. There was something else under that thin crust.

"And dirty cops. Start talking." I kept one eye on the clock.

"Oh, that. It wasn't even work, just something I learned on a house call." When I gave her a blank look, she smiled, a thin tight curve of lips that brought the hardness out and made her look a lot less sex-kitten. "I'm one of Shen's dogs, hunter. We're available for reasonable rates if you have . . . desires, and the money to pay for them."

That was nothing new. And neither was the way her face changed. Even paranormal hookers learn how to calculate, and they learn how to try and hide that calculation. She wasn't very good at it. Maybe she hadn't had a lot of practice yet.

"About two weeks ago I had a client, a police officer. Normally run-of-the-mill detectives can't afford us, you know. It's mostly the brass we service, and the politicos. But this one was flush, I guess, and paid up front." A gleam touched her eyes at the mention of money—a ratty little gleam I wasn't sure I liked.

"How much?"

"Seven thousand to secure the appointment, another five for the standard consultation, and four for . . . extras." Faint dislike tinted her voice, swirled away. She shifted her weight, licked her lips again.

Those heels must be murder. I waited for the rest of it.

"He wanted the usual, and my specialty. Most of all, though, he wanted to talk. His conscience was bothering him. That's what I do, I provide . . . discipline."

I got the feeling she wanted to call it something else. That gleam in her eye turned into a hard little diamond, assessing how much of her story I was buying. I still waited. Silence is the best weapon in conversations like this.

"Anyway," she continued, "he was really upset. Kept

repeating that he hadn't signed on for murder. He'd just wanted to make some money, some of the money he was spending on me. It was getting too big. He wanted out, but couldn't see any *way* out. I just gave him the usual and left. I didn't tell Shen about it—it didn't seem important, the man wasn't Trade material. Too guilt-ridden." Her shrug was soft poetry, like a Venus flytrap just waiting to close. "Anyway, tonight *this* detective shows up and asks for me. He stinks of human and doesn't seem to notice the place isn't safe for him. Turns out he had access to my client's credit card statements and traced me from there. We're independent contractors, you see, and—"

"Names. Your client, anyone else he mentioned."

Her eyes flickered from side to side, and a pale tongue-tip crept out, touched her glossy lower lip. "I don't know, the confidentiality—"

For fuck's sake, what are you, a psychiatrist? "I don't give a shit about confidentiality, I want names. That table in there can hold a Trader down, you know. You've been cooperative so far, I'd hate to have to *convince* you to give me what I need."

She shrugged again, satiny flesh moving against the velvet of her gown, and I had one of those irrelevant flashes of memory that happen when you've been going for too long on not enough rest. I'd been idly trying to figure out who she was dressed to resemble, and I had it now. She looked *just* like Jessica Rabbit in real life, right down to the high wide forehead.

I hadn't seen that movie in forever.

"It doesn't make much difference. Shen will kill me anyway." Her gloved hand flicked nervously and produced a long thin brown cigarette with a gold band. The pulse ran high and hard in her throat, despite her show of indifference. "The name on his credit card was Alfred Bernardino. Italian, greasy, built wide and hairy. Do you want to know what he wanted me to do?"

Bernardino? Why does that sound familiar? Most cops' names do sound familiar, since I put every rookie through the obligatory orientation class. But this sounded *more* than familiar—it sounded like I'd heard it in the past couple days.

My memory's normally like a steel trap; I only have to concentrate for a second or two to make a connection. The tip-of-my-brain feeling around the name hovered and, maddeningly, retreated. *Shit. Goddammit.* "I don't much care. What did he tell you about the organ trade? Is Shen involved?"

"All I know is that they're getting them somehow. There's a buyer from out of state, they pack them up and send them in shipments from a private airfield out of town. There are lists, you know, people too rich to stand in line like the rest of us." Another shrug. Her voice quivered, but I didn't blame her. Facing down a hunter in a bad mood should give anyone the shakes. Especially a Trader with something to hide.

And she was most definitely hiding *something*.

Jesus. "What do the cops do?" *I should have dug harder to find the clients that Sorrows bitch was shipping organs to. I should have kept an eye on Sullivan and the Badger and their case, too. God*dam*mit.*

Hindsight is twenty-twenty, but no hunter likes that sort of vision.

"They find the donors and cover everything up. It's

just under the table, he said. Like hiring illegals for yard work."

What a lovely way to look at it. "He told you all this?"

"He had a lot on his mind." She waved the cigarette. "Can I get a light?"

"No. Galina doesn't like people smoking in here, and you're not going outside. At least, not until I know you're telling me the whole truth." *This is a nice neat little story, but something's off. It just doesn't make enough sense.*

"Come on. Shen's going to kill me, this is the only chance I've got. I'm trading this for some kind of protection. They say you're fair."

Goddamn Traders. "Who says?"

"They. You know, *them.* Everyone."

"They say I'm fair?" *Now that's news. Traders saying I'm fair?*

"Mostly. I'll tell you something else if you protect me."

I eyed her in the gloom. The taint of Hell on her aura and that ratlike gleam in her pretty eyes told me not to trust her as far as I could throw her over my shoulder with a broken arm, but I was holding most of the cards here. She was right. Shen An Dua wouldn't take this Trader back unless it was to make an example of her, both for consorting with me and for being party to Shen's humiliation.

Which made Irene officially my problem. Except she was a *Trader.* And there was still a very significant unanswered question.

"Does it have anything to do with one of Shen's people trying to kill me in my own house?"

For a moment, something hunted flashed in her dark, liquid eyes. She lowered the unlit cigarette. "To kill you?"

Bingo. She knew something about it. This was looking up. "Yeah, a blond scarecrow. I'd be insulted, except it's easier when they send stupid-ass kids to kill me instead of people I'd have to work up a sweat over." My fingertips tapped the whip's handle, a solid comfort. "So, any light you can shed on this?"

"A blond . . . Fairfax? Why would she . . ." Now her hands were limp as boned fish at her sides. Her mouth loosened a little, and the shock made her seem more human. "He's . . . dead?"

Fairfax? What a name. "I don't play pattycake when murder comes calling, sweetheart." It answered a question—Shen had wanted me dead, but not enough to send a 'breed with the balls to do it. Or maybe she just wanted me looking somewhere, and the blond 'breed was supposed to send me in another direction. I hadn't given him enough time to lie to me.

Irene actually staggered, as if the heels had been too much for her. "He was . . ." It was a bare whisper. "He wasn't there to kill you. If he managed to get out he was there to warn you. One of the higher-ups wants you dead for interfering with an experiment."

Huh? Then why did he jump me? "What kind of experiment, and why would Shen warn *me*?"

"Maybe he escaped. But Shen might send him, if she didn't need him anymore. And she's got a grudge against the owner of the Monde."

"Perry?" *Well, who else?* "He's involved? What kind of experiment?"

The air swirled with darkness and the scar on my wrist tingled. Irene actually flinched when I said his name.

I didn't blame her one bit.

"I don't know. Fairfax is dead?" The green tone was back under her paleness, pronounced even in the dark. And the hard, calculating gleam had fled her face. "My God."

Well, at least that solves one mystery. Why are there other hellbreed at my house, though? "Sorry." I didn't *feel* sorry, but she looked so lost for a moment I almost couldn't help myself. "Look . . ." *What are you about to do, Jill? This is madness. She's a* Trader, *goddammit!*

But still, she'd made the right choice, taking Carp to the hospital. Sure, she'd done it because I told her she was next if he died—but still. It had to count for something, didn't it?

"Do you have what you want?" Her shoulders sagged, she dropped into her heels. "If you do, I'll be going back to the club."

What? "What the hell for? You just said Shen's going to kill you."

Her shoulders hunched. "If Fax is dead, I don't care."

Say what? "Oh, please. We're talking about a hellbreed, right?" I watched her flinch, dropping her gaze to the floor as her lips twitched. *Can it, Jill. Stick to the matter at hand.* "What kind of experiment, and who was running it?"

"Fax might have known. I don't." She glanced at me sidelong. A bleeding, shifting light had lit far behind her eyes. Did she actually look relieved? "Are you done?"

All my chimes rang at once. *Not even close. Not until I'm sure you're not hiding anything. And not until I'm sure you're telling the truth.* "You're staying here for the time being. How far is Perry involved in this? Is he the one who wants me dead?"

"No, it's one of the *other* higher-ups." Irene shivered. Now tears glimmered in the corners of her wide eyes. One had even tracked down her cheek, and I couldn't tell if it was grief or relief, her face was changing so fast. "But if you, say, owed Shen a favor, she could use it to her advantage against the owner of the Monde. She'd like that."

I eyed her. The idea that she might know a few things about how Perry interacted with the other hellbreed in Santa Luz was . . . intriguing, to say the least. Not to mention the "higher-ups." That was worth a good hour or two of hard questioning.

An hour or two I didn't have. But Galina would keep her here for me, all safe and warm.

"Jill." Leon stepped out into the shop's main room. "Everythin' even, darlin'?"

I don't know if you could call it that. "Even-steven. Want to go kill some scurf and find out why someone's shipping them?"

"Can't wait." His eyes narrowed as he took in the Trader, who slumped, splay-footed, on her high heels. "What are you gonna do with that?"

"She may be useful." I hated the words. It was the sort of thing a hellbreed would say. "How's Carper?"

"If he can pull through, Galina will pull him through. He seems okay." My fellow hunter shrugged. "We going?"

"Certainly." I weighed every priority I had, found each one jostling with the others, and wished wringing my hands was an option. "Let's roll."

21

The aftermath of a scurf fight isn't pretty. There's slime all over everything; most of it breaks down into powder but it will steam on any night under seventy degrees. The footing is treacherous, and everything that can be broken probably is. Weres are very rarely messy, but scurf are not the neatest kills in the world.

They just won't stop wiggling.

We arrived too late for any of the fun, and the Weres were gone. Instead, the warehouses were a shambles, the rail doors dented as if stroked a good one from inside by a huge hammer. There was a smell of fur and clean fury lying over the choking terrible candied sweetness of scurf, and Leon was pale as we started checking, covering each other.

Nothing living remained. The Weres had done a good job, and I could see where the battle had been particularly fierce. I hoped nobody *else* had died.

"Huh." Leon lowered Rosita. "Would you look at that."

The slime was merely a thin scattering near the rail doors—a spur here joined a yard about a hundred feet away. One of the doors was half-open; we ducked out into the cold and examined the tracks.

They weren't brand spanking new, but they weren't disused either. Our eyes met, and Leon's mouth firmed. We slid into the warehouses and he held Rosita pointing straight to the ceiling, gapping his mouth a little bit as he breathed to try and relieve some of the stink. "You thinkin' what I'm thinkin', darlin'?"

I pointed. "Pens, to hold them? You could herd them out through here. . . . If you were stupid enough to do so, I guess. But *why?* And where the fuck are the Weres? There should have been one or two here hanging around, waiting for stragglers—or for me."

He nodded, curling dark hair flopping into his face. "Yeah. And look here."

Part of the wreckage was metal gates, chain link knocked down in sheets—and a row of pegs holding slim black cattle prods. Some of them had been knocked down.

"Oh Jesus," I whispered, nausea biting under my ribs.

"Yeah. This definitely qualifies as big fuckin' problem." Leon shuddered like a horse scenting a snake. "What the *fuck?*"

I touched one of the cattle prods, lifted it down. The end crackled slightly when I depressed the trigger. One hell of a magic wand. "This is getting weird. Where are the Weres? One or two should *be* here."

He shrugged. "Suppose we look around after we give the rest of this the eye. Maybe . . ." But there was no way to make the situation any less odd. Neither of us said what we were thinking.

This has got to be a trap.

Nothing happened as we checked the rest of the building. Three interconnected warehouses, an L-shaped nightmare; we'd check the bottom of the L next. Even the roof was spattered with powder-slime.

Why weren't there more disappearances? This much scurf, there had *to have been something, someone else missing! Unless they were shipping them in quantity—but how were they feeding them? Scurf need* the *hemoglobin or they go into brainrot.*

There was a foreman's office up a rickety, smashed staircase neither of us could trust our weight to. Leon scabbarded Rosita and gave me ten fingers, lifting with a grunt, and I caught the edge of a window that might have sliced my fingers down to bone if glass had ever been put in it. For once, cheap shoddy work was to someone's advantage.

It was a moment's work to muscle myself through into the office. The light was uncertain, the few unbroken fluorescent fixtures buzzing like Helletöng through broken teeth.

The office was torn to shreds too, claw marks dragged into the cheap rotting drywall. Were claws—and *others.* Once you've seen them a few times, it's easier to differentiate claw marks than normal people would ever believe.

"Shit," I breathed, and started casting around. The candy-reek of scurf covered up the rotten smell of hellbreed, but once I scented it the aroma of Hell moved front and center.

And I hadn't been here to protect my Weres, god-dammit.

Drifts of slime-spattered paper covered the floor. A metal desk sat in one corner under a refrigerated cabinet; I looked it over and gingerly swung the powdered door open. Bottles of a rusty-dark liquid stood neatly on the shelves.

My gorge rose, pointlessly. Blood. But not nearly enough for the number of scurf formerly housed here.

Not to mention the obvious question—who were the donors, and were they willing? "Leon? Any refrigerators down there?"

"I'll look. What's up there?"

"Blood canisters stacked like Bud Lights. And a desk. There was at least one hellbreed here."

"Sheeeeee-yit." Maybe it was the Texas in him, but he could put an incredible amount of disgust in two stretched-out syllables.

The desk drawer was locked, but a simple yank took care of that. It was almost frightening, how casually I tore the reinforced metal apart.

The scar skittered with unhealthy heat, flushed and full. It was getting disturbingly easy to rip things up. I yanked a handful of folders up out of the drawer and flipped one open.

Nothing but shipping manifests. I eyed them, a sick feeling beginning under my breastbone. The informa-tion in them started to click over into the coldly rational part of my brain, and intuition kicked in. I scattered more papers, found pictures—eight-by-tens of an airfield. The picture started revolving inside my head, and I began to feel sick.

Oh, God. I spent at least ten minutes moving around, digging through paper. Bureaucracy is a bitch. You can't run an operation without it, but it leaves slimy little paw-prints all over everything.

"Jill?" Leon, moving downstairs. "You should come take a look at this." Sound of movement. "Jill?"

My throat was dry and my hand actually trembled. "Jesus," I whispered. "Jesus Christ."

"Jill, get the fuck down here, darlin'." Leon's voice didn't tremble, but it was firm. "Come on."

"One second," I said around the rust in my throat. The pattern was clear. Infrequent shipments from down south and slightly to the west, Viejarosas way. Mostly regular shipments from due south, with notations attached to the irregularities that I could well imagine. Smaller, more frequent notations in another column for shipments to ARA, wherever that was. I had a sinking, chilling feeling that I knew.

Oh, Jesus. Jesus God. No wonder there haven't been disappearances I could track.

"Goddammit, Jill! What the fuck's going on?" Leon looked relieved when I appeared at the window. He looked a little less relieved when I landed right next to him, boots thudding and the force of the landing almost driving me to my knees. The jolt was a bitch—three-quarters of a story isn't enough for me to brace myself, there just isn't time.

"I've got an idea. What are you bellowing about?"

He pointed. "This way."

As we worked our way down into the bottom of the L-shape, the pens got more and more reinforced—and more terribly shattered. How many scurf had been here, rattling against the chain link, tearing at the metal that held them?

Jesus. I had a good idea what we'd find around the corner.

Leon had already checked it, but we still covered each other as we slid around into the bottom of the L-shape. The light was a little better here, not so many fixtures damaged, but it wasn't the sterile white glare it would have been before the fight tore through.

More pens on one side, not torn apart, but with each cage door open. These weren't reinforced like the other ones. At the end was another rail door, with a line of tasers hanging along the side.

On the side opposite the cages were huge industrial refrigerators, their slick chrome sides dewed with scurf slime . . . and blood. The scurf powder was running in thin crackling trails across the tacky-wet handprints and whorls of human claret. I knew what fridges this size were used for, but I was still miserably compelled to open one cautiously, with Leon and Rosita covering me.

Racks and racks of bottled blood. Hanging corpses, just like sides of beef, swaying gently when I touched them. Each fridge could hold about twenty bodies on neat rows of hooks, each cased in crackling plastic—and each with brown skin, an undertone of gray death to them. When I approached I could see the neat excisions—organs taken out, the cavities of the belly and chest opened with surgical precision, the rest of the body just plain muscle mass to be disposed of. The thighs were flayed, probably for bone marrow harvest.

"What the fuck?" Leon was having a little trouble with this.

So was I. "These are probably all illegal immigrants. The manifests up in the office have them shipped over the border by *coyotes,* by the truckful. They're transferred to a rail line and shipped in. Held in the pens with the doors there. We'll find surgical facilities here—"

"For what?"

"Organ donation, *definitely* unwilling. The scurf take care of the remains. They were in the other pens. There's hellbreed involved, and cops. The organs are taken to an airfield about twenty miles out in the desert if the gasoline receipts are any indication. With the initials ARA. Shouldn't be too hard to find."

"Huh." He didn't ask the next question, knowing I'd answer it anyway.

"Selling to rich people who don't like waiting in line for transplants." My stomach twisted again. Each crackling plastic bag was a *life,* goddammit, someone who had wanted the American dream badly enough to risk being shipped over the border one way or another. If they hadn't ended up here, they probably would have ended up working dead-end jobs, trying like hell to keep their heads above water. Maids, construction workers, fruit pickers, yardworkers, carwash hands—all those jobs people with my skin color couldn't be bothered to do for themselves or pay someone decently for.

And this is where it ended up. Used and discarded one way or another, human beings reduced to empty soda cans.

"Why the scurf, though?" Leon shuddered. "There has to be more. *Has* to be."

"Getting rid of evidence? And it's a good way to keep

me occupied and off their back. Not to mention if some-one has a grudge against me."

"And the cops trying to kill you?"

"Probably without the hellbreed's knowledge, whoever it is. If the 'breed knew they'd have 'em use silver bullets and I'd've been in much worse shape." My own shudder ran below the surface of my skin. "Let's finish checking and get the hell out of here."

"You got it, darlin'."

Checking the other fridges was a matter of minutes and nausea. Leon was definitely green by the time we finished, and I wasn't far behind.

I stepped out of the last fridge, my eyes on the pen op-posite, its gaping door. The padlock was busted—proba-bly Weres. If anyone survived this mess, the Weres would test them for scurf, and probably try to get them home.

Not that it mattered much. Whoever was locked in these cages would have nightmares the rest of their lives, survivor's guilt, and probably be back over the border within a month working at a low-paying dead-end job be-cause their family had to eat.

Jesus.

"I've heard of some goddamn stupid things in my life, but *this* takes the cake and the whole fuckin' picnic too. What sort of shortsighted idiot would ship scurf into a clean territory? Even hellbreed ain't that stupid." Leon touched a busted padlock, watched as the whole chain-link cage shivered.

I closed the fridge door. The sound of it clicking shut was loud in the stillness. *Something still isn't right here. Something—*

I'd opened my mouth, but Leon and I both froze, our eyes meeting. I didn't have to ask if he'd heard it.

A footstep, sliding and soft, and definitely not human. Instinct placed it—around the corner of the L, someone had come in the main door and was picking their way, quietly, over the rubble.

I slid a gun easily from its holster. Drew silence over myself like a veil, and started considering my options just as other sliding sounds told me our guest, whoever and whatever it was, had brought company.

22

Down!" I yelled, and Leon dropped as I opened fire, silver-laden bullets punching through the shell of the third hellbreed. Two down, six to go, and things weren't looking good even before the whip crackled; Leon rolled and I already knew he was going to be too slow, *too slow* as the 'breed snarled, thin black ichor splattering in a high arc as I brought the whip around, the strike uncoiling from my hip as chain-link rattled under my boots. Not the best footing in the world, but the chance bounce propelled Leon on his way as I leapt, my focus narrowing to keeping them *off* him.

It was a mistake, one I realized even as I was in the air, committed to the movement and turning to present as small a target as possible, my boot solidly cracking against the 'breed's already-lacerated face. Kinetic force transferred, I stopped dead and dropped down to land splay-footed. The brunet 'breed went flying back, crashing into two of his fellows with a sound like sides of beef flung together hard enough to crack steel-reinforced bones.

I caught my balance and heard Leon scrambling to his feet behind me. My lips peeled away from my teeth, a silent snarl that shook the whole building, light fixtures swaying and making the shadows do a knife-edged dance.

No. It wasn't my snarl. It was someone else's, thrumming subsonic like tectonic plates grinding together.

"Hold!" The command spilled darkness like wine through the air, and the 'breed all dropped, cringing, flattened under a wave of Hell-tainted power. "Stay your hand, avenging one. We are not your enemies."

Of all the things you could say, that's probably the biggest, fattest lie. I froze. I knew that voice.

"Shit," Leon whispered, and I wholeheartedly agreed.

The whip coiled, stowed safely in a half-second. I had both guns out and trained on the corner when he stepped into view, his cream-pale hair catching the light. It wasn't the hip super-short cut he'd sported last time I saw him but slightly longer, just as expensively trimmed, and it still did nothing for his expressively bland face.

Most of the damned are beautiful. The owner of the Monde Nuit is merely average, and that dries up the spit in your mouth like desert sun dries up a single lone drop of water.

Especially when his eyes are eaten alive by an indigo stain swallowing the whites, leaving the irises burning gasflame-blue. Eyes should not look like that.

He held his hands up, a classic *hey man I'm harmless* stance that didn't fool me for a second. His suit was pristine, gray wool instead of his usual white linen, sharply creased in all the right places. His shoulders were a touch broader than I remembered, and something new glimmered at his throat—a metal chain, with a small gem set in iron filigree flashing under the swinging, dancing light. It was a red-tinted diamond, and I would have bet everything I owned that it held a flaw like a screaming face in its blood-gleaming depths.

I swallowed dryness, settled my guns—one covering him, the other one covering the group of hellbreed, spilled or standing, he'd brought with him. "What the fuck are you doing here, Pericles?"

His hands dropped a fraction, the indigo swirling through his eyes like ink through water. "Why, my darling Kiss, helping *you*. What else would I be doing?"

"There's hellbreed stain upstairs, and this is right up your alley. Give me one good reason I shouldn't ventilate you now. Didn't you learn *anything* from last time?" *Calm down, Jill. You're sounding like a fishwife instead of a goddamn hunter. Chill out.*

He didn't shift his weight, but all the bloodless shark's attention was on me. "Oh, I learned, my sweet. It was a truly regrettable series of events, but so far in the past. I think we have other problems now, don't you?" A slight, expressive movement, indicating the shambles all around us, and the indigo stain retreated from the whites of his eyes, like the tide along a wreckage-filled beach. "You have not been keeping a clean house."

"You have ten seconds to tell me what the fuck you're doing here, Perry. And even less than that to convince me you don't have anything to do with this." My guns clicked, a nice piece of theater. Leon's breathing evened out, and I knew without looking that he was covering the other 'breed. The one I'd shot lay moaning on the floor, and Perry didn't spare him a single glance.

"This place is *mine;* it belongs to me. Why would I invite such filth in?" A shadow of distaste crossed his blandness. "They foul the carpet and stain the very air. Give me some credit for business sense, as well. There is no profit in having such things contaminating my territory—as I would have told you, had you bothered to speak to me."

Don't, Jill. He's just trying to get inside your head. The scar chuckled wetly, my pulse hammering as a wave of heat jolted up my arm. He liked doing that, fiddling with my internal thermostat when he was in the same room.

Another of those physical efforts to regain control and get my priorities straight made stress-sweat prickle along the curve of my lower back. The guns, however, did not waver. "You're just as much an infection as scurf, hellbreed. Start talking."

He opened his mouth—probably to taunt me—and visibly reconsidered, calculations crossing his face like the shadows of airplanes over baking sand. "I have been engaged in finding the source of this . . . corruption . . . for some time. No hellbreed claims to know about it, and each small marker I sent to be my eyes vanished. Three promising young ones gone without a trace, and I have decided to take personal interest in the matter. I have traced the corruption this far, and arrive to find you here and the work of Weres all over the walls—and the smell of my last protégé's untimely death upstairs." He folded his arms, still not sparing the hapless, bleeding 'breed on the floor a single glance.

One of the higher-ups wants you dead. I eyed Perry. "You wouldn't be the only one sending hellbreed after me, would you? What about skunk-haired idiots busting in on a nest-cleaning and trying to kill me?"

"Skunk-haired? His eyebrow lifted. "None of my protégés deserve that appellation."

"What about a 'breed sent to kill me in my own home and whisper someone else's name?" I pressed. I got a half-second of some other emotion flickering across his face. Did Perry look, of all things, *surprised?* "So you ride in to my rescue, huh? You're *helping* me. How very congenial of you." *Like shit you are. You're probably neck-deep in this too, God knows you always are.*

My tone must have warned him. His eyes narrowed a fraction, and instead of looking at me like a prize entrée, he eyed me like a cobra eyes a mongoose.

It was a welcome change. Still, it bothered me. What had calmed him down enough that the staining on his whites retreated?

I holstered both guns, though my entire body fought it. They were my protection, and these were *hellbreed,* for Christ's sake. "You can start by telling me which of your little hellbreed friends wants me dead."

"And what will you pay for that information?" He cocked his pale head, still regarding me with that cautious, unblinking reptile stare. His coterie cringed even further.

Jesus Christ, Jill, what are you going to do now? There was only one thing I *could* do. "I don't need to pay you, Pericles. You were in violation and we renegotiated. And you can threaten all you want, but if the scar goes sour, I'll be well within my rights to erase your sorry little ass from the face of the earth and send you screaming to Hell. Your choice."

There it was, as plain as I could make it. If he made trouble, better it was here with Leon backing me up and the scar still mostly workable.

"And that would reduce your power by an order of magnitude or two." Perry was very still, a statue carved of gray ice and platinum hair. His eyes had half-lidded, their gasflames burning down.

Why isn't he angrier? "Maybe I'm willing to risk it. What other hellbreed wants me dead, Perry?"

"There are many who wish your death, hunter. Aren't you happy we have such a marvelous little agreement?"

Oh no you don't. "The only *agreement* we have, Pericles, is that you trade information for your continued survival. You're in this city on my sufferance. This is the last time I'm asking, hellspawn."

Leon didn't move, but I could almost *feel* him tensing. Had I been backing up a mouthy hunter, I would have been getting a little itchy too. This was wrong. *All* wrong.

Perry didn't move, but there was a general scurrying and his hellbreed scrambled away like roaches once the light's on. The moaning hellbreed on the floor tried to scrabble away from Perry's slow, even footsteps.

Perry stopped, looking down at the mess of thin black-welling ichor and torn flesh. *"Haasai,"* he rumbled in Helletöng, and the injured 'breed drew in a huge hissing breath, as if preparing to scream.

The owner of the Monde didn't even seem to move. One moment he stood, hands in pockets, looking down at a wounded member of his species.

The next, his foot came down, and the injured 'breed's skull shattered like a watermelon dropped on concrete. I skipped away, guns clearing leather again, and braced myself. Preternatural flesh steamed, scurf slime cringing away from the deeper contagion of hellbreed ichor, and Perry made a short satisfied sound. A low chuckle, to be exact, as if he had just been surprised by something enjoyable.

My stomach turned over hard, rebelled against its moorings, and then I was too busy to care, because Leon let out a short sharp garbled word and Perry had taken three steps in a rush, with that same eerie darting quickness.

My left-hand gun spoke, a brief muzzle-flash and a roar. The bullet whined and pinged, and Perry stopped short. The sleeve of his suit coat smoked; a crease not intended by the tailor along his shoulder.

It was my night for trick shots, I guess.

"The next one goes in your head." My heart thundered, the scar snapping and twanging with pain like a rope in a high wind, puckering the flesh of my arm. *It's not doing anything, Jill, you know it's not, goddammit* focus! "Settle *down,* hellspawn."

Perry's head cocked like a lizard's, a flicker of tongue too red and wet to be human showing between his white, white teeth. Once before I'd seen what lurked under the pretence of bland humanity he wore, and my brain had shunted that memory aside, refusing to hold it. I was goddamn grateful at the time, and even more so now.

We stood like that, Perry's head not six inches from my right-hand Glock's muzzle, my left gun settling slightly lower, zeroed in on his mouth.

"Argoth," Perry whispered. The rumble of Hell's mother tongue under the word made the shadows turn angular, the lights buzzing and crackling. "Argoth is coming. You should be thankful, my dear one, that I've kept this little ant farm safe. You should get on your knees and pray to your bloodless Savior. I can only hold the tide so long."

"What tide?" *Argoth? Nobody I've heard of before. I'll bet I don't have time to run by Hutch's and set him to working on it, either.* The 'breed behind Perry drew back, with scary nimble quickness, making little inhuman sounds wherever they stepped.

"Silly, stupid little hunter." Perry leaned forward on his toes, for all the world as if wanting to tango and waiting for a dancer unwary enough to join him. "You truly think you owe me nothing? You think we *renegotiated?*"

Don't fall for it, Jill. But I did. My fingers tightened on the triggers, and the little clicks sounded very loud, especially when echoed by another, sharper, more definite click from Rosita. "Take one step closer, Perry, and *fucking find out.*"

We stood like that for five ticking seconds, the scar working a red-hot coathanger up the channels of my nerves and veins, but my arm never wavered. It was only pain, and if it got too bad, I would shoot him now and keep shooting until I was sure the fucker was dead.

If I ever *was* sure, that is. And it wouldn't stop me from parting out the body and burning each steak and hamhock down to ash.

And scattering the ash.

Miles apart, *continents* apart if I could.

The owner of the Monde stepped mincingly . . . away. He retreated, his eyes still bright blue, and it unnerved me more than if they *had* been turning indigo with fury.

Six feet away he halted, came back down on his heels,

and pointed to the 'breed on the floor, a quick sketch of a movement. "He was becoming troublesome, you know. You killed him just in time."

"I only wounded him, Perry. You murdered him all on your own. What's Argoth?" *Have I heard that name before? Don't think so. Shit. Never rains but it pours.* My pulse was struggling to thunder again, but control clamped down. The switch inside my head trembled— the one that could flip and make the world into a chessboard, every move clear and clean, with nothing even resembling hesitation to keep me from what had to be done.

The uncomfortable thought arrived right on schedule. *Like bashing a hellbreed's head in? Did that just have to be done? Does Perry think of it that way?*

"Not *what*, but *who*. He is Death come calling, and you will see him soon enough." Perry smiled broadly, his teeth gleaming. "You think you can manage without my help? Go and see, my dearest."

"Don't even think of welshing, hellbreed." The switch trembled again, I forced it to stay still. I had never even told Mikhail about that part of me, the way I could lift out of my own body and just do what was needed.

What was necessary.

"Oh, you may have rope to hang yourself and to spare. Have no fear of that." Perry took a gliding step away, and another, as if it was a dance. Chain-link rattled under his feet like metal bones. "Enough rope, and a noose as well. Goodnight, sweetheart."

He all but vanished into the sudden darkness, the lights at the bend of the warehouses failing utterly, and there was a sound like pipe organs chuckling in some deep subterranean cavern while a madman pounded on the keys. I let out a long shaking breath, forcing my arms to come down and rest stiff at my sides, weighed down by the guns and their cargo of deadly silver.

"What. The fuck. Was that?" Leon spoke for both of us.

"I don't know." I sounded tired even to myself. "This does not look good."

"Every time I see that motherfucker he looks like he just won the lottery."

Just like any other hellbreed. "He can't cash the check as long as I'm around, Leon." My eyes dropped down to the quick-rotting 'breed on the floor. The stink had just officially gotten worse. Runnels of decay poured from the smashed head, down the neck and through the chest cavity, fouling the clothes—a pale blue shirt that was Brooks Brothers, unless I missed my guess, and a pair of high-end designer khakis. Alligator wingtips, too.

I felt a momentary flash of guilt. It hadn't been necessary to kill them, if Perry was telling the truth and he'd come here to help.

Get real, Jill. What kind of "help" do you think Perry's going to offer you? Nothing you'd want to accept. You made the deal with him because Mikhail said it was a good idea, and now you're sitting pretty.

As pretty as you can sit with a hellbreed mark on your wrist and Perry laughing at you. Cold fingers touched my spine as I stared at the collapsing face.

It was a relief it didn't look human. Well, much.

You're not thinking straight. Focus.

Just as I prepared to make another of those gut-clenching physical efforts to tear my mind out of a psychological dead end, I froze and tipped my head back, staring up at the fixtures slowly losing their dangling momentum.

"Jill?" Leon was getting to the edge of not-quite-frantic-but-definitely-uncomfortable. "I'd like to buy a fuckin' vowel, please."

Me too. But I think I just got one. "Shhh." The thought circled, returned, and I leapt on it.

Irene's voice floated through the cavern of my skull. *The name on his credit card was Alfred Bernardino. Italian, greasy, built wide and hairy.*

Echoing against it came Carp's voice, from a few days and a wide shoal of darkness away. *They won't talk to me or to Bernie—his partner—but it doesn't seem possible that one of them pulled the trigger on him.*

Bernie, in Vice. Italian, built like a dockworker, with a foul mouth—always an asset in the Vice department—and stubby fingers always holding a filterless cigarette. Pedro Ayala's partner.

The insight hit me in a flash of blinding white, the fluorescents overhead beginning to buzz again, the warehouse brightening as hellbreed contamination ebbed.

"Holy shit," I breathed. "Leon, I'm an idiot."

He magnanimously refused to comment on that. "Can we get the fuck outta here now?"

"Sure thing. Let's go back to Galina's, I need to talk to Carp."

23

_D_awn leached gray through the sky. Galina's eyes were smudged with sleeplessness. "Thank God you're here," she greeted me. "Your detective's all right, but that Trader—"

Oh, Jesus. What now? "Do I have to kill her?" I only sounded weary, which was a bad sign. Leon sighed, leaning against the door, and Galina handed him a cold can of Pabst.

That's your local Sanc. On tap with whatever you need. Galina made a slight moue of distaste. "She's up in the greenhouse, crying. Tried to get out, but you said you wanted her here. Something about Fairfax, and—"

"I can kill her," Leon volunteered hopefully, popping the top and taking a slurp. The eyeliner turned his eyes into dark holes, and made the smudges of exhaustion under them deeper. "Put a real capper on my night."

It's not like a Trader to cry, unless there's an advantage in it. Still, she saved Carp. Under threat of death, but still. I let out a sigh that was mostly weariness, with a soupçon of irritation thrown in. "Not yet." *Not tonight, at least. Or today, since it's dawn.* "Where's Carp?"

"In bed. He's sedated. I think he'll be fine, if he can get over the nightmares." Galina sighed, too. She really was a gentle soul.

It made me wonder sometimes. If I'd ever been a gentle soul, would my life have knocked it out of me? Would I have survived hunter training and the nights afterward if I'd had any gentleness left in me?

Stay with the here and now, Jill. "Can he talk?"

Galina shrugged, slipping her hands in the pockets of her gray knit hoodie. She looked like she could use a night or two of rest as well. "Depends on what you want to talk to him about. He's not going to be doing quadratic equations, but he's coherent."

Upstairs, in the spare room over the shop, Carp lay still as death under a vintage yellow counterpane. He was cottage-cheese pale, his sandy hair a bird's nest, and even though the blood had been washed off the wound on his head was glaring. He stared at me through the gray light spilling through windows humming with a Sanctuary's powerful defenses, and I knew that look in his eyes.

Carper was now haunted. He'd seen the nightside up close. Not just the fragrance of difference that hung on a Were, not just the bodies left after a nightside eruption into the civilian world. He'd been in the nightclub for forty-five minutes or so—more than enough time for him to see up close what lurked under the fabric of reality.

They just wanted to play with him before Shen came down, Irene had said. God alone knew what game they had played. One that involved taking a bite out him, apparently.

I dragged a straight-backed chair over to the side of the bed. "Hey." Even though I needed words out of him, needed them quickly, I spoke slowly, softly. "How are you?"

He managed a harsh little thread of a laugh. "Kismet." It wasn't an answer. "Jesus."

"Just the former, Detective." A little humor, to set him at ease.

Who was I kidding? No way was Carp going to be set at ease. He'd seen under the mask.

I decided to get down to it. I couldn't make the shock any less, but I could at least get usable information out of him if he was coherent. "Bernardino, Alfie Bernardino. Ayala's partner. What do you know about him, Carp?"

Still, even as I said it, I hated myself. He needed sedation and a therapist, not me digging around and reminding him of things he was probably goddamn eager to start forgetting.

He blinked. Made an internal effort, things shifting behind his eyes. "Ayala. His partner. Slippery fucker."

Man, this just keeps getting better. "He's in it up to his neck, and probably deeper. But then you know that, right?"

"Credit card statements about this waitress— Irene. She—" He coughed, weakly, his eyelids falling down. "Kiss, their eyes. Their eyes were glowing."

They always do, Carp. I laid a hand against his forehead—my left hand, since the right was humming with fever-hot hellbreed-tainted force. "Just rest. It'll fade."

I was lying. Things like this don't fade. They come back in nightmares and in waking dreams, flashbacks and stress disorders you need antidepressants for—or something stronger.

Something like a steel-cold barrel in the mouth, or the bottle in the hand, or pills you can't get in the States. Something, anything, to make it go away so you can face the normal world.

Except sometimes you can't.

"Do you have anything else on Bernardino?" I didn't want to push him . . . but I had to know. I *had* to.

"File. Maybe in the file . . . their eyes. And the teeth . . ." His eyelids drifted down, and Carp took refuge in the sedation.

I didn't blame him.

I sat there for a long few moments, gray gathering strength through the windows, dawn coming up. My left hand lay human-cold and limp on Carp's sweating forehead, under the gash that ran along his hairline and jagged into his temple, sutured up and quiescent under a dabble of green herbal paste running with the clear gold of Sanctuary sorcery. Galina's work, fine and gentle, stitching together damage.

I wished she had something that would stitch up the damage inside him. I'd have to get him to a trauma counselor; there were a few on call that took care of things like this and billed the police department.

What comes next, Jill? Come up with a plan. Your brain works just fine, now for God's sweet sake, use it.

I took my fingers gently away from Carp's feverish, damp, *human* skin.

It took longer than I liked, breathing deeply and staring at the gray filling up the cup of the window, for my mental floor to clear. I needed sleep, and food, and a good few hours of hard thinking.

So many things I needed. What I was going to *get* was a long mess before this was all through.

When I finally pushed myself up, leather creaking, I stood looking down at Carp's slack face. He was still shocky-pale, but breathing all right. He might wake up not remembering much, the brain outright refusing, to keep the psyche from being further traumatized. Or he might wake up reliving every single second of it, replaying it like a CD on repeat until he had a psychotic break.

It was too soon to tell.

"Jill?" Leon stood in the door, the copper tied in his hair clinking and shifting as soon as he spoke.

"Where's the Trader?" I kept staring at the planes and valleys of Carp's unhandsome face, as if they would turn into a map that would lead me out of this.

The amulets around Leon's throat jingled a bit as he touched them, his version of a nervous tic. "Up in the greenhouse, Galina says. Are we sitting tight or moving out?"

I swallowed hard, juggling priorities. *Rest easy, Carper. I'm on the job.* "Moving in fifteen, Leon. Get what you need."

"Where we going?"

The next step is to find Bernardino—after we visit Hutch. "Hutch's, to find out what we're up against. Then we're going cop-hunting. Leave your truck here."

24

*H*utch pushed his glasses up on his beaky nose. "Oh, Christ." At least he didn't try to slam the door in my face. I pushed past him and into his bookshop, the familiar smell of dust, paper, and tea enveloping me. "I hate it when you do this."

"Hey, Hutch." Leon grinned. "How you doing?"

"Not you too." Hutch backed up to give both of us plenty of room. *Chatham's Books, Used and Rare,* was painted on a weathered board out front as well as in peeling gilt on the front window, and he did a good trade in repairing old texts. Most of his business is done over the Internet, which is the way he likes it.

Still, the place would've probably gone under if it wasn't for the back room. That room gets Hutch a subsidy from the resident hunter *and* resident law enforcement—a room with triple-locked doors, long wooden tables, and high narrow bookcases stuffed with leather-jacketed tomes on the occult, the theory and history of sorcery, accounts of the nightside, and just about every useful book a hunter needs.

Hey, we're not savages. Sometimes research is the only thing that keeps a hunter's ass from being knocked sideways by the unexpected. Ninety percent of solving any nightside problem is figuring out exactly what you're up against.

And if it wasn't in books, Hutch could *still* probably find it for you. He'd discovered computers in the dark ages when they still used floppy disks; they were still talking about his raids on government databases in law-enforcement classes.

He hadn't wanted to use the information, Hutch always pointed out. He'd just wanted to prove it *could* be hacked.

Nowadays he collects information the resident hunter might need—enough of an exercise for Hutch's skills to keep him out of trouble. If he did anything more, at least he didn't get caught. Which is all I *or* Mikhail ever really asked for. In return, we kept him out of trouble with the law when he went a-fishing and a-hacking on our behalf.

Today Hutch wore a Santa Luz Wheelwrights sweatshirt and a pair of khaki shorts, his thin hairy calves exposed. His beaky, mournful face twisted as he locked the front door and flipped the sign to "closed." "I *really* hate it when you do this. What is it now?"

He isn't one for excitement in the flesh, our local nightside historian. Wise man.

"Internet trace, Hutch. Find me the vitals on one Alfred Bernardino. He's in the Precinct 13 Vice squad. Hack if you have to, but don't leave any fingerprints." I barely broke stride. "And make yourself some tea, we're going to be here a while."

"Why aren't you asking Monty to do this? Or someone else?" Hutch pulled all his angles in, from his thin elbows to his knobby knees, and I considered telling him we had a scurf infestation and all sorts of trouble boiling into town.

I erred on the side of mercy, for once. "Because this time it's the police that are the *problem*, Hutchinson. Find the cop for me, and we're spending some time in the back room. I need to know about something."

"About what?" He didn't quite perk up, but any chance of poking through dusty old books brightens him considerably, even if he's allergic to the idea of seeing *anything* abnormal up close.

I'm not the only one with personality quirks.

"Something called Argoth. And something about an airfield just outside of town."

The milky pallor under his freckles deepened. *"Argoth?"* He actually squeaked.

I halted next to the counter with the antique cash register. A brand-spanking-new credit card reader sat next to the old brass machine. I turned, on the balls of my feet, my coat swaying with me, and met Hutch's eyes, swimming behind their thick lenses. "You know something about Argoth?"

"Only that he's a hellbreed, operated mostly in Eastern Europe. The last time he surfaced was 1929, he went back down in 1946." Hutch's thin shoulders came up, dropped. The bookstore breathed all around me. "You can guess where he was stationed."

And indeed I could. Both World Wars created enough

chaos, pain, and horror to blast the doors between here and *other places* wide open; the battlefields and camps were playgrounds for all sorts of nastiness. Some places on earth still haven't recovered—like Eastern Europe, the hunter population out there is *still* scrambling to get a lid on some of what was let loose decades ago.

"Christ." Leon sneezed twice. It *was* dusty in here.

I'd heard rumors about the war before, but this was unexpected. "Pull me the basic references on Argoth, then get me that cop's vitals. And I need you to find me everything you can on an airfield out of town, possibly called ARA."

Hutch had produced a small steno pad, a mechanical pencil, and was scribbling furiously. "And after that I change water into wine, right?"

If you could, I'd ask for a bottle or two of a nice pinot noir. "Don't get cute. After that you're going to Galina's while I poke around in here some more."

His eyebrows shot up and his pencil paused. "Again?"

Yes, again. Because if they know I'm alive and they know I go to Galina's, they probably know I come here too. "Yes, again. Unless you want to get a severe case of lead poisoning."

"What have you gotten me into now?" But he went back to scribbling. "Okay, come on into the back room. Christ on a crutch, why did I ever take this job?"

"Because you thought it would be interesting, Hutch, and Mikhail saved you from being locked in a six-by-nine." I really must have been feeling savage, because for once even mild-mannered Hutch shot me a dirty look and I realized that was a really, really bitchy thing to say to someone who had risked his ass over and over again to help me. "I'm sor—"

"Oh, shut up. Get into the back room. I just got a new machine, best way to break it in." He made little shooing motions with his hands, for all the world like a farmer's wife herding chickens. "Come on, kids. Let's go see what Uncle Hutch can dig up."

It's certainly something to see an underweight, glorified librarian poke and prod two fully trained and armed hunters around like a chicken herder. If I was less tired, I might even have been amused.

Hutch left about an hour later. I should have taken him to Galina's, but there was precious little time. The next half-hour passed slowly, both Leon and I up to our eyeballs in reading material. He'd taken the Argoth references; I took Carp's file and Bernardino's stats as well as whatever Hutch could dig up on the airfield.

"We are looking at some serious shit," Leon said quietly.

I glanced up from Carp's file. "How bad?"

He tapped the thick, dust-choked leather-bound tome sitting open in front of him. "Bad enough that I've got the heebie-jeebies, darlin'." Copper clinked in his hair, and he took a pull off the only beer Hutch had stocked—a brown-bottled microbrew Leon wrinkled his nose at but took down three of. "Says here that Argoth surfaced earlier than Hutch thought. First recorded instance of him is in 1918, something involving a batch of three hundred shell-shocked soldiers in a hospital ending up with a serious case of dead and half-eaten."

"Charming." I didn't quite shudder, but it was close. "Any verification?"

"Some British hunter thinks it was him, anyway. Then he shows up in Germany in 1924. A couple of Alsatian hunters living in Munich ID'd him hanging around with an Austrian wannabe rabble-rouser who came to power a little later."

I let out a slow whistle, air bleeding between my lips. *Ugh. Nasty.* "A *talyn?*" I hazarded. It certainly seemed likely. When they come out of Hell, they come hungry. And shell-shocked, vulnerable humans would be a nice snack.

"Could be. Sources ain't specific enough. Went through the hunters in Germany like a hot knife through butter all the way through the war; the Allies had to bring in their own hunters attached to the armies just to stay afloat of all the nasty." Leon's mouth pulled down like he tasted something sour. He probably did.

I dimly remembered hearing about that time from my own training, one of the long sessions with my head on Mikhail's chest and his fingers in my hair, his voice tracing through the history of what we know—and even more important, what we suspect. "Mikhail mentioned that."

It was a bad time all around. Here in Santa Luz there had been the great demonic outbreak in '29, and the few hunters remaining stateside during the war years had been overworked almost to death. The Weres suffered high casualties too, and pretty much the only thing that kept any kind of lid on the situation was the Sanctuaries letting hunters move into their houses and training halls, quietly taking sides even though they were supposed to be neutral.

Patriotism isn't just for normals, you know.

Leon looked down at the page, tapped it with one blunt fingertip. "Says here Jack Karma—the second one, that crazy fucker—takes credit for killin' him, in February of forty-five. In Dresden. That must've been a goddamn sight."

"Jack Karma, huh?" I eyed the book speculatively. "He moved to Chicago after the war, didn't he."

"Think so." Leon didn't need to say any more.

I had Jack Karma's apprentice ring, blackened and vibrating still from the incident that had killed him, tucked safely away in the warehouse on a leather thong with five other silver rings. Each one was a story, passed along the way family history is.

Mikhail hadn't spoken much of his teacher, and I supposed it was normal—as normal as a hunter ever gets. Losing your teacher is much worse than losing a mother or a father. It's almost as bad as losing an apprentice.

And I still could not think of Mikhail's death without an ache in the middle of my chest. "Huh. So we don't know exactly how high-up in the hierarchy this Argoth is. But Jack killed him or sent him back, right?"

"Probably just sent him back, if that blond 'breed is talkin' him up now. Which means he's worse news than a fuckin' *talyn*. But there ain't been anything in the news lately big enough to break anything big out of Hell. Not on this continent, anyway." Leon sighed. "There ain't nothin' else of any use here. What you got?"

In other words, Perry could be leading us down the garden path. Even though I didn't think it was very likely. Still, first things first. "A whole pile of not very much," I admitted. "Carp's right. The file's a bunch of dead ends.

There's only initials in witness statements, and witnesses have a habit of disappearing. Want to bet they all ended up as scurf chow?"

"Now why do you want to take an old man's money, darlin'?" Leon rolled his shoulders in their sockets, easing tension, and pushed the book away, leaning back in his chair and eyeing me.

"There's one common note in here—someone high up in the police structure, identified only as *H*. Pedro Ayala told Carp that he knew who H was, that it was bigger than Carp thought, and suspected wiretapping so bad he wouldn't even talk on a pay phone. Then he ended up dead." *And I still have to find time to find out who took him down. Christ.* "Sullivan and the Badger had four different leads who referred to a big-time cop as ringleader, but all four of them petered out, mostly with the people giving the leads disappearing."

"There's an almighty big mass grave out somewheres, then."

And a cop so dirty he makes Perry look almost clean. I swallowed hard. "Not if it's scurf-related. Listen to this. Twelve murders of illegal immigrants, organs stripped. Then everything stops—just when that Sorrows bitch moved in last year. Want to bet this little organ ring came to the attention of someone on the nightside once the Sorrows started putting their fingers in?" I cocked an ear, listening. Traffic on the streets outside. The shop was dead quiet. All was as it should be, hot sunlight trickling away with every moment we spent in here. Prickles of sweat touched the curve of my lower back even through the air-conditioning. Last year had been bad in more ways than one.

And somewhere out there in the world was Melisande Belisa, the Sorrow who had killed my teacher. Free as a bird, again.

Get it together, Jill. Belisa's not your problem right now. Scurf are your problem, and whoever is killing your people is your problem. Even Argoth isn't a problem— yet. Prioritize.

I took a deep breath laden with the smell of paper and dusty knowledge. Forced myself to pull it together.

"Huh." Leon thought it over. He sneezed twice, lightly. Took another swallow of beer.

It felt good to say it out loud, to string the events together. It's always handy to have someone else to bounce things off. "The scurf we've found have all been too old. If they're escapees from that warehouse on Cherry, they're communally sharing kills. Which means the disappearances we've had fit a pattern. If you dropped a mature nest in the middle of a populated area you'd have exactly the sort of disappearances I've been seeing lately."

"So it's a pattern." He nodded. "Good fuckin' deal."

"Amen to that." If it was a pattern, it could be anticipated—and interrupted.

"So we're gonna go find this cop? Bernardino?"

I gained my feet, pushing the chair back. "Yup. Let's just hope he hasn't gotten twitchy. Or a case of the vanishings."

Leon hauled himself up. "Never knew you was an optimist. What you gonna do about this Argoth character?"

Pray? Hope he's not hungry? "I don't know yet. But it might be time to visit the a few hellbreed dives and twist some arms—*after* I find out who's shipping scurf into my town."

"Sounds like a plan. I'm gonna piss."

"Thanks for sharing." I didn't say what we were both thinking. If hellbreed were connected to the scurf, and a major hellbreed's name was being bandied around, and one of Shen's Traders said a "higher-up" wanted me dead . . .

Well, it wasn't looking good. But at least we had something to look *at* now, instead of a maddening half-baked mass of weird occurrences with no rhyme or reason.

I sat staring at Carp's file while Leon vanished. Shut my eyes, breathed deep, and tried not to think of Carper lying in bed, his mind at the mercy of suffocating terror. Or of Jacinta Kutchner's body hanging like a rotten fruit from a blue and white nylon rope. Or of Saul and how much I wished it was him I was bouncing ideas off.

It was looking like the Kutchner case was my sort of case after all.

25

Bernardino lived on a quiet little street, not quite suburban but close enough. He had a nice ranch-style, freshly painted, and his yard was greener than many of his neighbors'. I wondered if he had a landscaping service staffed with illegals out to take care of it, and spent a good few moments wrestling with nausea at the thought as we slid through a neighbor's yard and up to his front door, seeking maximum cover. It wasn't easy, with a high-noon summer sun beating down.

He had no alarm system on his house, and he was probably at work in the Vice department.

Dear God, the irony.

I held my right palm in front of the doorknob and concentrated, a thin thread of etheric force snaking out and bifurcating. One thin thread slid into the doorknob, the other quested blindly and found the keyhole for the deadbolt. A moment's worth of the fierce, relaxed concentration peculiar to sorcery, and the deadbolt eased back, the doorknob lock clicking as it cleared.

"You'd make a great housebreaker," Leon mouthed.

Yeah, that's just one of the many career options open to a hunter. "You think?" I whispered. I eased aside, toed the door open while Leon covered me, and slid into Alfred Bernardino's home—only to recoil and straighten, the reek so intense it scorched the back of my throat.

Dead, decomposing human tissue. "Goddammit," I whispered, my eyes watering, and plunged into the house. Leon swept the door shut behind us, and we cleared and checked every room, working through a place that had obviously been searched. Drawers were pulled out, cushions slit, paper scattered everywhere—and that horrible, nose-eating stench.

And the smell of hellbreed or Trader, a subtle, sweet-sick corruption. "There's been 'breed here," I whispered. The kitchen was torn to shreds, a drift of takeout containers and cheap dishes. The living room was a shambles, the dining room smashed too. Bernie's taste had run to cheap mismatched bachelor furniture, but the huge state-of-the-art plasma flatscreen on one wall was new, and the stereo system still smelled of its packaging. That is, through the fume of smoky violence—even these toys bought with blood money had been broken.

I don't know if it was a fight or a hell of a search. Leon covered me down a hallway, we checked a bathroom and a room that had been left empty and bare except for a stain on the carpet and a silver tangle of handcuffs. The reek of sex fought briefly with other varied stenches; Leon's eyebrows went up and I shrugged, moving on. I pushed a door open softly with my foot and saw the source of the worst smell.

Alfred Bernardino lay spread-eagled on his bed, his

body bloated by several days' worth of decomposition. His ribs had been torn free and wrenched back, the lungs carefully pulled free and shriveled by exposure to dry outside air. His legs were flayed and his belly opened; a feast of insect life swarmed in the cave of his entrails.

If I'd had any gag reflex left on this case, the sight would have done it.

"Jesus," Leon breathed.

Another fucking dead end. "This is *ridiculous*."

Leon moved past me, checked the closet. Neither of us put our guns away. Bernardino's clothes were tumbled off the hangers, his cheap white-painted dresser drawers pulled out and disemboweled, and I leaned against the wall, silver tinkling sweetly in my hair.

"You think . . ." Leon glanced at me. "How long would you say he's been dead?"

I glanced at the window. It was suffocatingly hot in here, and the bedroom window was open a crack, the screen slit. Easy enough for insects to find their way in. The air conditioning wasn't on, and a cool bath of dread touched my spine, working downward from my nape. "With that window open and the critter buffet sign out? Couple days to a week. But we have his credit card run by Irene . . ." *A Trader, the last known contact we have with this man. Huh.*

"Four days ago," Leon supplied.

Looks like there's more here than meets the eye. My brain gears turned, meshed, caught. "It could fit with the widow's death. We have someone killing the cops to cover this up. Jacinta's account books are missing. Bernie's having second thoughts . . ." I sighed, then winked, shutting my dumb eye. The smart one, the blue one, showed me a room swirled with the etheric contamination of violent death and desperation. But nothing for me to latch onto, no thread that I could pull to unravel the mess.

Leon let out a gusty sigh, one he probably immediately regretted because he had to take a breath. "Someone tore this fuckin' place apart. And I don't like it—why hasn't anyone come by to check on him? He's a cop."

"A cop with a dead partner. If there weren't cops trying to kill me I could call in and find out if he was on administrative leave or something. Though if this is *el pendejo gordo* they were talking about, he can't have called in the gang hit on me." I lowered my guns, thinking, and my attention snagged on something.

On the bed, actually. It was stripped down to bare mattress and boxspring, but both of them were new, blue with pink flowers, a matched set of Sealys. Intuition tickled under the surface of my brain, and I stared at the mess of Bernardino's body, unseeing, for a long half-minute before Leon moved, checking the master bathroom again. Copper chimed in his hair, a deeper sound than the silver in mine. "Screen's slit in here, too. Window's open."

"The screen was cut in the widow's place. But the window wasn't open." I replayed the Kutchner scene in my head, walking through mental rooms taken in by a hunter's ground-in, thorough training in observation.

Yes, there above the bathroom window, two patches in the paint.

Curtain rod, ripped down. The screen hurriedly cut. The space between the screen and the window, just the right size to hold . . .

I let out half a soft breath, opened my eyes. "Come on."

The garage held two cars—a puke-green 1971 Dodge Charger that had seen much, much better days and was drifted with fast-food wrappers inside, and a brand new red Mustang with none of the grace or fluidity of the old models. A fiberglass piece of shit and a horribly mistreated piece of heavy American metal. There was detritus stuffed everywhere; Bernie had been a terrible slob.

But leaning against the wall next to the Mustang was an old mattress, dingy yellow and broken-in.

"Pop the hood on that and check the engine." I indicated the Charger with my chin and slid between the Mustang and the wall, reached the mattress, and started looking.

Twenty seconds later I found what I was looking for—a long slit in the fabric sheathing. I held my breath and reached in as Leon rummaged under the hood.

My fingers closed on something. Hard plastic, book-shaped, and thick. "My God," I whispered.

"What? What is it?"

I yanked the ledger free, tearing the tough material. It must have taken some doing to get the goddamn thing into the mattress, but the hiding place had done its job. "Leon, my dear, we have a break." I ripped it the rest of the way free and flipped it open, riffled through the pages, then fished around again inside the mattress and yanked another one free. "We've just found Jacinta Kutchner's account books. Cooked and *un*cooked, I'm betting."

"Is that so. Looks like this car will run, too. I ain't no mechanic, but nothing seems wrong with it." He dropped the hood.

"Let's find the keys, then. And get the hell out of here." Something stopped me, looking at the Mustang. For some reason I wasn't even considering taking it—for one thing, it was too red. We'd left Leon's truck behind for the same reason—it was too conspicuous a vehicle.

And for another, the Mustang reeked of hellbreed. Or Trader.

My instincts tingled again, and I looked for license plates. Nada. Not even a dealer tag. The Charger was registered to Bernardino, all its papers in order. "Someone's lying to me."

"You think?" Leon sighed. "The shit's just getting deeper. I'll look for car keys."

I wasn't looking forward to it, but we had to go to Micky's. I expected to see the regular Were waitstaff and I expected Theron at the bar. What I did *not* expect was to be almost-mobbed by Weres as soon as I set foot in the door. It looked like a regular lunchtime crowd, but it was full of cat Were and bird Were, and I was hugged, slapped on the shoulder, fingers brushing over my face and touching my hair. A very big, very angry Theron came pushing his way through the humming, thrumming crowd.

Even the framed pictures of film stars on the walls vibrated, glass and wood chattering. Theron grabbed me by the shoulders, gave me a once-over, and shook me twice, sharply, so my head bobbled and my ears rang a little.

I let him. A tide of sound rose through them, swirled, and Leon was clapped on the shoulder a few times. A bird Were breathed in his face, greeting him, and he nodded and grinned, giving a thumbs-up, especially when someone passed him a cold, foaming can of Pabst.

"God*dam*mit, Jill!" Theron shook me again. "What

am I going to tell Saul about this, goddammit? Where have you *been?* There's hellbreed all over your house—"

"Settle down." My tone sliced through the hubbub. I shifted Carp's file and the ledgers under my left arm. "There's not much time."

The rumbling swirled down, and I caught sight of an anomaly—a human face among the Weres.

Gilberto Rosario Gonzalez-Ayala leaned over the counter, watching the Were cooks as they moved around the kitchen. Amalia passed him, handing off a bottle of microbrew the kid looked far too young to drink, and the kid turned around, his eyes sweeping Micky's interior and stopping on me. "What the hell is he doing here?"

"Showed up. The 51s sent him to check with us, since you got firebombed on your way out of their territory. Then the guys that blew up your car moved into the 51 slice of the barrio. Things have been hopping down there."

Shit. How was I going to sort that out too?

Priorities, Jill. As much as I hated it, gang warfare wasn't my problem. I had bigger fish to gut *and* fry.

Someone flipped the "closed" sign and Weres crowded close as I commandeered a table near the back of the dining room, away from the windows. "Pipe down, everyone." I took a deep breath as they settled, eyes shining expectantly. "What we have here, ladies and gentlemen, is a situation. We have a hellbreed operating inside Santa Luz, shipping in scurf with the help of several members of the police force, and using them as the cleanup crew after a nasty little organ-stripping campaign. Illegal immigrants are being shipped in by *coyotes,* parted out like junked cars, and the remains disposed of. The organs are sold— and the scurf are *not* just here for cleaning up what's left.

There's experiments." The quiet had become dead heavy silence, pressing against my skin. "Experiments on scurf, with scurf tissue, and funded by this organ operation."

"What kind of experiments?" Amalia balanced her tray on spread fingers, tense and alert, not even the feathers in her hair stirring.

"I don't know." I set down the ledgers and Carp's messy, stuffed-to-the-gills file. Taken together, they were a pretty damning picture of corruption, at least from the organ-theft side of it. Looking below the surface, there was another shape, something looming over my city like a hand about to crush a struggling ant. "Corruption in the police department goes high up. I'm not sure how high just yet. The cop we thought put out the hit on me down in the barrio's been dead for a few days." I let my eyes travel past the Weres to the fringe of the group, to where Gilberto stood, leaning hipshot against the long lunch counter where truckers sometimes sat—or anyone who didn't mind their breakfast slid to them along the counter like a hockey puck. His dead eyes narrowed.

I held his gaze for a long moment. "Señor Gilberto?" *What does this kid know about the nightside? He knows about Weres, that much is certain.*

Gil stepped away from the lunch counter, and the Weres parted to let him through. Leon took in the kid with a swift glance and sucked another long gulp off his beer.

"He's representing the 51s," Theron didn't twitch, but he was tense at my shoulder. "They . . . feel bad, that you were attacked."

And they don't want to piss off a witch allied to the Weres. "It wasn't their fault. I wasn't on 51 territory. I'm worried about them catching flak from associating with me."

"They had you marked the minute you crossed off our turf, *chiquita*." Gilberto paused, took a sip. He was sorely out of place, a human kid with bad skin and the smell of neglect hanging on him like mildew amid the crackling hum of perfection from the Weres. "Now how you suppose they did that?"

I shrugged, my tattered coat flapping. "I'm a *gringa?*"

It was the right thing to say, because he laughed, a reedy little sound. "*Si, bruja.* But nobody knew you come down to see us but *el gato* here. Right?"

And Carper. "There was one other person—the cop that gave me the lead on Ay. Gil, your brother's partner killed him."

Gil's utter stillness might have fooled a human, but not a roomful of Weres. Theron sighed. I held the boy's dark soulless gaze, watching the color bleed out from under his cheeks until he was sallow instead of Hispanic.

"His partner's dead too," I continued. "His house was torn apart, but I've got a rough timeline. He had the widow's ledgers, and—"

"Hold up, *bruja.* Ay. His partner, you say? Bernie kill him?"

Silver clinked and shifted in my hair as I nodded. "It appears that way. I'm going to keep digging, though. Until I find out everything about this, I'm still on the job."

"Then the 51s stay on the job too." He darted a glance to Theron, sweat sheening his forehead and upper lip. He'd lost the hairnet, and his hair was surprisingly soft-looking, with a hint of childhood curl. "I go to Ramon. *Es un traidor en nuestra casa, bruja,* because there was no way they should know you visit us." Another silence rose, uncomfortably, between us.

I had to say it.

"The traitor may not be among the 51s, Gil. Because if Ay's partner was dead, my contact sent me into the barrio. But he's not fat. The name *el pendejo gordo* mean anything to you?"

The kid thought it over. "Lot of *pendejos gordos* in *el barrio, bruja*. Lot of them."

"Don't declare war on the cops." It came out harder and faster than I intended, and Gil stiffened slightly, his wiry shoulders coming up. "The last thing we need is a bloodbath in the barrio." He shrugged, the kind of evocative shrug street kids learn early. I pressed a little harder. "Do *not* fire on the cops." *Why do I feel like a den mother?*

The kid seemed to feel comfortable enough in a room full of Weres, and had only given Leon the same passing glance he gave me—measuring, calculating, and not frightened at all. Curiouser and curiouser. "I take it to Ramon. He decide."

Good enough. Ramon's smart enough to keep things quiet down there—I hope. "Can someone go with him?"

Two of the Weres—a lean cub whose face looked very familiar and a bird Were with sleek black feathers knotted in her straight dark hair—volunteered for the job. Gilberto left without a backward glance.

"Nice kid," Leon said, sarcasm tinting his tone.

He'd just as soon kill someone as look at them. Nice kid my ass. Still, Gilberto was smart enough to see my point about firing on cops. And if the 51s had sent him here, he couldn't be entirely lacking in brains *or* discretion. Still. . . . "How much *does* he know about the night-side?"

"Enough, Jill. They all know enough, down in the barrio." Theron folded his arms, leaning against a table. "You want to tell me why there's hellbreed swarming your house?"

I suppose I should be grateful he held off grilling me for this long. "If I knew enough to fill you in, I'd be gunning for the 'breed behind all this. So far all I know is . . ." I ran up against the wall of incomprehensibility, glanced outside to gauge the fall of sunlight. There was a pattern, sure, but it wasn't clear enough. "Any more scurf? Anything?"

"Not a whisper. We cleaned them out."

Thank you, God. "Did we lose . . ."

"Two more." Theron's jaw firmed, and a rumble swirled through the assembled Weres, drained away.

Goddammit. Futility clawed acid at the back of my throat. Two more of my Weres dead, and I didn't even know their names. "Were there hellbreed there? At the warehouse site?"

He shook his dark sleek head. "Not a one. We would have held back and waited for you awhile if there had been."

So the smell of 'breed up in the office had been *after* the fight? I chewed at my lower lip, considering. The cold dread had turned into a hard rubber ball in my stomach, and the smell of food taunted me. No Were strategy session is without munchies, but if they were closing down Micky's and feeding people for free the situation was dire indeed.

Weres can eat a *lot*.

I stared at the stack of paper on the table as if it might tell me something I didn't know instead of just taunting me with half-seen connections. "I want two or three Weres on Montaigne. Watch him, don't let anything get to him. He's a target now too. I also want some of you watching Galina's house. They tried to kill me onsite before and I've got a wounded human and a Trader in there. Hutch will be there too, for the duration."

Which meant only one thing. I expected serious trouble and didn't want anyone else to get burned. In other words, war. A fresh tension spilled through the Weres, a tautening of attention.

Good allies to have, Weres. But if something bigger than a *talyn* was coming down the turnpike, it might be time to evacuate them.

Deal with that when the time comes, Jill. For right now, get going on what you know *you have to deal with.* I glanced up to gauge Theron's reaction. He nodded. Then I dropped the bomb. "Tell the 51s we want a meet with the gang that opened fire on me. If we can find out who *el pendejo gordo* is I'll feel a lot better about this."

Of course he didn't think much of the idea. "Oh, for Chrissake, Jill, the barrio—"

Shut up, Theron. "You'll be standing in for me, I'm not going into the barrio again. Leon and I are going to make a run on this airfield where they transport the organs out. There's bound to be something out there."

"We'll go—" the Were began, but I shook my head, silver chiming. Rested my fingers on the butt of a gun.

"No, you won't. No Were will get within ten miles of that place. It's hunter business, Theron, the kind that doesn't mix with Weres. There's rumor of a hellbreed involved with this." *More than a rumor. This has sticky little hell-fingers all over it.*

Theron digested this, looked up at the other Weres. "Maybe that bastard that runs the Monde?"

They were quiet, watching us. Apparently Theron had been elected to talk to me about that. "Not him." Of that much, at least, I was reasonably certain. "Another hell-breed. Seriously bad news, if the sources are right."

Which was the understatement of the year. My brain returned to the problem, probing at it like a sore tooth. There is a strict hierarchy in Hell, and we usually only saw the lower orders, it being too goddamn hard for the biggies to come through into the physical plane. The biggest we usually see is a *talyn,* and they're mostly insubstantial anyway.

Except Perry, who might or might not be one. Which I didn't want to think about right now. He couldn't be a *talyn,* he was all-too-substantial on a daily basis.

I didn't want to think about that either.

If half, or even a quarter, of what Hutch had in moldy books about this Argoth was true . . .

"Leon and I will take care of it." I even said it with a straight face. "But I need every Were watching the city. Keep the barrio from boiling over, and see what you can do about finding out exactly *which* cop gave the kill order on me. Got it?"

"I don't like this," Theron said. "You should have backup."

Shut up. "I *have* backup, Theron. He's standing right here. What I don't need is you second-guessing me."

Another rumble rippled through the Weres. Theron

tried again. "This is Lone Ranger shit, Jill. You know how—"

I interrupted him, rude by any standard but especially by Were etiquette. "Shut *up,* Theron!" I rounded on him, both hands loose, and felt the tension in the room tip and shift. "Leon and I will *handle* it. You have no idea what's about to go down, goddammit, and I need my city kept safe while we avert a goddamn apocalypse or two!"

The Were studied me for a long moment, orange light shifting in his eyes. Dressing down a cat Were in public isn't a safe thing to do.

But goddammit, this wasn't a democracy. Weres function by cooperation and consensus—they *have* to. But when the city's under fire, with scurf and 'breed and God knows what going on, it's the hunter's call.

Still, Theron was my friend. And good backup. I shouldn't be taking out my frustrations on him.

The Were slumped, his shoulders going down. "All right." It was a submission, a virtual baring of the throat. "You got it, Jill. We'll keep the city together."

Leon was downing his third beer. I considered telling him to take it easy, decided not to. If the quick, strung-out jerkiness of his movements was any indication, he felt exactly how I did about this whole thing.

"Good deal." I pointed at the ledgers and the file. "Keep that for me, will you? I don't know where else to put it."

"Anything else?" He was suddenly all business. I didn't blame him.

"Just keep Santa Luz on the map and spinning like a top, Leon and I will take care of the rest." I nodded sharply, turned on my heel, and headed for the front door. Leon grabbed another Pabst from Amalia and fell into step behind me, the sound of him popping the ringtab loud in the stillness.

We got almost to the door before Theron spoke again. "Jill."

I didn't turn, but I did stop. *Don't hassle me now, furboy. Just don't do it.*

"We can't afford to lose a hunter." Which is as close as he would ever come to telling me to take care of myself. *And* Leon, for good measure.

Goddamn touchy Weres. You can't even get mad at them when they're so concerned about you. The thought of Saul rose like choking smoke in my chest, I shut it away.

"We won't," I tossed over my shoulder, and made it out the door. Leon followed, guzzling for all he was worth.

The green Charger sat across the street, in a rare bit of shade and free parking in front of a whole-foods store and a video rental place. I got behind the wheel, Leon slammed his door, and I looked at my fingers on the steering wheel. Bernie's keychain, a heavy brass Playboy bunny head, swung through the hot stillness of the interior.

"You just lied to a roomful of Weres." Leon took another hit off the can. "Jesus, Jill."

"The shipments should stop now that we've hit their distribution center." My fingers moved restlessly, Mikhail's apprentice-ring glinting on my third left finger. *In other words, Leon, you can go home. You don't have to see this through.*

Yeah. Right. Like he was going to go for that. I shouldn't even have thought it.

"I been curious all my life." He shrugged, finished off

the can with a long slurp and a massive belch that threatened to fog the windows. "Ain't gonna stop now."

The unspoken lingered just under the day's heat. *And if this Argoth is closer than we think, I'll need all the help I can get. Since neither of us is Jack Karma. Not even close.*

I twisted the key. The Charger roused, nowhere near my Impala's sweet purr. Bernie hadn't taken care of this car. *I could fix that, if I hang onto this hunk of metal after the case ends. Have to clean it out, too.* "We need ammo, but I don't want to draw any more attention to Galina's. I've got a cache in the suburbs. We should get to the airfield in about two hours."

The sun would be past its highest mark, the day hot and still in its long afternoon; blessed, safe sunlight everywhere. With a bit of luck, we could disrupt anything going on at the airfield and be home in time for dinner.

I was hoping I'd finally be feeling hungry by then, too.

"More ammo." Leon nodded sagely. "And I'll be praying my ass off, Jill. This is suicide."

You don't think I know that? "It beats sitting in front of the TV." I checked traffic and pulled out, sedately for once. I didn't know how far I could abuse this engine, and I didn't want cops marking this car. Not for a while, anyway. With Bernie's partner dead and me driving like Granny Weatherall, there shouldn't be a reason for anyone to run the plate number either.

If we were lucky.

"Amen." Leon belched again, dropping the can on the floorboard, and I rolled my window down.

26

The Anabela Rosenkrantz Memorial Airfield sits about twenty miles outside the city limits. It's a dusty, claptrap place, hangars set on one side of a long strip of pounded-down desert, leveled by a wheezing bulldozer after every gullywasher. Hutch had done his digging well, and now I knew all about it.

ARA was where prop-plane enthusiasts stored their machines and the Santa Luz Police Department trained their two or three helicopter pilots. The county fire department trained out here too, sometimes, rather than at the bigger airport situated halfway between Santa Luz and the state capital.

All in all, the dusty little place saw a lot of activity. That is, until last year.

Hutch had discovered ARA had been "closed for repair" last winter, and never reopened. The amateur enthusiasts had moved closer to the county seat, and the cops hadn't been out here at all this year.

At least, not the honest ones.

Which is why I wasn't surprised, when we crested the rise on a Forestry Service road cutting off the highway at an angle and heading into the canyons, to see more tin roofs throwing blinding spears of sunlight at the sky. It was the eight-by-ten I'd found in the Cherry Street warehouse. That picture had been taken recently, for some reason—probably to familiarize a pilot with the layout so the cargoes could be flown out.

The drug runners move through further east, trucking things up through the border, carrying them through with illegal immigrants, and paying flyboys top dollar to play tag with Border Patrol. The last time I tangled with serious drugrunning into Santa Luz had been that hellbreed motherfucker selling tainted E, but most of that had been cleaning up the pipeline for ingredients, since the actual drug had been made in the basement of an apartment building at the edge of the barrio.

"What?" Leon glanced up through the windshield as we rolled to a stop below the top of the rise.

I gestured briefly, switched the radio—AC/DC moaning about the highway to hell, since we're both classic rock fans—off. Heatwaves blurred the distance and poured in through the open windows. "They've built more onto the airfield."

We exchanged a long meaningful look. Rosita was in the back seat, out of sight but close at hand should he need her. "Shit." He leaned over the seat to grab her.

I agreed. Coming in this way we had some cover, but the airfield was . . . well, an airfield, and out in the middle of nowhere where you could see somebody coming. We would raise a roostertail of dust into the stratosphere, and if they had assault rifles—

We'll deal with that when we get there. I tipped my shades down my nose, looking over them and memorizing the layout. Light stung, water wrung out of both my smart and dumb eyes. And yes, friends and neighbors, wasn't there a plucking in the fabric of reality around the airfield? Little dimples of swirling corruption lifting like pollen on the air, rising with the heat, and a brackish well of contamination centered right over the airfield, welling up like crude from a deep, dark secret place.

Leon eyed it too. "Gives me the willies," he said finally, a world of hunter's intuition boiling down to four little words.

"Contamination. Can't tell what it's from, yet." Baking, sand-smelling wind scoured the inside of the car. Junkfood wrappers rustled and blew. *Thank God we're downwind.*

"Yay." His blunt fingers touched Rosita the way they would touch a lover's hand. "This ain't gonna be pretty, darlin'."

"I know. If half of what Hutch has archived is true we're stuck hoping he hasn't found a door yet." *That's a hell of a run of luck we're expecting.* "This bothers me, Leon. It bothers me a *lot.*"

As usual, he took refuge in understatement. "You get the feelin' we're bein' led by the nose?"

"All through this goddamn thing. I just don't see how anyone would think Monty would call me in to look at his ex-partner's 'suicide.' And I don't see how anyone could expect me to find scurf and take them out, even if I was looking into disappearances on the east side. Those were probably escaped stragglers, unless the 'breed was outside to watch over them. It was probably luck pure and simple, and . . ."

"And anytime we get that lucky, someone has to be planning something." He shifted uneasily in his seat. "So what we gonna do?"

"We find out what's going on at this airfield, and what those new buildings are. And with any luck, they won't be expecting us to hit them *here*." *Luck. Again. Never a substitute for proper planning, ammunition, or intelligence, as Mikhail would point out to me.* The nagging feeling of something missing, of a trap about to spring, hovered over me again, retreated. "Fuck."

"My sentimentals 'zactly. So what's the plan?"

"What would you do?" *Since you'd do exactly what I'd do.*

He sniffed, tasting the air. Made a face. "Drive this piece of shit straight in and keep my eyes open. Then I'd send you out to draw their fire, darlin', while I bulwark myself in and Rosita covers you. That's assumin' they have guards."

"I don't see anyone moving, but that's no assurance." Headache pounded behind my eyes, and I slipped my shades back up my nose. The world took on a better contrast, but I'd have to take them off for the last few miles of approach. "This baby's heavy metal, like my Impala. Should be good as long as nobody hits a gas tank. After blowing up one car already on this case, I don't think I want to blow up another."

"Amen, darlin'." He sighed, copper clinking as he settled himself in his seat. The look on his face told me he was wishing for another beer.

I waited for him to add more, but he didn't. So I

dropped the car into "drive" and hit the gas, glad to have him with me.

Dust rose in a choking swathe as I worked the steering, swinging the rear end out and standing on the brake. I bailed out as Leon did, and we both scrambled for the defensible angle between the back of the car and the farthest hangar. From here we had a straight shot down the runway or a good chance of cover while bobbing and weaving to the new buildings.

When no shots rang out and nothing happened, it was absurdly anticlimactic.

I crouched, my coat hanging behind me. The copper in Leon's hair chimed. "Go," he whispered, Rosita socked to his shoulder, his keen eyes alert down the alley for any muzzle flash.

I *moved,* etheric force pulled through the humming scar on my wrist, almost faster than I could control. *It's acting up. Dammit, Perry.* The thought was gone in a flash. I reached cover, pointed my guns down the way, and found no breath of anything stirring. It was as quiet as a grave.

Get it, Jill? Quiet as the grave? Arf arf.

I whistled, and Leon tore down the same path I'd taken. We covered each other, leapfrogging, because it was goddamn evident there was nobody here. I couldn't even hear a heartbeat. Just the rasp of sand sliding over the desert, carried on the back of an oven-hot wind.

Just like scales moving in a dark hole.

"This is creepy," I muttered. Then I shut up, brain working overtime. It had to be a trap. *Had* to be.

The largest of the new buildings crouched under a shiny tin roof, and Leon and I both stopped, considering it for a moment. There was a door, a nice double-reinforced number, on the side of the prefabricated trailer. A brand-spanking-new set of wooden steps and a ramp large enough to wheel a forklift up led to the door, its latch and padlock glimmering like fool's gold.

"Are you—" he began.

I noticed it too. "No windows." I answered. "And locked on the *outside.*" Just like the Winchell murder site. Gooseflesh rose cold and hard under my skin, and I made another one of those wrenching mental efforts to stay clear. Leon was depending on me, dammit. So were my Weres and my city.

But what's behind that door, Jill? Hm? You're so smart, what's behind that door?

"Yeah," he breathed. "You go first."

"Sure you don't want to take this one?" Black humor at its finest, I glanced at him and Rosita. The spark was back in Leon's eyes, and high hard color stood out on his cheeks. Otherwise he was dead white. A sheen of sweat not from the incidental heat of the day—because as a hunter you learn to regulate your body temperature pretty thoroughly—touched his forehead.

"Aw hell, darlin', ladies first." His attention never wavered from the padlocked door.

I grinned, a fey baring of teeth Saul would recognize as my *get ready* face. "Age before beauty."

"Pearls before swi—"

But I was already moving, bolting out of cover. The sun lay in a white glare like a hot sterile blanket over a corpse, and I hit the door like it had personally offended me. It gave, buckling, built to withstand more than ordinary pressure, but the extra force I pulled through the scar blazed through my arm and it crumpled like paper. I landed hard, weight on the balls of my feet, and swept with my guns.

The Trader hit me just as hard, knocking me ass over teakettle down the three wooden stairs I'd just bolted up. I landed on my back, already firing, and heard Rosita roar.

At the apex of his leap, the dirty-blond Trader, wearing an eerily gleaming long white coat, was tumbled sideways by a load of silver ammo punching into his side, curling up like a spider dropped into a candleflame. His screech tore the simmering air, and I was on my feet again in a moment—pull the knees in, *kick,* use the momentum to jackknife and get your feet under you, then leap sideways as well, *get on him Jill, take him down are there more Leon cover me goddammit—*

"*Mercy!*" the Trader yelled, and I landed with one gun trained on him and the other on the door of the trailer. "*Mercy don't kill me Kismet don't kill me please!*"

Whafuck? I replayed it in my head and decided that yes, he *had* really said it. "How many more?" I shouted. "Who else is in there?" I felt naked, horribly exposed, no cover, if they wanted to open fire on me like they did at Galina's I was right in the crosshairs.

No heartbeats. There's nobody here but this Trader. But you didn't hear him, you might have missed someone else, dear God—

The Trader moaned. Bright blood welled between his fingers, clamped to his side. The white was a lab coat, now grinding into the dirt and fouled with blood. Lots of blood, only faintly tinged with black corruption.

"Mercy . . ." The sibilant at the end of the word trailed between a ridge of triangular teeth sharp as a shark's. "Irene . . . Irene—"

What the hell? I eyed him. Nothing happened for a long taffy-stretching moment. Hellbreed crawling all over my house and now this Trader moaning a Trader waitress's name.

Hang on a second. Hold the phone for just one god-damn minute here.

"Fairfax?" I hazarded, not lowering my guns. Every hair on my body stood on end, quivering, scouring the air currents for the next weird happenstance. *Wait a minute. I thought I killed you. But I just said blond, and Irene . . .*

Caught assuming. Again. Goddammit. And Irene had looked relieved when I insisted the blond was *hellbreed—* I hadn't said *Trader.*

The Trader froze. His eyes, blue under the flat shine of the dusted, half-opened. "Nobody . . . here," he gasped, and took in a huge sucking breath. "Just the . . . the sub-jects. And me."

"Jill?" Leon was getting nervous.

That made two of us.

"Subjects?" The hammer on the gun pointing at the Trader clicked up. "And how the *fuck* do you know Irene?"

"The *subjects!*" He whisper-screamed it, losing air. "She's my *wife*, goddammit!"

I holstered a gun and hauled him up from the crum-bling dirt by his lapels, dragged him toward the blown-out door, his body in front of mine like a shield. "Move." I prodded him, both guns back out. "Inside. And if there's someone in there, *you die first.*"

"They say you help—" He stumbled. He was losing a lot of claret through that hole in his side. When Rosita talks, she's not to be taken lightly. "Help . . . people."

They certainly say that. What they don't say is that I'm a right bitch. "Sometimes." I stepped in front of the open door, prodded him again. He stumbled, took two steps inside, and dropped down in a heap, his eyes rolling up inside his head.

The smell boiled out and hit me. Candied, foul, rotting sweetness. My hackles rose, adrenaline dumping into my bloodstream like pollution into a river.

"Jill?" Leon, getting even more nervous.

I scanned the inside of the building. "Jesus," I whispered. "Jesus Christ." Then, over my shoulder, "Come on, Leon!"

And I plunged into the smell, stepping over the unconscious Trader. I didn't even cuff him. He was losing blood too fast to need it.

27

The tanks were huge glassy cylinders of greenish liquid. In each clear tube, a scurf floated, in varying stages of maturity. The smell was enough to make my eyes run even with the door blasted open and sunlight scouring a rectangle of yellow linoleum.

There were two rows of the green tubes, each lit with ghostly non-UV light. There were dissection tables, and a long bookcase along one wall, stacked with reference works and binders.

Leon helped me drag the Trader to a table and bandage him. Leon also snapped silver cuffs on him, just in case. Meanwhile, I stared at the closest tube full of green viscous stuff, and the scurf floating, eyes closed. "They're preserved." My gorge rose, hot and hard at the back of my tongue. "Jesus."

Leon gave them barely half a glance and turned an interesting shade of pale. His amulets clinked. "What the fuck is going on?"

"Check the books." I tipped my head at the bookcases

and holstered a gun, then set about trying to wake the Trader up. It was hard—he'd lost a lot of blood, but he was tougher than the average human. Then again, it didn't look like he'd Traded for anything good, like superstrength or invulnerability.

But then, there were those teeth. And his hands looked funny, bonelessly flopping and too delicate. Strangler's hands.

"Virology. Chemical composition of antidepressants. *The Anarchist's Cookbook,* even." Leon snagged that one, it vanished into his coat pocket. "Looks like a first edition too."

"Kleptomaniac." One whole wall of the trailer/hangar was taken up with chem-lab equipment. They'd been cooking something up, out here in the desert. The Trader started to come around, his eyes rolling back down in his head. He shifted uneasily, the silver cuffs clanking, and cringed when he caught sight of me. "He's waking up. Check that stuff over there, will you? Didn't you take chemistry?"

"Once in m'benighted youth, darlin'. Left as soon as I figured out how to make beer and fertilizer explosives."

"Now *there's* a combination." Both of us took care not to turn our backs to the door. The scurf floated eerily in their green tubes. They didn't look dead, just . . . sleeping, caught in a moment of rare immobility, like during daylight when they pack themselves together like sardines.

I shuddered. Leon was all white now, pale even under the fishbelly of "night-walking hunter." His eyeliner had turned garish against the new pallor. From the cold feeling in my cheeks, I probably wasn't far behind.

The smell was incredible. Fresh tears trickled down

my cheeks—and the scar puckered itself up into a tiny mouth, a thrill of painful heat running up the branching channels of my nerves.

"Irene . . ." the Trader moaned. He woke up all the way and blinked at me, like a six-year-old coming out of a nightmare.

This is goddamn ridiculous. "Hey, Sleeping Beauty. Start talking."

"You're her." He gasped in breath again. He really did sound awful, but then he'd taken a load of silver in the side from Rosita. I wouldn't be too peppy myself under those circumstances. "Kismet. You're actually *her*."

"No shit." *Who else would be doing this?* "The question is, who the fuck are you? But that can wait. Is there anyone else here? Anyone at *all?*"

"J-just the subjects." He winced and the cuffs clanked, blue sparks running just under their surface, responding to the contamination of hellbreed on him. As Traders went he was a lightweight. "They're in the east building, two down. It's not due in the s-south building for another week—"

Another week? "What's in another week?"

Blond stubble covered his cheeks. He looked like a watered-down version of Hutch, weak-eyed as a mole. The lab coat covered a frame that wasn't even wiry-strong, just wiry.

Still, he knocked me over. Must be something in there. Looks can be deceiving, especially when it comes to Traders. And what's the story with him and Irene?

"The Summoning," he whispered. "They're not due for another week. When the moon's dark. Then they . . . they—"

Oh shit. A summoning? "They what?" I had a sneaking suspicion I knew.

Argoth. Or other seriously bad news.

"They won't tell me." He cringed against the surgical table we'd laid him on, instruments rattling. It took me a moment to figure out why he looked familiar—there was the same ratty little gleam in his eyes as in Irene's, a gleam I wasn't sure I liked. "Only that *he* is coming, and *he* wants this place. I keep my ears open, so does Irene. When *he* comes . . . they have the formula, they'll make as much of it as they want—"

"*Formula for what?*" *And why do I have this sinking feeling like I know who "he" is?*

"For the sickness." He cringed again as I loomed over him, even though I hadn't moved. "For Dream."

I frowned. "What sickness?"

He made a short sketching motion, arrested when I twitched, a hair away from breaking his arm. "Bioweapon. They came to me with samples. I thought they were from the government. They said, what can you do with this? It was a good job, I took it—and then they took Irene. Said I had to start working, and working quick, or Irene would be dead before—"

Bioweapon? Oh Christ Jesus. "Samples?" *Keep him on track, Jill.*

"From—" His eyes flicked nervously to one of the green tubes. But his face had lit up, just like a mad scientist talking about his monster. "From them. They got live ones from somewhere, a lot of them. Finally figured out to put 'em in the xarocaine and the cellular burn stops, they die but don't rot. It's a preservative. Used the same process for—"

"There's some Day-Glo purple powder over here, Jill." Leon's tone cut through the Trader's babble. "All in little Ziplocs. Looks ready for shipment."

The Trader nodded jerkily, his hair flopping. "It *is* ready. It starts changing on the first hit, you can deliver it through the water supply; it could possibly go airborne if I had enough time. But I can't figure out how to stop the replication yet. The side effects—"

Dear God. The smell was worse now, because drafts of fresh air were spilling in the open door. A fresh gout of stench hit each time the wind shifted, and the breaths of not-so-bad air only served to underscore the reek. "Side effects?" It was like questioning a waterfall, hard to keep him on one topic, words spilling out past those sharklike teeth.

Oh yeah. Definitely Dr. Frankenstein material.

"These things, whatever they are . . . the viral replication is just endless, it remodels the genetic code and eats up hemoglobin like nobody's business. So the Dream— that's what I call it—hits hard and fast like a Mack truck, but the side effects, they can't go out in the sun, their pupils get all dilated, and they get thirsty. They tear each other up, and when one of them starts to bleed—" His shudder echoed mine. "It's in the blood. I could engineer the effect for just a quick death and stop the mutation if they would give me more *time*. But they said—I thought they were from the *government*. Who else would want something like this?"

"Holy shit." I eyed him. *Is this for real?* "You're kidding."

"Once it's perfected—"

"Shut up." *Men like you made the atom bomb, you*

waste. I didn't need any help putting together the consequences. No wonder hellbreed were crawling all over this, it had all the things they like in a weapon. But what was the connection, where was the other half of the puzzle? The sense of a missing puzzle piece returned, nagging.

Was it just because it would cause enough death to feed a hungry high-class hellbreed just out of Hell? Something even worse than a *talyn?*

I hate those sorts of questions.

"I say we put a fuckin' bullet in his head and burn this place to the ground." Leon racked Rosita, but his eyes were steady.

The Trader squealed like a rabbit in a trap. *"Nooo! Please, no don't kill me, please—"*

"For Christ's sake." I'd heard enough. "Shut the fuck up. I'm not going to kill you yet. You said something about subjects. What subjects?"

"The test subjects. Some of them just get addicted to the Dream, they don't die. They exhibit side effects. They're in the east building." He flinched again, cowering, even though I hadn't moved. "They had Irene, I had to do what they said, I *had to!*"

Fax might know, I don't, I heard Irene say, in her flat little voice. *Definitely* more to this than what Mr. Skinny was telling me. On the other hand, Irene wasn't the most dependable source either. So, two lies to choose from?

That's not the issue, Jill. The issue is what we're going to do now. Leon and I locked eyes for a long moment, weighing the situation. When he nodded, fractionally, I knew his mental calculus was the same as mine.

I stepped back from the surgical table. "Cover him. I'm going to check the other buildings."

"Have fun." Leon drew a Glock from a hip holster. "If I hear any ruckus, Doc-Boy here gets one in the *cabeza*."

"I'm sure there won't be anything." I lookcd down at the Trader. "Am I right?"

As good-cop-bad-cop routines go, it was a good one. If Fax could have lost any more color without turning transparent, he would have. "Just the subjects," he whispered. "They . . . you won't believe it until you see it."

Leon snorted. It was unintentionally funny, and I found myself wanting to smile too. Dispelled the urge. *You have no idea what I might believe, kid.* I turned on my heel, sharply, and headed for sunlight. The water on my cheeks dried as soon as I checked the angles and stepped out into the harsh glare of daylight. The fresh air was a balm after the reek of scurf, hellbreed, and lies.

28

Ten minutes later I stumbled back out into the glare and made it, then grabbed at the side of the building and retched, my eyes spouting water. Again, a tearing heave that came all the way from my toes. One last time before control clamped down, stomach cramping, aware I was making a low hurt sound and hating it.

Focus, goddammit! It wasn't Mikhail's voice in my head this time, it was my own, harsh as if I had a throatful of smoke. *Get a handle, Jill. Any handle will do.*

I made it to the laboratory. Leon barely glanced at me, did a double take. "Jill?" For once, all Texas bluster and drawl was erased from his voice.

I had to try twice to speak. "Get him in the car. Take him to Galina's and *chain him the fuck up*." I wiped at my cheeks. "I'm going to stay here and rip this fucking place apart."

"We been havin' a little chat in here." Leon's eyes were watering from the stink too, and he looked none-too-happy. "It's worse than you think. Some guy named Harvill—"

My brain shuddered with what I had seen inside the south building. *Dear God, their eyes . . . their arms, and the smell—*

I lunged into the present. *Harvill. The District Attorney. Big fat redhaired good ol' boy. Ran last year on a tough-love, three-strikes ticket. You voted for the guy, remember?* "The DA is in on this?" *The H. in the file. A big-time cop, one of the witnesses said. But I didn't think of the DA's office. Jesus. It makes sense. It makes too much goddamn sense.*

That's the trouble with hellbreed. Sooner or later they find someone high-up to seduce. It never fails.

"I don't know who he is," the Trader whined. "Just that he was a bigshot, he came in with—"

I found myself at the side of the table, the Glock out of its holster and pressed to his forehead. "Shut. Up." *He did this. Willing or not, he did this. He made those . . . things. Dear God.* "I should kill you now, for what you did to those people."

The weak blue eyes shimmered with tears. But under the gleam there was that hardness, the animal calculating how to survive. I've seen it too many times in Trader eyes—the little gleam that says everything is disposable to them, as long as they get what they want.

I've seen that gleam in ordinary people too. I grew up with that avid little light shining at me from the faces of people who should have loved and protected me. I hit the street to get away from it and found out it only got deeper. I *hate* that queer ratlike little shine in people's eyes.

And sometimes I wonder if my own eyes hold that

little gleam. When I'm considering murdering someone, Trader or criminal or hellbreed. When I've got my toes on the cliff edge and am staring down into the abyss.

Get a hold on yourself, Jill.

Tremors ran through my arms and legs. *Don't kill him.* The voice of reason in my head was Saul's, and I was grateful for it.

If it had been any other voice, I'd've spread his brain and bone all over that fucking table.

"Hellbreed," I rasped. "Who came with Harvill? Which one of the motherfuckers is behind it? Who did you Trade with?" *I think I already know. And if you lie to me, so help me God, I will send you to Hell right now.*

Cringing and sobbing, he told me, and quite a few things fell into place. *Don't kill him, kitten,* Saul's voice repeated. *You know what you have to do.*

"Jill?" Leon asked again.

Daylight's wasting. I had too much to do, not enough time to do it in. Story of my life.

"Those things in the east building. Are they vulnerable to UV light like—" I tipped my head back a little, indicating the scurf floating peacefully in their green tubes.

Oh Jesus. Jesus and Mother Mary. The urge to vomit rose hard and sharp under my breastbone again. I shoved it down.

"Y-yes—" He looked ready to plead for his life again, but something in the geography of my face changed. I felt it, skin moving on bones, from somewhere outside myself.

The Trader shut up. Wise of him.

"And this stuff, Dream, fire destroys it? It doesn't become toxic in midair?" *It better not. If it does, I don't know what I'm going to do.*

He nodded, a quick little jerk of his head. The movement ended with a flinch, because the gun's blind mouth was still pressed against his forehead so hard I felt the trembling running through him.

"One more question." Every muscle in my body protested when I took the gun away from his head. *They know it's possible now. Some hellbreed somewhere is going to do something like this, unless I can cut it off at the root.* "Is this *all* of it? All the weapon, the drug, whatever it is? Everything you've got onsite here? Is there a backup to your research?"

"Everything's here—my work, all the computers. No backup, nothing. The first shipment is in planes in the hangars—"

That was all I needed to know. I dismissed him, looked up at Leon, who stood cradling Rosita. The bright spots of color still stood out on his cheeks, and his aura sparkled through my smart eye, the same sea-urchin shape as mine. A flicker of disgust crossed his face, and I was terribly, sadly grateful that it wasn't me he was disgusted with.

My voice didn't want to work properly. "Get him the fuck out of here. Now."

He didn't think much of the idea. "Jill—"

I was not in the mood. "If you don't get him out of here, Leon, I am going to lose my temper." Flat, quiet, just as if I was telling him what was for dinner. "Stay in touch with the Weres and keep my city together. If I'm not in town by dawn tomorrow—"

"What the fuck are you thinking of doing?" But Leon was already moving, racking Rosita, sweeping the Trader off the table and onto his feet with a gun pressed to his side. "Give me a vowel here, darlin'."

"First, I'm burning down this building." *I have to erase every trace of this, or it'll be used somewhere else.* I holstered my gun with another one of those physical efforts that left me shaking, shook out my right hand, and drew on the scar. A hissing whisper filled my palm, and pale-orange, misshapen flame burst into being between my fingers.

I barely felt the burn against my skin, I was so cold under my leather and weight of weapons. It was the absolute chilling freeze beyond rage, beyond pain, and beyond fear.

I could wish it didn't feel so familiar. "Then I'm burning down *every* fucking stick of this place, and consigning every soul in that east building to God." I paused. "If He will take them."

Leon had the Trader, was dragging him toward the door. Their shadows moved in the ragged rectangle of clean sunshine, and the flames dripped from my fingers, scorching the floor. The sorcerous flame hunters are trained to call on—banefire—devours all trace of hellbreed and leaves a blessing in its wake, but for this, I needed something more.

I needed pure destruction.

The hellfire made a sound like strangled children whispering. Like dead souls filling up a room with angry cricket-voices. Like the click of a bullet loaded into a magazine, over and over again, with a feedback squeal as my fury escaped my control for a single moment, a breath between thoughts.

The bookshelves burst into oddly pale orange flame.

The hellfire laughed, wreathing my fingers, and I flung it in a wide arc, smashing against the beakers and shelves on the back wall like napalm. Glass screeched and exploded, and I backed toward the door, fire scouring wetly in a trail from my right hand.

The frightening thing wasn't how easy it was to pull that sort of power through the scar, or even the agonizing plucking against every nerve running up my right arm and into my shoulder, branching channels full of magma played like dissonant violin strings.

The frightening thing was that the hellfire turned yellow, a clear pure yellow like sunlight, and I jerked my hand away from me, toward the green columns of floating dead scurf. Glass shattered and slime flooded the floor, bodies falling with wet thumps as the backdraft pushed me out the door, just in time too. I landed sprawled on the wooden ramp, hearing the Charger's engine rouse itself just as the first explosion—of course, there were stocks of chemicals in the building, I was basically torching an ammo dump of viral weaponry—rocked the desert air and the fire took a deep, vast, hot breath. A belch of greasy black smoke rounded itself like bread dough rising and flared for the sky.

Burn, someone whispered inside my head. *Burn it all.* And this last voice sent me scurrying, trying to shake the yellow hellfire away from my hand like hot grease, because it was Perry's voice, and I knew that for once I was going to do exactly what it said.

Smoke rose in a huge black smudge, a beacon underlit with bright yellow leaping flame. I shot the last mewling, crawling, burned-black thing skittering in the ashes in its approximation of a head. My gorge rose again, point-lessly, receded with a sound like a choking-dead laugh. The hangars were burning, sharp guncracks of explosions sending flaming debris arcing across the runway.

The entire place looked like a bomb had hit it, except the last building. The sun hung low in the west, a gigantic bloody eye. *Someone has to have noticed this by now.* A tired sound escaped my lips, sounding suspiciously like a giggle.

The only building I'd left almost untouched was the southerly new one. The Trader said the evocation was due in a week, and a glance inside the kicked-in door had shown me a fresh concrete floor with a pentagram carved deep—and it was definitely a penta*gram,* not a penta*cle*—inside a circle and square, candles ranked on fluted iron holders, and the reek of hellbreed so strong and thick it almost knocked me over despite all the varied and won-derful stenches that are a hunter's life.

The hellfire, burning steadily on my fingertips now, running from the scar like greasepaint, had turned green at its tips. Most sorcerous flame works on a spectrum, and I shouldn't have been able to produce more than red flame tinged at the edges with a little orange.

Instead, I was cycling up through the spectrum. I'd seen Perry produce blue hellfire once or twice, and it made me wonder. How much of this could he feel, sitting in his office in the Monde? Was he curious about what I was doing? Was I using up all my stock of preternatural power in this one futile gesture?

If I was, I'd cross that bridge when I came to it. There were more immediate problems to solve. *They have a backup somewhere. They would be stupid not to. Or this is a backup.*

Still, the statement I was making might make any hell breed think twice before visiting my town. Even the ones still burning in Hell's embrace.

Even one who had killed my teacher's teacher? Wasn't that the sixty-four-thousand-dollar question? If they released Dream—drug, bioweapon, whatever it was—on my city as this Argoth climbed free of Hell, the massive suffering would be a huge banquet. It would *feed* him, and with that sort of energetic jolt he'd become a very serious proposition indeed.

And I wasn't a Jack Karma, capable of containing that sort of thing. Not even close. Not even with Perry's scar on my arm—a scar that might turn into a liability if Perry was ordered by a much stronger hellbreed to Do Something About Me.

Get cracking, Jill. There's work to do.

In the center of the pentagram the altar stood, a chunk of wood probably from a hangman's tree under draped black satin stiff with noisome fluids. Various implements, hissing with malice, scattered over the altar's surface. I took them all in with a glance, shaking my hand. The hellfire didn't want to go away. It kept popping and hissing, chortling at me, drawing strength from the contagion in the air.

Each piece of silver I wore spat blue sparks. I shut my eyes, my smart eye piercing the meat of my eyelid to show me the shape of things under the surface of the world. The evocation was indeed very close to being finished. Had this continued, on some night under a dark moon the walls between the physical plane and Hell's screaming, shifting flames would have gapped for just the tiniest moment, and something could have slipped through, not just as a bad dream or a walking shade like an *arkeus,* only able to coalesce into physical form when someone bargained with it and gave it a toehold.

No, something real would step through. It only took a moment, a knife's-edge worth of time. And what would a creature like Argoth want with my town? Revenge on a hunter of Karma's lineage? Something coincidental? A darker purpose?

Always assuming Perry was telling the truth and it *was* Argoth waiting to come through.

If it wasn't that hellbreed in specific, it was probably one just as bad. And its corruption would spread until burned out, fueled by the suffering of my people. My civilians. *My* city.

Not in my *city.*

The sharp clarity of my rage was comforting, but I couldn't stay there. It took a long while, me wrestling with the scar, a battle of wills that ended with sweat breaking out all over my body and my eyes snapping open to see that darkness had gathered in the corners. A dry lion's cough of an explosion sounded. *Did I really do all that?*

I held up my right hand.

In the uncertain light, the puckered lip-print on my inner wrist was just the same. There was no mark on my skin of the power I'd pulled through it. It felt flushed, obscenely full, pulsing in time with my heartbeat.

"God," I whispered. Blue sparks hissed.

The banefire came slowly, whispering around my fingers in wisps, almost drowned by the pressure of

hellbreed contamination in the ether. It tingled, like a
numb limb right before the pain of waking up starts.

The prayer rose inside my head. *Thou who hast . . .* It
circled the rage, came back. *Thou Who hast given me to
fight evil, protect me; keep me from harm.* The prayer,
skipped, skidded, and returned to the most important
part. "O my Lord God," I whispered, "do not forsake me
when I face Hell's legions." My voice cracked; I licked my
dry lips. From some deep place inside me the idea of calm
rose, and I grabbed for it with both mental hands. The last
sentence fell into a well of silence. "In Thy name and with
Thy blessing, I go forth to cleanse the night."

I opened my eyes.

Oily, pale-blue banefire wreathed my hand in living
flame, whispering to itself, a cleaner sound than hellfire's
greasy chuckling. It boiled up, sheathing my skin, and I
threw it at the altar with every ounce of hellbreed strength
my right arm possessed.

It hit, dimmed, and roared up, a sheet of avid blue flame
crawling over cursed implements and scouring the black
satin. The curved knife, the twisted claw of no animal
that crawled under the sun, the chalice full of noisome,
clotted scum, other things that had no other purpose but
to hurt and wreak havoc—all wrinkling like paper in a
flame, the banefire gathering strength as I stumbled back
on legs as weak and rubbery as noodles, hit my shoulder
on the wrecked door, and almost went down in a heap out
in the dust beyond.

Jill, you're in bad shape.

I let out a hard jagged sound. Better shape than
those . . . *things* . . . in the east building. If hunters were

allowed to go to Confession and Communion I might have turned a priest's hair white, sharing the horror.

It was worse because they'd been human once, and worse even than scurf because of the—

My mind reeled violently away from the thought. There are only two or three things in my life as a hunter that have that effect—memories so terrible the fabric of the brain itself refuses to hold them, human comprehension shying away.

Good, you can't remember. Which means it's over. Which means you need to get on your fucking feet and finish the rest of this job. Monty. Theron. Carp. They're all in danger, and it's up to you. So quit your bitchmoaning and figure out how you're going to get the hell back to your city.

I came back to myself on my knees in the dust with my head down, hair hanging in dark strings starred with blue-sparking silver, and the hissing of banefire behind me underlying the crackle of other flame. If anybody was giving out prizes for laying waste, I'd have won one. The entire airfield looked like a picture of an artillery attack I'd seen in an old magazine. Every hangar was a roaring shell, and the new buildings were burning merrily, mostly with orange and yellow flame.

I struggled up to my feet, taking harsh deep barking breaths. The crimson stain in the west was the sun finally dying. And the plume of black smoke stretching up into the gathering dusk was a huge fucking neon sign.

Priorities, Jill. Your city's in danger. They could have another evocation site, and you're stuck here without a car. What are you going to do?

Why weren't there news helicopters circling? Someone

had to have seen this from the highway. Out here in the desert, you could see forever, couldn't you? A pillar of smoke during the day, miles from the city—

Instinct, and instinct alone, made me raise my head. I wouldn't have heard the car's tires over the snap and crackle of flame. Behind me, banefire exploded, and the heat of it against my back was comforting enough to make my knees sag again.

Or maybe it was the green Charger, slid into a bootlegger's turn and sending up a great spume of dust that did it. Because the passenger door opened, and I ran for the car as if my soul depended on it. I assumed it was Leon, come back to pick me up.

That assumption was my next mistake. A muzzle flashed, and something hit me in the chest like a padded hammer, and all of a sudden it was burning, my heart was a lake of fire inside my chest.

This time, they used silver. They shot me four times, and the last thing I heard was the crunch of feet on gravelly dirt as blackness closed over me, shot through with lead and redness. And a voice that was familiar, a woman's voice.

"We've got them by the balls now. Give me that rope."

29

_T_radeoff for being a helltainted hunter: silver fucking *hurts* to get shot with. The wound closes slowly, not poisoning me the way it poisons a hellbreed, but at about three-quarters the usual speed. I lose blood I can't afford, too, thick trickles of trying-to-clot claret.

I came back to consciousness slowly, in patches. Something hard was against my back, my head lolling, eyelids fluttering. My hair hung down in greasy wet strings, silver charms hanging like odd, blue-glowing fruit.

"They'll be here. They can't afford not to." The woman's voice was familiar. Slight smacking sounds—a wet, openmouthed kiss. "Relax, sweetheart."

"You didn't see what she did." Male. Sounded familiar, too, and scared of his own shadow, with a whining edge that set my teeth to clenching together. "She almost shot me. And the *entire* place, just like a bomb hit it. Jesus."

What the hell? Grogginess receded, and the scar prickled, a pucker of skin, still feeling full and obscenely flushed.

"I saw enough. Even Shen's scared of her. Don't *worry* so much. We have the only samples left, I saw to that. You have the formula, and we have the hunter to trade in. Everything's going to be okay." Another soft, wet kiss and a small moan. *Someone* was having a good time. "Just as long as you do what I tell you."

The world resolved around me, my consciousness sharpening.

I was in a chair. The air pressure was still, swallowing sound, echoing, telling me I was underground. Rope crisscrossed my chest, holding me in the chair. My hands were tied behind my back, fingers swollen, my elbows tied together, my ankles lost in coils of blue and white nylon rope.

I shifted my weight a little, looking for slack in the ropes. Found some.

Whoever had tied me up had done a goddamn messy job of it. I stilled, watching the silver in my hair run with blue sparks under the smooth metal surfaces. Hellbreed contamination in the air, but not a lot of it.

I saw concrete, a crumbling wall threaded with thin trickles of dried nameless fluid. I was in the dark, but electric light played over a vertical edge, a corner with teeth where the concrete had been worn away.

My eyes fell shut again. I was so tired. Even my toes hurt. Even my *hair* hurt. And I was starving. I would have given about anything for a chicken-fried steak right about then. And a nice cold beer.

Jill, wake up. My own voice, soft and urgent. *Wake the fuck up. Something's happening right in front of you.*

The scar ran with wet heat. My wrists rubbed against each other, and the hunger shifted under my breastbone, turned steely and sickening. I heard nylon rubbing against a cross-beam as a body shifted below, dead fruit. *You're tied up with the same type of rope. Wake up, Jill.*

It was like a bucket of cold water. I snapped into full consciousness silently, my wrists rubbing, the scar turning hot. It burrowed in toward the bone, and I wondered if it would slip my control and fill with yellow flame again.

The idea of burning expanded my chest with unsteady glee. I clamped down on it, reflexively.

Can't afford to do that, no matter how good it feels. I blinked crusted something out of my eyes, felt the tingle along my skin as the last bullet hole in my chest closed over, the silver-coated slug pushed free and no longer hurting me. The scar hummed, the strings of the physical world thrumming like a violin touched by a master's fingertips. Just the slightest plucking, making subtle vibrational music.

Something was about to happen.

Too late. It's too late.

Hopelessness threatened to scour the inside of my head. *Bullshit it's too late,* I answered that whining little voice. *Get out of these ropes, Jill. That's the first step. Everything else comes from that.*

I rubbed my wrists together like Lady Macbeth. The skin on my entire body tautened. They hadn't even taken my trench off, the dumb bunnies. And the rope had plenty of give in it—enough for my purposes, anyway. Etheric force tingled in my swollen fingertips, my concentration falling into itself like a rock down a bottomless well, and tough nylon frayed, parting.

It took all my waning energy to keep the state of fierce relaxation so necessary for sorcery. Strand by strand, the rope parted. Nervous silence ticked on the other side of the wall, broken only by the sound of breathing and the occasional wet kiss or moan.

"What if they don't show?" the male said, fretfully.

"They have to show," Irene said, with utter mad certainty. "We're holding all the cards, Fax. Just relax."

I wondered, for a few seconds, how she'd gotten free of Galina. Either she'd tricked the Sanctuary—hard to do, but Galina had that core of blind decency that made her able to do what she did—or there had been violence. It was vanishingly possible that she might have overwhelmed Galina physically for long enough to escape, but treachery was more likely.

Inside a Sanctuary's house, the owner's will is law. It *had* to have been a trick. But if she'd hurt Galina, the Trader bitch was going to pay in blood.

That's not the only thing she's going to pay for, Jill. Get out of the rope.

My concentration slipped. Sweat trickled cold down the valley of my spine, a flabby fingertip tracing. I regained myself, felt more strands slip, fraying loose under the knife of my will.

"They're late," Fairfax whined.

If it hadn't been so critical to keep quiet, I might have laughed. *They're expecting hellbreed they've double-crossed to be on time. Silly them.*

"They usually are. Will you just *relax?*" Irene's tone held less fondness and more command now. Movement in the light told me someone was pacing, sound of high heels clicking. No more kisses, and no more soft words.

The air pressure changed like a storm front moving over the city, pushing thunder in front of it. These two

Trader idiots were about to get a huge surprise, either from their visitors—or from me. Copper coated my palate, adrenaline dumping into my bloodstream to sharpen me and deaden the edge of exhaustion. *This is about to get real ugly real quick. Hurry, Jill.*

A general rule of sorcery is that more haste equals less speed—but the rope fell loose, and I eased my shoulders out of its coils. My hands were numb and tingling, but they worked. I just couldn't pull a trigger for a little while. Pins and needles raced up my legs, and I almost blacked out when I bent over to take care of the rope messily looped and pulled tight around my ankles.

Rule one of tying up a hunter: you'd better be *damn* sure she can't wriggle out. Nylon's useless. Hemp's better, but it stretches too. Orichalc-tainted chains are the best, but even those are workable if the hunter's left alone and conscious long enough.

I've only been chained up so bad I couldn't get out *once*. That was enough for me.

They'd taken my guns. But my knives were still all present and accounted for, along with my whip and everything else, even all the ammo in my pockets.

Jesus. People this stupid shouldn't be playing with hellbreed. The air sharpened, the swelling in my fingers going down too slowly, *way* too fucking slowly, and I heard them arrive.

The air was suddenly full of hissing like laughter, the subliminal reverberation of Helletöng rubbing painfully against my ears. I eased myself off the chair, quiet, quiet, stopping when my right thigh cramped viciously. I kept my breathing soft and even. Raised my hands over my head to help my fingers drain. I would need them soon.

My hands turned into fists. Rivers of sparkling pain ran down my arms. I eased them open, and made a fist again. It would help the edema drain. *Come on. No time, Jill.*

On the other side of the wall, there was a wet crunching sound. A sudden impact, like a side of beef dropped three stories onto simmering pavement.

Funtime's over, kids. Everyone out of the pool.

Irene let out a shapeless, garbled yell.

In the ringing silence afterward, Shen An Dua spoke. "Oh, I am sorry. I was supposed to negotiate, wasn't I."

There was a slobbering wet noise, and another crunch. "Dear me." Shen giggled, a little-girl sound. "So sorry. I just keep making mistakes."

"You *idiot*." Irene's voice trembled. "Now you've killed the only person who has the formula!"

Another chill giggle, edged with broken, freezing glass. "Oh, I haven't killed him. He'll heal, with the proper care—care I can provide, as your liege. Besides, now I know what is *possible,* and it is easy enough to find more scientists." The hellbreed's tone darkened. "Where is the hunter?"

I dropped my hands. *So glad I'm not tied up right now.* My fingers curled around knifehilts, clumsy and aching. More copper adrenaline dumped into my blood, enough to sharpen me, not enough to blur. I'd pay for it later, when my body's reserves finally gave out.

I let out the soft breath, took another, my lungs crying for oxygen I couldn't take in. No use in gasping and advertising my position and status as awake and reasonably ready to kick ass.

"Fax?" Sounds of material moving, probably her long

sequined dress. The hardness had left Irene's voice. "Fax, hold on—*Fax! Fairfax don't you leave me!*"

She sounded like a victim. Maybe like one of her *own* victims. I doubted she'd see the irony if someone else pointed it out, though.

"Oh, shut *up*." Another impact, and the wall in front of me quivered imperceptibly as something human-sized was thrown up against it hard enough to crack bones. Shen let out a little satisfied sound. "Whining. Always *whining*."

I tensed all over. The scar thrummed against my wrist, a high-voltage wire.

Shen suddenly turned all business. "Spread out. Search for the hunter. She's close, I can smell the bitch's shampoo."

Lunatic laughter bubbled up in my throat. I swallowed it. *What's wrong with my goddamn shampoo?*

"That's the last order you'll ever give," Irene snarled, and I crouched reflexively as gunfire rang through the small space, echoes tearing and re-tearing at my sensitive eardrums.

Maybe I could stay right here and let them sort it out. But something hit the other side of the wall again, bone-crunchingly hard, and I was out of my little hole and in the light of a swinging, naked electric bulb before I even noticed moving. The flap of my abused coat followed me like the smell of burning, clinging to me in tatters.

Four of them, and all you've got is knives.

Well, that wasn't quite true. My left hand had been smarter than me, curling around the whip handle and jerking it free. I guess Irene and Fax had thought I was tied up too tight to use a whip.

Fucking morons. They shouldn't have been playing with hellbreed.

Confined space, a concrete cube, the smell of blood cooking on an incandescent bulb as it swayed crazily, making the shadows dance. A slight hiss of steam echoed the longer hiss of hellbreed.

Shen An Dua stood, incongruous in a pale-pink kimono patterned with plum blossoms, her narrow golden hands folded and her eyes running with yolk-yellow flame. Her hair was piled atop her head in a complex patterned knot, held in place by lacquered shine and chopsticks with dangling things reflecting hard darts of light. And here was my first piece of good luck. In her monumental arrogance, Shen hadn't brought full 'breed to the party.

No, she'd brought four Traders, all male, and the whip smacked across flesh and dropped one, screaming, to the floor, clutching at his face and howling loud enough to shake the entire concrete cube.

Shen screeched, but the knife left my hand, flickering through the dance of shadow and blood-dappled light, and I had a second piece of good luck. It buried itself up to the hilt in her right eye as the whip crackled again, catching the next Trader at the top of his leap. I moved aside, spinning on feet gone numb and scraping-slow, and my hand flicked again, coming up full of steel.

Move move move! The screaming inside my head was no match for the noise bouncing off the walls until I tuned it out, focusing instead on the Trader closest to me, a cute little number who might have been Puerto Rican while he was human. Now he was small, brown, and unholy quick; the mirrored surfaces coming up from his cheekbones and inserting into his eyebrows gave him permanent sunglasses. He was right next to me before I realized it, but instinct saved me again—my fist, full of knifehilt, blurred forward and his trachea collapsed with a crunch.

Guys always expect you to go for the nut-shot. They never expect a rabbit-punch to the throat. And no matter how good you are, if you can't breathe, your fighting effectiveness is numbered in bare seconds.

Just to be safe, I slid the knife between his ribs, high in the left side of his chest, punching with a generous share of hellbreed strength to get through the pericardium—if I was that lucky.

Shen hit the floor, wailing, and I got a glance up her kimono skirt. If I'd eaten anything recently I would have thrown it all up, again, but the animal in me was concerned with survival first, snapping me aside with a half-skip and a clatter of steelshod bootheels to free my footing from the Trader's spasming legs.

Gunfire echoed again, and the third Trader—a stocky motherfucker in motorcycle leathers, his ears coming to high bristling points—collapsed, a neat hole appearing in his forehead and the back of his head vaporizing. Irene was picking her shots.

Let's just hope I'm not her next target, eh?

I hit the ground, rolled, and kicked the knees of the last Trader, he went down in a heap and I fed him a few knives to keep him quiet.

I lay there for just a second and a half too long, my sides heaving and my body suddenly failing to obey me. *Wait just a minute, bitch,* my muscles informed me. *We're declaring mutiny. You've fucked with us for too long.*

The body will do what the will dictates, yes. I learned that in my first year of training. But sometimes, even the will isn't enough to get the body up off the floor, when you've forced flesh past the point of no return. Even a berserker will eventually get tired.

Shen landed on me, tentacles swarming, thick black gore slicking her right cheek. Probing, flexible hairy pseudo-fingers bit hard, helped along by tiny vicious suckers, each rimmed with sharp cartilaginous protrusions resembling teeth. *Peeked up the skirt of destiny, did we?* the merry voice of impending doom snarled inside my head. *About to pay for it, Jill. And pay for it big.*

Slim strong human-shaped fingers tightened around my throat, and if my cervical spine hadn't been hellbreed-reinforced, my neck would have snapped. I kicked, my knee sinking into fleshy pulsing warmth nesting under her kimono and finding precious little bone to bounce off. My abraded wrists swarmed with tentacles, and she exhaled sicksweet foulness in my face, squeezing harder now, black ichor dripping from her pointed chin and splashing my face.

I spat, defiant to the last, and heaved up. No dice. She had too much leverage. Judo doesn't teach you how to fight off *tentacles,* goddammit.

The gun roared again.

The unwounded half of Shen's head disintegrated. Silver grain loaded in hollowpoints will do that. Black ichor spattered my face, stinking as it rotted.

The tentacles spasmed. Her hands bit in once more, terribly, but I wriggled free. My own fingers tore hers away, and I took in a gasping, whooping breath.

Irene was sobbing. The Trader whose larynx I'd crushed was suffocating to death, thrashing on the floor, a knife-hilt protruding from his chest. Someone else was dying in leaps and spasms. I scrabbled through the crowded space, noticing for the first time that I was bleeding. Someone had clawed me in the side, my wrists were wet and dripping, my legs ached savagely, and I was blinking away both crusted and fresh blood. Not to mention the hellbreed-stinking gore dumped all over me.

There was the click of a half-depressed trigger, and I looked up. *Ohshit.*

But Irene stood, straddle-legged, over the Puerto Rican Trader. "Bobby," she whispered, and pulled the trigger. I tried not to flinch. "You should have listened to me." She let out a sound like a choked sob, and again the gun spoke.

Silence descended. There was a smear of thick crimson beginning near the ceiling, on the wall I'd been tied up behind. It looked about the size of an adult male, as if a man-sized canvas bag of blood had been flung at the wall and slid down, sopping-wet.

I gained my feet in a convulsive movement. The entire goddamn place was only about ten by ten, too small a space for the carnage it held. Pipes clustered at the far end. The naked, blood-spattered bulb swung in ever decreasing arcs.

Irene hunched over something near the wall. The gun dangled limply in her hand. "Fax," she whispered.

I coughed, deep and racking. Fax wasn't going to mix any more bioweapons for anyone. Pretty much every bone in his body was broken, and the odd shape of his head meant his skull was crushed. Thin red blood, only a little tainted with hellbreed black, slicked his face and spattered his now-grimy lab coat.

I tried to feel something other than hot nasty satisfaction. *Got what you deserved.* Bile whipped the back of my throat as the thought of his "subjects" crawled under the surface of my consciousness, refusing to surface fully.

Thank God for small mercies. It wasn't much, but I'd take it.

I found my other guns near the ruins of what looked like a wooden chair. It had been smashed to splinters, and it looked like the chair Winchell had been beaten in.

Shen must have thought I'd be easy to take out. My, isn't this tying up nicely. Three guns, Irene had the fourth, and I had a bead on her even while my left hand picked up the two leftover Glocks and holstered them independently of me.

I coughed again, tasted blood and the bitterness of exhaustion. My neck was going to be bruised.

"Fax," Irene whispered again. "Oh, God."

I checked all the other bodies. They were twitch-rotting, fast, contagion spreading through tissues and loosing a powerful stench into the air. I kept the gun trained on Irene.

Dead and rotting meant they were no threat. But God, it *smelled*. If there's anything I hate about my job, it's the varied odors of rot and corruption.

Not to mention almost getting killed on a regular basis. Or getting lied to so frequently I barely even trust *myself* anymore.

Or how even a job that ties itself up can feel almost like a failure. I'd been caught assuming too often on this one, and how many people could have died if I hadn't been lucky? Or if I'd been just, simply, too late and a high-class hellbreed had stepped through to sit down and have himself a feast?

I took two steps forward, over the tangled ruin of a body. Fury worked its way up inside me, I blinked more blood out of my eyes.

Irene didn't move, crouched on her high heels, her knees splayed. The green tint to her skin was pronounced under the bloodspattered light.

"What did you do to Galina?" I husked.

"I threatened to shoot the detective unless she let me go." Her slim fingers opened. The gun clattered, came to rest right next to Fairfax's dead, crushed hand. "Goddammit."

"You're playing out of your league." The gun barrel met the back of her head, through that blood-colored hair. She didn't move. "Who else is in on this? Harvill, Shen, who else?"

"They're mostly dead." The words were colored with a sob, but I didn't miss her shifting her weight slightly, very slightly. She froze when I shoved the gun against her skull again, harder. "Fax and I, we were trying to fix it, once we realized what they were planning. Bernardino killed the widow and I took care of Winchell, but we didn't find the ledgers. We couldn't pressure Harvill without them. Shen sold me to Bernardino to keep him quiet, he was a pile of filth. I *enjoyed* killing him, but he didn't have the ledgers and it all went . . . Fax. He was . . ."

Yeah, you were trying to fix it, and blackmail a few people in the process. A nice little nest egg, there for the taking, but Bernie had plans of his own. Enough double-crosses to make everyone dizzy, all of you little fucking rats scurrying once the lights turned on.

It might have been funny if it hadn't been so pathetic. Or if so many people hadn't died, used like Kleenex and discarded without a thought. And now she was sniveling over her dead bioweapon-making boyfriend. *I'll bet it never even occurred to you to look in the garage, either. Even with the car you arrived in sitting in there.* "What other higher-ups were involved? *Who,* goddammit?"

She kept talking. Maybe she thought that if she kept going, she'd find a way out of the hole. Or maybe it didn't matter to her now. "Just Shen. She wanted to ingratiate herself with the *big* guy, he wanted a way through, into this city. She thought the owner of the Monde knew and sent you to blackmail her so he could get in first."

Perry? Evoking Argoth? I don't know, he likes being the biggest fish in town too much. I cleared my aching throat. "Was there a backup for the evocation?"

"I don't think so. Shen was always going out to the airfield, every dark moon for six months. It was the only time I was allowed to see Fax." Her voice broke again. But the calculation was back in it, the slightest hesitation masquerading as sorrow.

When you've spent a lifetime listening for that hesitation, it blares like a bullhorn.

"You realize I have to kill you." It didn't hurt to say it. Cold clarity had settled over me again, the part of me that didn't count the cost or hesitate when something had to be done.

It wasn't the same as the cold calculation or the ratty little gleam. It *wasn't.*

At least, I hoped it wasn't. What else was I doing this for, if it was?

"Just do it," she whispered. "Do it fast."

My hand tensed. I struggled to think clearly. This

wasn't like taking a life in combat. This was something else.

"Did you hurt Galina? Or Carp?" I pushed against her skull with the gun, just a little. Her head bowed, pliant. "Tell me the truth, Irene."

"What the fuck does it matter?" Cold weariness, now.

"Oh, it matters." *It's the difference between me killing you mercifully . . . or otherwise.* The scar plucked at my arm, humming to itself. It wanted me to kick the Glock near her hand away and beat the living shit out of her personally. It's a small step from knowing how to fight to knowing how to stretch out hurting someone.

It's an even smaller step between knowing how to do it and finding a *reason* to do it.

She sighed. "I dumped the detective at the end of the block and ran. He was okay enough to squeeze off a few shots at me."

Thank you, God. I don't have to hurt her. "You're going to Hell." I couldn't sound comforting.

"Fine." She shrugged, pale greenish shoulders smeared with blood and other matter. An exhausted rat in a cage. "Like it's so different from here. Just get it over with, Kismet."

I wanted to tell her Hell *was* different. That's why they call it *Hell,* for Christ's sake.

But in the end, I didn't.

Let her find out for herself.

30

When I surfaced on the street, I knew exactly where I was. Irene and Fairfax's little hidey-hole turned out to be the half-basement of a shabby little deserted office building on Rosales, less than two blocks from Winchell's murder site. Everything tying together into a neat little package. *Bumbling incompetents getting themselves killed. Avarice, arrogance, and envy are the hunter's friends; if it wasn't for that I wouldn't have found so many loose ends to tie up. And if not for monumental fucking arrogance, Shen would have brought hellbreed.*

And that would have been a goddamn clusterfuck.

I stood in the shadows in the lee of the building, night wind rising off the desert brushing the street and curling down the alcove. Did it smell like burning, or did I? I swayed, my fingers catching at the wall and leaving smeared prints behind. Blood and stinking hellbreed ichor, and more blood. Forensics would have a field day with that little room, if anything was left after a night's worth of decay. I hadn't been able to muster up the strength to force banefire off my fingers.

Think, Jill. Think.

What was my next move?

The Charger was easy enough to find, tucked into an alley across the street. One of them had topped off the tank with gas and done a passable hotwire job on it. Irene's work, I was betting—Fax hadn't seemed like he could tie his shoelaces, much less hotwire a car.

But he'd been enough of a genius to engineer a weapon likely to completely bash my city out of recognition, loosing a tide of darkness and corruption that would feed a huge hellbreed. *And* turn people into blood-hungry fiends or . . . those *things*. And he'd done it all without asking where his "subjects" came from. Probably talked himself into thinking it was real bang-up science he was doing, too.

I shouldn't have felt sorry for either of them. But a few more minutes of questioning Irene before I sent her on her way meant I'd found the link between Shen and Fairfax. An intent-to-distribute conviction for mixing up designer drugs to make some cash, and the concurrent threat to a promising career, had brought Fax into Harvill's—and Shen's—reach. And with him, Irene, who had taken to being a Trader like a duck to water. But then, when you're dating a mad chemist, I suppose you can get used to bargaining with Hell one slice of flesh at a time.

Just like I was mortgaging myself an inch at a time. I didn't have the energy to argue with myself over whether or not I was different.

The only loose end was the district attorney, the node-point of corruption. How had he gotten involved with

Shen? Had she gone looking for someone amenable or had he committed some indiscretion that brought him to her attention? Did it matter?

It was probably the latter. The happy little organ-theft ring that had intersected with Melisande Belisa's plans last time had intersected with Shen's *this* time, and I had a chance to pull it up by the roots.

I rested my head on the steering wheel and breathed in, breathed out. The crusted blood in my eyes irritated me, I blinked it away.

It wasn't just the crusties. It was hot water filling up my eyes and trickling down my cheeks.

Jesus. I'm in bad shape.

The wind rattled and rolled down the street, deserted because it was after dark. So much of a hunter's life is played out on an empty street, or in places where no light shines. Places nobody can share with you, or wants to share. Not if they're right in the head at all.

Saul. He would be worried. I wondered if his mother was sliding over the dark edge into finality.

Theron would be climbing the walls too. Leon, if he knew Irene had slipped the leash, would have gotten the situation at Galina's under control and would be coordinating the Weres in my absence. Faithfully keeping the city under wraps. I wondered how long I'd been unconscious. My bet was on not very long, since Shen would have been anxious to get the formula and her pet chemist back.

And kill me, of course, both for interfering and for making her look bad while I did it. And probably to make points with this Argoth guy.

I lifted my head, peered blearily out the windshield.

The old moon hung, a nail-paring, low in the sky. It was approaching midnight.

I knew Harvill lived in Riverhurst, the tony part of town, north and a few minutes out of the downtown sector. Keeping tabs on high-level law-enforcement personnel in your town saves a lot of trouble when you're a hunter, whether you need heavier bureaucratic guns to take care of a case—or the case itself involves them.

What are you going to do, Jill? You're in no shape to take anyone on.

It didn't matter. This was mine to finish off, and by God, I was going to.

I stroked the Charger into starting. It was an automatic, so I didn't need to worry about shifting the way I would have in my Impala. Which was good—my legs were still weak and my fingers painfully swollen. The headlights came on without any demur, cutting a swath through the night.

You're not even in any shape to drive. Find somewhere to rest, get to Harvill tomorrow.

Fat fucking chance. I slid the car into drive. Eased my foot off the brake and the car slid forward, the engine sounding overworked and underpaid.

Just like the rest of us, honey. Never mind about that. We'll fix that right up. I always wanted a Dodge.

A roaring sheet of darkness beat at the edges of my vision. I blinked. The tears slicking my cheeks came faster, dripping off my jaw and wetting the ruins of my shirt.

It's about a twenty-minute drive, Jill. Do it in ten.

The Charger nosed at the street, I turned, and reached for the little tingle of precognition along my nerves. It didn't happen for a long thirty seconds, so I cruised along the dark street, my fingers still swollen and aching. The wheel slid smoothly under my hands, and I turned left on Twelfth. I could zig crosstown and avoid the major cop activity, which at this hour would be around the bars and nightclubs as they hit their stride. Drunks would be getting rowdy just about now, and domestic disturbances reaching their peak for the night too.

The Kat Klub won't be reopening anytime soon, folks. I done put that bitch out of business, as Leon would say.

And I would be lying if I'd told myself it didn't feel good to know Shen An Dua was dead. The only trouble was, her replacement was likely to be an even bigger bitch. Cogs in a wheel—one corruptor rolls out, another clicks in. Way of the world.

When the tingle came, I shook myself. I was weaving, and one tire kissed the curb before I snapped into my own skin, each new ache in my overstressed muscles not just a weight against the nerves but a balm, keeping me awake.

Come on, Jill. Just one more thing. Then you can rest.

I was lying to myself and I knew it. But I tightened my dirty hands on the wheel, shook my hair back, and jammed the pedal to the floor. The Charger had some life left in him yet, and he lurched forward like someone had just stuck a pin in him. Speckles of streetlight ran up the hood, and the buildings on Twelfth all yawned at me, sliding past as if greased. I let out a painful, half-hitched laugh; it sounded rusty under the wind from the rolled-down window rustling all the fast-food wrappers. First thing I had to do, when I had time, was clean this god-damn car out. It was a dirty crying shame for a good piece of American metal to be so filthy inside.

Complain about my driving now, goddammit. I dare you.

He had the wrong house for a DA. It was a nice ranch-style pseudo-adobe, all done up with red tile roof and everything. The garden, what little there was of it, was immaculate, and he had a lawn that probably guzzled a winter's worth of water every week.

The Charger looked sorely out of place in Riverhurst. It's the rich section of town, well insulated both from pesky downtowners and from the stink of the industrial section. The rule here is wide sidewalks, lovely expanses of thirsty grass, and more often than not a wall and an iron gate. And trees. This is the only place in the city, other than the parks, where you find honest-to-God trees, mostly left over from the quiet neighborhoods of the twenties and early forties.

Harvill's house was easily the shabbiest, but still worth a nice chunk of change in property tax alone. The windows were all dark and deserted, only the porch light burning.

What are you going to do? Go up and ring the doorbell? Is he married, does he have kids?

I couldn't remember right now.

What are you going to get into if you walk up the path and knock on that door?

I was still considering this when another car approached, nosing down the street. It was a little red import number, and the engine sounded like an overworked sewing machine. Even more out-of-place than the Charger. I slouched down, keeping it in view. *What's this?*

The little red car—I could identify it now, it was a Honda—chugged to a stop in front of Harvill's house under a big old elm tree in full leaf. The engine shut off, and the door opened, squeaking. A slim male shape rose from the tiny front seat, and I smelled someone familiar. I had trouble matching it to a face for a few seconds.

Gilberto Rosario Gonzalez-Ayala went up the front walk. He checked the house number, then rang the bell.

Jesus. What the hell?

Two full minutes ticked by. He pressed the bell again.

A light came on.

Twenty seconds later the door opened, a rectangle of golden light. Harvill stood in the door, a man-mountain in pajamas. He looked ruffled and sleepless, and my blue eye saw a faint stain of Hell's corruption on him. He wasn't a Trader, but he'd been fucking around with a hellbreed.

Gilberto said something I didn't catch.

"Who the hell are you?" Harvill's voice carried across the street, the stentorian tones of a man used to the courtroom and television appearances.

The gun spoke, a faint pop. He had a silencer.

Harvill went down hard. I reached for the door handle.

Gilberto stepped forward, fired twice more. Stood watching. I heard a slight sound, like an exhale. Like someone sinking down into a bed. The breath of corruption intensified, taking hold as the soul fled the body and quit fighting to reclaim the flesh.

Do I have to kill him too?

"That was for my brother, you piece of shit." Gilberto's young voice broke on the last syllable. I slouched further in the seat. So Gil had been conducting his own little war, and found the hand behind his brother's killer in his own way.

It all made sense—Harvill putting whatever cops he was sure of on me, and using his position to start a little gang war on me too. I wouldn't be able to question him and find out *exactly* who opened fire on me, though.

Life's not perfect, Jillybean. Take what you have.

The 51 retraced his steps. He stopped by his driver's side door, eyeing the Charger. I touched a gun butt, ran my fingers over it, and was glad I was in deep darkness.

I didn't want to kill this kid, no matter how scary his flat dark eyes were.

"Eh, *bruja*," the young man whispered. "Still on the job, me."

I can see that, Gilberto. I turned into a stone, drawing silence over me like a cloak. Could he sense the change in the night, an absence where before there had been listening?

How much did he know about the nightside?

Just who was this kid, anyway?

He dropped down into the Honda. The sewing-machine engine started up again. He backed into Harvill's sloping driveway and pulled out, heading away down the street. Somewhere in the deep water of darkness a dog barked.

Before he turned the corner I saw a brief flare of orange light. Gilberto had just lit a cigarette.

Jesus. A shudder worked its way down my body. I stroked the Charger into starting again, watching the street. Not a hair out of place, except for that faraway hound. Everyone sleeping the sleep of the rich and untroubled.

Jacinta Kutchner's neighbors hadn't heard anything either.

I put the car in drive and pulled out. Took a right on Fairview. The city stayed quiet. Darkness beat at the edges of my vision again, my body reminding me that it had put up with a lot of shit from me in the last forty-eight hours.

I made it to Galina's, parked drunkenly crosswise in front of her store because I couldn't see well enough to do more than bump the car up against the curb. I fell sideways across the cushioned center console and darkness finally took me. I struggled on the way down—there was more I had to do, wasn't there? There was *always* more to do, and something I'd forgotten.

I dreamed of yellow hellfire chuckling and groaning to itself. I dreamed of scuttling, crawling things that forced themselves through cracks in the walls and licked up the corruption running from the corpses left stacked in a ten-by-ten basement room, runnels of foulness seeping through the walls. I even dreamed of the time before I'd become a hunter, curling up in a small space while adults fought outside and someone cried softly into a teddy bear's wet fur.

I struggled a quarter of the way into consciousness while someone carried me, the heat and a deep rumbling purr reminding me of Saul. But my body mutinied again and dragged me down, and in this fresh darkness there were no dreams.

31

Sunlight poured through the window. I lay and stared at it for a long time before moving, wincing a little bit as my head and body both protested. Even hellbreed strength has to be paid for, and I'd cycled enough etheric force through my body to give myself a *hell* of a hangover.

Get it, Jill? "Hell" of a hungover? Arf arf. I groaned, stirred slightly, and pushed weakly at the covers. I was tucked into Galina's own bed, the huge mission-style monstrosity she'd hung with white netting to make a sort of cloud to sleep in.

I heard footsteps. Voices. Nobody was yelling, and one of the voices was Galina, calm as always. So she was okay.

Good.

I lay in the bed a few moments longer, staring at the fall of sunlight through the window. My trench, battered and still smelling of smoke, was draped over a high-backed wooden chair. It was cool in here, air conditioning soughing through a vent near the door. Mellow hardwood shone through layers of polish and care.

My fingers were back to their regular size. I was still filthy with crusted blood and smelling of smoke, and my head ached, ached, a pumpkin on the stem of my neck. I felt the bruises from Shen's narrow delicate hands still digging into my throat.

How long was I out? Is it darkmoon yet? I killed that evocation site, but maybe Shen had another one. Irene didn't think so, but she could have been lying.

Coherent thought halted. I didn't have enough energy for it.

I blinked. My cheeks were hot and chapped. There was grime ground into my face and under my nails. I almost never fall asleep without washing my face, even if I'm covered in guck I like scrubbing my shiny little flower smile, as Sister Mary Ignatius called it in kindergarten.

I tried moving again. Rolled over on my back.

Get up, Jill. Get moving. You're not done yet.

Footsteps on the stairs. I listened—Galina's softly distinctive tread, and someone else's. Probably Leon, the way he pushed lightly off of each step was familiar. I pressed myself up on my hands, ignoring the shaking in my arms, and found out I was wearing a T-shirt reduced to bloodsoaked, bullet-holed rags, and my leather pants stank of hellbreed guck.

And here I was in Galina's nice clean bed. Why hadn't she put me in the spare room? Was Carp still in there?

Rest easy, Carper. It's all tied off. Well, mostly. I hoped he was sleeping. I hoped he'd pulled through.

"You're awake." The Sanctuary's sweet face was solemn. "I'll have to let Theron know. He threatened to kill you as soon as you woke up."

I cleared my dry throat. Leon came into sight behind her, expressionless, with a beer can in one hand and a bottle in the other. The copper in his hair gleamed, and Rosita was snugged safely against his back.

"Charming." My voice was a dried husk of itself. I coughed, and Leon slid past Galina, offered me the chilly bottle of microbrew. Why he drank canned piss when there were better things around was beyond me. "How long was I out?"

"Don't worry." My fellow hunter settled himself on the end of the bed with a sigh, easing down as if he hurt all over too. "We found a primary evocation site at that nasty-ass nightclub. I took care of it."

I sagged in relief. So the one at the airfield had been Shen's backup. One worry down.

"Jill—" Galina began, but Leon interrupted her.

"Why don't you go get her somethin' to eat, darlin'? I'll make sure she doesn't hurt herself. You go call Theron too, so he can stop worryin'." Leon's dark eyes were steady, and his mouth was drawn in a tight line.

Oh, shit. What's gone wrong now? "More scurf?" I hazarded, but Leon shook his head. Copper chimed in his hair. There were dark circles under his eyes.

"Naw. Town's clean as a whistle. Go on now, Lina." He toasted her absently with the Pabst can, and she made a face as if he'd told her to drink it.

"I'll bring up coffee." She cast one short, troubled glance my way, but I was too aching and muzzy-headed to decipher it. Instead I took a pull off the bottle and winced at the havoc it was going to play with my headache.

We listened to her go down the stairs. Leon shifted a little bit inside his clothes. Copper clinked, and he touched one of the amulets hung around his neck, then put his hand down with an effort. "Talked to that lieutenant. Your contact."

"Monty," I supplied. *Thank God he's okay.*

"Big fucking mess for him to clean up. I guess this Harvill asshole came down with a serious case of the dead." Leon's tone was a careful nonquestion, and my silence a careful nonanswer. "Dangerous, being in bed with hellbreed."

I shrugged. Took another pull off the bottle. Waited for him to get to the point.

"Your town should be clean, but you know how scurf are."

I knew. I nodded. One of my earrings was lighter than the other; it had probably broken sometime or another. My skin crawled. I couldn't wait to get cleaned up.

"That cop you brought in from that nightclub." Leon sank a little heavier into the bed, took another long swallow from his can. Condensation beaded on the aluminum, I could hear the liquid going down his throat. Downstairs a refrigerator door opened, and Galina began to hum.

My heart turned to a stone inside my ribs. *Oh, shit.* "Carper? Is he okay?"

Leon sighed. "He talked Galina into letting him go home yesterday. Waltzed out, went home, and ate his Glock."

No. Oh, no. "What?" I sat bolt upright, then wished I hadn't because my head immediately started pounding. "What the *fuck?*"

"Galina blames herself. Said she never should have let

him go. I was with the Weres, cleaning out that night-club." His shoulders hunched. "She said she figured the cop was up and walking around, and everything was tied off . . ."

"Carp?" I couldn't wrap my brain around it. "*Andrew? It can't . . . he wouldn't . . .*"

Leon's face set itself. "He wasn't too tight-bolted, Jill. Sometimes when civilians see the nightside, they go nuts. He was in that hole run by that Asian bitch for a while and they played with him, Lina said."

While I sat outside and worried over who would report me as not dead. "Jesus," I whispered. "You're sure it was suicide?" *Because Kutchner's death looked like a suicide too, but maybe someone pulled the trigger on Carp too. Because . . . oh, God. Carper. Why?*

But I knew why. Sometimes, when you pull a civil-ian out of a tangle with the nightside, they don't stay out. They go into the black hole. A peek under the surface of the normal world throws them off the back of reality, and they never return.

Leon spread one hand, made a helpless gesture. "I'm sure, Jill. That's where I talked to that lieutenant—Montaigne. Good ol' boy, that one. Worried about you."

"I'm sure he was." The words tasted bitter. I drained the bottle in a few long, long swallows. It was ashes going down. The carbs would give me a quick flush of strength, but I needed protein if I was really going to bounce back. "Jesus Christ. Carper."

"Funeral's this Saturday. I got it all written down if you want it." His shoulders slumped for a moment, and so did mine. Silence rose between us, under the safety of sunlight.

He knew what it feels like to lose one of your own. Only another hunter understands. We are here to protect, and when our protection fails sometimes we don't pay the cost. Others, less trained, less equipped to bear the strain, pay what *we* should.

And oh, God, it hurts.

There was nothing he could really say.

So he was quiet.

I rested the chill of the bottle against my forehead. The thick brown glass came away spotted with flecks of dirt and dried blood. A sharp bloody stone lodged in my throat, with beer carbonation trapped behind it. My eyes were hot and dry.

"He was a good cop," I finally whispered.

Leon eased himself up to his feet. The sun brought out highlights in his hair, made his copper charms shine. The amulets around his neck clicked as he shifted his weight, and Rosita's blued-steel barrel shone with a fresh application of oil. "I gotta get home. Some things to clean up back there. You gonna be okay?"

No. I guess so. What choice do I have? I made another one of those physical efforts to focus. It came a little easier now that I'd had some rest. "I'm not sure I'm done yet. Harvill might not have been the only bigshot involved. But I'll keep digging." *Andrew. You shouldn't have. Why couldn't you have waited?*

He balanced on the balls of his feet. "Good fuckin' deal." A nervous glance toward the door. Galina was still humming downstairs. "Thought you were a goner, darlin'."

"I could have been." *Two steps behind an arrogant hellbreed and a stupid-ass set of Traders the whole time, and Carp paid the price. I should turn in my badge. If I had a badge.* "Leon?"

He grunted, a truly male sound, and took another shot of his piss-masquerading-as-honest-beer.

I had to settle for two of the most inadequate words in the English language, words too pale to express what I needed to say. "Thank you."

"Aw, shit, girl. We all do what we can." His shrug was a marvel of indifference. "Be cool." *I'm sorry,* his eyes said.

"You too, Leon. Get your truck looked at, will you?" *Me too,* I thought. *I'm sorry too. I can't call this a win. Can't even call it a tie.*

"All right. Goddamn nagging." He waved his beer can, slopping the liquid inside, and stumped for the door. Stopped halfway there.

I waited, but he didn't say anything else. Just squared his shoulders and walked away without a backward glance. Classic Leon.

Then again, most hunters aren't much for goodbyes. You never know which time will be the last. Better to just walk away and carry on the conversation the next time.

If there is a next time. It's superstition, but you take what you can get.

I pushed the covers away. Someone had taken my boots off; they were in a puddle of stink right next to the bed. But I padded in sock feet across the room, stopping when my head started to spin or my legs threatened rebellion.

The bedroom window overlooked the street. Galina's humming stopped, and I heard low voices again. Leon's question, her soft reply. Then his footsteps, speeding up.

The door to her shop jingled a few moments later, and Leon headed across the street to his truck.

My entire chest hurt, a pain that wasn't physical. The copper in his hair caught fire. He got behind the wheel and the engine turned over.

I lifted my hand to wave, found it full of the empty beer bottle. He wasn't looking anyway.

The air in the room changed imperceptibly. I lowered my hand.

"Just like that," Galina said. "Jill—"

"He told me. It's not your fault." *It's mine. I was too far behind the game. Should have done something more, seen something more.* The heavy weight of responsibility and disappointment settled on my shoulders.

Galina sighed, the sound hitching in the middle. "I shouldn't have let him go. I thought the danger was past."

It was and it wasn't. "It was." The carbonation crept past the blockage in my throat, I exhaled beer and the taste of failure onto the glass. Faint condensation swirled. "Sorry about your bed."

She was quiet for a long few seconds. Nerving herself up to it, probably. "It's what it's there for. Jill—"

Christ, Galina, if you apologize one more time . . . "Did you say something about food? I'm starving."

"Coming right up." Mercifully, she left it at that. "Theron brought you some clothes. He says your house is clean, no more hellbreed. I've got to call him and let him know you're awake."

"That'd be good." I kept my stiff back to her. Exhaled again on the window and watched the condensation fade, like a ghost. My head ached. "You got any coffee?"

"I'll bring some up to you. You know where the bath-room is." Again, she hesitated.

"Food, Galina." I said it as gently as I could. "I'm not done yet."

"You got it." She turned quick and light as a leaf, and was gone down the stairs.

I tipped my head back, looking at the slant of the roof. Across the room, the mirror atop her antique cherrywood vanity held my reflection like a black stain. The plaster on her ceiling was in whorls, spiraling in and out.

The tears trickled from my eyes and vanished into my filthy hair. *Jesus. Carp, you asshole. Why didn't you wait for me?*

When the pressure behind my eyes faded a bit and the smell of something good frying began to waft up the stairs, I tipped my head back down. The street was full of hot liquid sunshine, and there was light traffic. The Charger sat across the street, behind the empty spot that had held Leon's truck.

It was a fine-looking piece of heavy American metal. It needed a bit of work to get it into shape, sure, and Monty would roll his eyes when I asked to requisition the car. But there was no reason to let it go into impound.

No reason at all. Except I didn't want to drive it, now.

I turned away from the window and hobbled on my stiff legs toward the other door. Galina had a shower in there, and I needed one. Then as much food as I could stuff into the bowling ball my stomach had become. After that, on to the next thing.

And if the tears came when I was standing under the hot water, if I made a low hurt sound like a wounded ani-mal, if I scrubbed at my flesh like it was an enemy with her pretty pink floral-scented soap, it was nobody's business but mine. It was between me and the water, and the water wouldn't talk. It would carry my tears along with the dried blood, the dirt, and the beer I vomited back up down below the city into the dark.

32

*I*t felt strange to walk into the precinct house again. Nobody said a word, but conversation failed when I appeared and turned into a tide of whispers in my wake. I stalked up to Montaigne's office, ignoring the nervous looks and whispers both.

Who among them was happy I was alive?

Who wasn't? Which one of them had a secret and an assault rifle? And access to a blue Buick? And a connection to Harvill?

I might never know now, if he kept his head down and his mouth shut.

Monty was out, so I stepped into his office and waited. When he stamped into view, armed with a load of paper and a scowl, I had to fold my arms and school my face. A relieved grin wouldn't help him in this mood.

He grunted. "Jesus fucking Christ. *There* you are."

"You don't look happy to see me." I stepped aside, let him lug his papers past me. "Are you okay?"

He gave me a look that could have peeled paint. "I got

to buy more Tums. I got a dead DA and two more dead cops—"

I winced internally. "Leon explained it all?"

He swept the door closed with his foot and dropped the pile of paper on his desk. "You see this? These are the forms I have to fill out. You burned down an entire goddamn airfield, Kismet. You're a menace to property."

"It's better than the alternative." I didn't mean to sound harsh, but each word was edged. *Better than some sort of poison engineered from scurf taking over my city and a high-up hellbreed waltzing through.*

"Jesus, don't you think I know?" He dropped down behind his desk and regarded me. "He saw something, didn't he. Carper."

You could say that. "He got tangled up in nightside business. There was a connection after all." I swallowed. Galina's steak and eggs still weren't convinced they wanted to stay down. "How much do you want me to tell you, Monty?"

He considered it for a long thirty seconds, then reached down in his desk drawer. "You want a drink?" He brought out the Jack Daniels, amber liquid shaking inside the bottle. There was half of it left. Bully for him.

Oh, Monty. I nodded, not trusting my voice.

He actually rustled up two almost-clean coffee mugs, one with a badge in worn gold foil and the other with a picture of a disgusted-looking hippo on it. Both were probably from his house. He poured me a generous measure, himself a little less generous one, and we both knocked back without waiting.

That way, I could pretend the slow leaking from my

eyes was a result of the booze scorching my throat and uneasy stomach.

The short silence between us no longer had sharp edges. "Ballistics on the DA didn't come up with a goddamn thing. It's a clean gun. Goddamn .22s are like fuckin' cell phones, everyone's got one." He set his cup down. "No more disappearances on the east side. The papers are calling Harvill a fucking saint and the airfield's blamed on a propane tank explosion." Monty rubbed at his tired eyes.

Nice and neat. Everything smoothed over. "Bernardino's car is parked out front. Stick it in impound." I set my own mug down, balanced carefully on the messy stack of paper.

"You sure? I mean, what with your car and all . . ."

"I'm sure. I don't want to clean the fucker out." I licked the last traces of whiskey away. "Carp was clean, Monty."

"And Marv wasn't?" He set his jaw.

I opened my mouth to tell him the truth, shut it. He already knew. There was no point in putting salt on that wound. Instead, I looked past him, to the picture of his wife propped right next to a dormant computer monitor. "How's Rosenfeld taking it?"

A single shrug, his shoulder holster peeping out from under his jacket. "Dealing, I guess. The funeral's Saturday."

Tomorrow. I nodded. Silver shifted in my hair. "I'll be there. Anything else?" My cheeks stung, but I didn't wipe at them.

"Not much. There was a warehouse fire down near the railyards. The 3700 block of Cherry. Whole place was burned down. Some interesting wreckage in there, but not anything to go on."

"Hm." I contented myself with a noncommittal noise. Cold air blew against my wet cheeks, drying them.

"Other than that, quiet as the western front out there. No weirdness. Just garden-variety rapes, murders, and larceny."

"Glad to see everything's back to normal." I straightened. "Thanks for the drink. I'll be in touch—I need another pager, too." *Since my last two have died inglorious deaths.*

"Jesus H. A menace to property." He waved me away. "Go burn down something else, will you? I'd hate to get bored."

"Have a nice evening, Monty." I turned on my heel and headed for the door.

"Jill?"

I stopped, one hand on the doorknob. The noise from outside—phones ringing, people talking, breathing, working—faded. "What?"

I don't know what I expected him to say. Why would he thank me? But at least he knew, now. There wasn't the nagging doubt.

It's cold comfort. Sometimes knowing doesn't help. Sometimes *understanding* doesn't even help. It just drives the knife in deeper.

He cleared his throat. "Glad you're around. Now get the fuck out of my office."

A police funeral has its own etiquette. In some places, bagpipers play. Here in Santa Luz there's the official ceremony, and then the wake, usually in the back room at Costanza's Pub downtown.

Hunters don't go to those.

Saturday dawned bright and fresh. I hadn't slept yet, but I'd made sure I was wearing my tiger's eye rosary and my dagger earrings. I'd hosed off my trench coat, so it was at least clean, if torn and a bit shabby.

He had a full escort of blues, and they laid him to rest in Beacon Hill's lush greenness, under the trees. I stood in the shadow of a century-old oak in the south corner of the cemetery, watching, my hand against the treetrunk.

Monty was there, and Rosenfeld. Rosie's hair was on fire under the fierce desert sun; she wouldn't stand under the portable awning. The glitters of her dress uniform were sharp enough to cut diamonds.

The scar puckered hungrily, tasting the tang of misery and grief riding the air. Mikhail's headstone is in the northern half of Hill, where there was a good view of the rest of the valley, a light scum of smog lingering against the rising towers of downtown.

I know that view like the back of my hand.

There was Lefty Perez from Vice, and "Fuckitall" Ramon. Other familiar faces—Anderson, McGill, "Shooter" Kirby and Rice, all from the Vice Squad. Sullivan and the Badger from Homicide, the Badger's gray hair pulled severely back, shoulders square. Carson and Mathers from Homicide too, and Frank Capretta. Some rookies, and some blues, all dressed their best. Piper and Foster, from Forensics. Other faces I put names to, matching them up slowly.

I knew them all, and drew deeper into the shadows under the tree. The chaplain's voice reached me in fits and starts, carried by the faint wind from the river, smelling of greenness and mineral water.

There was no blue Buick parked on the single strip of asphalt cutting through the rolling green. I hadn't expected it, but it was a relief.

Soft footsteps behind me. I didn't turn around.

"I should kick your ass," Theron murmured.

Just try it, Were. My hand tightened, loosened on the treetrunk, Mikhail's apprentice-ring closed around the third finger. "Show some respect."

"Sorry." And he was. "You gave me a scare, Jill."

It was my turn to apologize. "Sorry."

Silence. The chaplain stopped, then the recital began as the coffin lowered slowly into the waiting darkness.

I duly swear myself to the service of the citizens of Santa Luz, to protect and to succor. I swear to act without fear or favor, to protect the innocent and to safeguard the living. I swear to be honest and true, to be a servant of the law, and to do my best each and every day, so that the citizens who place their trust in me are well and truly served by the power of Justice.

I mouthed it along with them. Hunters have their prayer, I suppose cops are no different.

A few of them said *Amen* afterward. Very quietly.

My chest hurt, a sharp tearing pain. Something too sharp and smoking-hot to be grief loaded the back of my throat. My fingers tightened on rough treebark, I dropped my hand to my side, shook out the fingers so they were nice and loose.

"Gilberto sends his regards," Theron said softly. He stood so close I could feel the heat of his metabolism, but he carefully didn't touch me. "He says he owes you a beer."

I nodded. "Tell him . . ." *What, that he's safe? That I watched him commit a murder and didn't interfere?* "Tell him I understand." *And that he'd better not get in the habit of killing people in my city.*

Rosie stepped forward. Neither of Carp's ex-wives were here, and even if they had been Rosie probably still would have been the one to take the small shovel and scatter the first handful of dirt into the hole.

I heard it clearly, small pebbles striking the roof of the coffin. A hollow sound of finality.

"The warehouse on Cherry is cleaned out," Theron continued, in a monotone. "No sign of scurf. We found an evocation altar downstairs in the Kat Klub. Looked pretty nasty."

"Leon told me." I swallowed sourness. This morning's breakfast had been a few mouthfuls of vodka, the sting relished before I hit the door running. "You're good backup, Theron. Thanks."

He let out a sound that might have been a dissatisfied sigh, smothered in respect for the dead sleeping all around. "Saul's been calling. He's pretty upset. I haven't been home much."

Shit. But it was a Were's tactfulness, asking me what I wanted him to say. If he and Leon had thought I was in serious trouble, or dead, Theron would have been the one to bring Saul the bad news.

It would not have been pretty.

I braced myself. "Neither have I. But I'll get hold of him soon. Let me talk to him." *In other words, Theron, this stays between you and me.*

He absorbed it. "How close was it, Jill?"

What do you want me to tell you? "Close enough. I can't count this one a win." I stared unseeing at the tableau around the open, yawning grave, a mound of dirt covered with Astroturf sitting neglected to one side. Rosie's chin was up. Monty had his arms folded, his shoulders slumped. Sullivan looked down at the ground, Piper's cheeks were wet.

"City's still standing. And that 'breed who ran the Kat Klub—"

"She's dead." I said it too quickly, on a breathy scree of air. *Carp, I avenged you without knowing. I wish I could do it again.*

Sometimes avenging isn't enough. They don't tell you that when you're training. You have to learn it on your own. It is one of the lessons that makes you a hunter, not an apprentice.

The service began to break up. The honor guard marched away to their flashing vehicles; the knot of uniforms and suits at the graveside fraying. Theron watched with me, in silence. Monty stayed while car doors slammed and engines started.

So did Rosie.

The chaplain, an unassuming, balding little man in a black suit, exchanged a few words with Monty, who neatly cut him away from Rosie. She stood in the sun, her hair throwing back its light with a vengeance, her hands knotted into bloodless fists at her sides. She stared at the hole in the ground, then lifted her head, scanning the cemetery's rolling greenness.

I made a restless movement. Theron was still, the peculiar immobility of a cat Were.

The chaplain headed off toward his own car, a sunny yellow Volkswagen Beetle. I stepped forward as he drove away. Picked my way with care around headstones and plates set in the ground, passing wilted flowers and the occasional shrub. The last twenty feet or so were the hardest, because I could feel Rosie's eyes on me and the grave opened like a mouth. Strata of sprinkler-wet earth striped its sides.

I came to a halt outside the awning's shelter. The sun beat down.

Monty clapped me awkwardly on the shoulder and handed me a new page. "We're going to Costanza's." The words hung in still air, the breeze had died.

I nodded. Silver clanked as my hair moved.

Rosenfeld sounded steady enough. "Give me a minute, Monty?"

"Sure." He shifted his weight, awkwardly.

I could feel his gaze on me, maybe he was trying to tell me something. I didn't look up. There were a few handfuls of dirt scattered across the coffin's lacquered top, and someone had dropped in a rose. Probably Piper.

Monty retreated. I steeled myself, raised my gaze, and met Rosie's head-on.

Rosenfeld was crying.

Oh, hell.

"He was Internal Affairs." She lifted her prizefighter's jaw a little bit, as if daring me to make something of it. "Jill . . ."

So she knew.

She was his partner, and probably knew him better than he knew himself. Of course she would at least suspect he was IA.

"He was clean, Rosie." The words came out in a rush. "I did my best. He saw something, something awful. I didn't get there in time."

"Oh, Jesus." Her mouth gapped a little, her nose inflamed—redheads can't cry gracefully, at least not any redhead I've known. Then again, the whole point of crying is that nobody does it gracefully. "I thought . . . his ex-wives, and the case he was working. I thought . . ."

"I got the people responsible." My voice didn't seem to work quite right. "I tied up the case."

"They're dead? The motherfuckers that did for him?" She searched my face.

Do you even need to ask me that? "They're dead." *Except the other dirty cops Harvill had on a string. But sooner or later, I'll get to them. I swear it, Rosie.*

It would be vengeance, and it wouldn't help. But it was the least I owed her.

She glanced at the grave, her mouth firming and twisting down, bitterly. "I've been thinking, I should have seen it. It was all there. He's been withdrawing all year. Just sinking deeper and deeper into the pit. I should have nagged him into something. Counseling. *Something.*"

Oh, Rosie. "It was the nightside, Rosie. Not him." *Give her that much, at least. Don't let her blame herself for this.* "I should have kept him under tighter wraps, made sure he was okay. It was on my watch. I'm . . . sorry."

"It isn't your fault. He was already cracking."

I smelled the sweat and the misery on her. The heat was immense, Biblical, no shred of air moving to break the bubble of silence laid over us. We stood in the sun and watched each other.

Once, Rosenfeld had checked herself out of the hospital and marched into my warehouse, all in order to apologize to me. Seeing the nightside up close had put a streak of white in her hair she had to dye and given her nightmares she'd needed two years of therapy to face. The guilt would eat at her, because she had seen the naked face of darkness and survived.

And Carp hadn't.

I broke the silence. "He was a good cop. A damn good cop."

The air started moving again, flirting and swirling as the breeze came up the hill, laden with heavy green rainsmell. We'd have thunderstorms as soon as the season started changing. Fall would ride in with afternoon rains, and winter. And here, sleeping under the earth, would the dead take any notice of weather?

There was never any rain in Hell. I knew that for a fact.

"He was," Rosie agreed. "Don't . . ."

Don't blame myself? "If you won't, I won't."

"Deal." She held out her hand. I took it gingerly, and we shook the way women accustomed to men shake—a brief squeeze, eye contact, and a half-embarrassed smile.

The scar throbbed, sensing the misery saturating afternoon scorch. I let go of her hot fingers. A thin trickle of salt sweat oozed down my spine. "You'd better go on. Monty probably needs a drink."

She let out an uneasy half-cackle of a laugh, choked off midway as she glanced toward the scar cut in the green earth. "I feel like I should stay with him."

"They'll be along in a few minutes to fill in the . . . to fill it in. I'll stay." *It's my job. It's the least I can do.*

She nodded once, sharply, her spiky hair drooping,

plastered to her skull. We stood there for a few more moments, nothing left to say hanging between us.

Her shoulders finally dropped. "I guess I'll see you
around?"

Why did she make it a question? "I'm not going anywhere." *This is my city. And when I find the other dirty
fucking cops, I'll serve vengeance on them too. I promise.*
"Rosie? Take care of yourself." *Please.*

"Yeah. You too, Kismet." Military-precise, she turned
and headed for Monty's car, running now. I thought of
the air-conditioned comfort inside and breathed out softly
through my mouth, since my nose was full.

Monty pulled slowly away. Theron approached, and I
heard a golf cart buzzing along. The diggers, two broad
Hispanic men in chinos and blue button-downs—*of
course,* I thought, *white would show the sweat and the
dirt, and we can't have that*—arrived, and gave me a nervous glance.

I headed for the strip of asphalt and paused there,
watching. One of the diggers had shucked his button-
down and was in a black wifebeater. The other was still
eyeing me. They began filling in the grave. Heat bounced,
shimmering, up from the black asphalt, clawed at me in
colorless waves. Still, I didn't sweat much, even under the
leather.

I did wonder, standing there and watching them work
with their shovels, if they had come over the border. I
wondered if they'd been born in my city. I wondered if
either of them had any idea who they were burying, or if it
was just another job to them. I wondered if they resented
the fact that they were cheaper than a machine, or if they
were grateful for the work.

And I wondered if they would ever want to know how hard I tried to keep them safe too. I couldn't fix economic inequality, but I could stop hellbreed from preying on the poor and marginalized. One at a time and piecemeal, but it was better than nothing.

They call us heroes, Mikhail sneered inside my head. *Idiots. There is only one reason we do it, milaya, and it is for to quiet the screaming in our own heads.*

One of them said something in an undertone. The other laughed, replied with a snatch of softly-delivered song. It sounded oddly reverent. Even if it was just another job, they spoke quietly around the dead.

"Jill?" Theron, at my shoulder again. "Come on. I'll buy you a drink."

"Hunters don't go to police wakes, Theron." *It hurts too much. Far too much.*

"At Micky's. I'll spot you some lunch too. If I know you, you haven't eaten."

I waited in the sun for another ten minutes. It didn't take them long to fill in the grave and tamp it down. The taller one elbowed his partner, and they glanced at me again before loading their shovels and the Astroturf into the golf cart. They buzzed away. Maybe they had other holes to fill.

Sleep well, Carp. My chest ached with all the things I could never say.

I wiped at my face again. *Jesus, Jill. Quit it.* "I didn't have much breakfast," I admitted.

Theron manfully restrained himself from commenting. "I'll drive."

33

The sun went down in a glory of red and orange. Wind shifted, veering in off the baking desert, but it carried a breath of something other than sand and summer on its back. A faint tang that meant autumn was coming. Not for a while, but still coming.

I'd considered calling Perry. I'd even considered waltzing into the Monde Nuit and questioning him about Argoth. And about just what he'd known about Shen's little bid for a bigger slice of domination in the city.

Questioning him *hard*.

In the end I dragged the cut-down discarded end of a metal barrel from the railyards behind my warehouse and fed it a mound of barbeque charcoal. I doused the briquettes with lighter fluid and wadded up bits of waste paper, lit a match.

When the coals were glowing red to match the sun's nightly death I dug in my pocket and pulled out the little Ziploc baggie.

The purple crystals inside were slightly oily, giving

under my fingers with a faint crunching through the plastic. I'd searched both Irene and Fax pretty thoroughly, but only Fax was carrying a sample and several folded sheets of paper covered with arcane notations.

I never took any chemistry in high school, so they might as well have been Greek. They burned just like any ordinary paper.

When they were ash I tossed the Ziploc in. There was a brief stench of burning plastic, and flame flared like the yolk-yellow light in Shen's eyes.

It still bothered me. Why hadn't she brought other hellbreed to finish me off? Then again, if she was trying to make points with one of Hell's higher-ups, she would have been greedy for the credit and unwilling to share. A big drawback to being hellbreed—they can't trust each other, and barely even trust Traders mortgaged to their eyebrows.

Which meant that maybe, just maybe, nobody else knew about this little foray into experimental chemistry.

Dream, he'd called it. More like a nightmare. A nightmare nobody would wake up from. Cold sweat prickled along my arms, along the curve of my lower back. With this shit to provide a banquet, Argoth could have stuffed himself to the gills on death and destruction. He could have made an entire continent a living hell.

Hey, he'd done it last time.

The only thing about averting a goddamn apocalypse is that it happens so routinely. None of the civilians have any idea how close the world is, *all the time,* to going up in smoke.

Sometimes I wonder if that ignorance is really a blessing.

The purple crystals sizzled, I poked at the fire with Saul's barbeque tongs to make sure every little scrap was consumed. Sparks rose, and I kept my face well out of the hot draft. Who knew what this shit could do to you?

I did. I'd seen it.

Argoth is coming . . . I can only hold the tide so long.

How much had Perry known? Only as much as he'd told me? Or was he hoping I'd disrupt Shen's plans?

I didn't want to know badly enough to let him fiddle with my head again.

Getting cowardly in your old age, Jill?

It didn't matter. If another hellbreed was crazy enough to try following in Shen's footsteps, they'd get the same treatment. I knew what to look for, now. And even if Perry hadn't been involved . . . well, we'd just have to see.

I hate just waiting to see.

The scar pulsed under a copper cuff, one of the old ones Galina had dug up for me. With Saul gone I was back to the copper, since I can't work leather to save my life.

The sun finished sinking below the horizon. My city trembled, waking up to nightlife.

The phone shrilled. I made sure every scrap of chemical and paper was gone, then stamped inside and scooped it up right before the answering machine would click on. "Talk," I half-snarled. *What now? Goddammit.*

"Hey, kitten." A familiar voice. He sounded sad, and bone-deep exhausted. "Glad to hear you."

Oh, God. "Saul." I sounded like all the air had been punched out of me. "Jesus. Good to hear you too. What's going on?"

"I was about to ask you that. Can't get hold of Theron. Everything okay out there?"

I closed my eyes, throttling the sigh of relief in my chest. "Just fine. Been a little busy, is all. How are you? What's going on out there?"

"You sure you're okay, kitten?" The rumble hid behind his voice. Distress.

"Just fine. Fine as frog's fur." *I just fucked this thing up six ways from Sunday and almost lost my whole city. But it's cool.* "We had a scurf scare and some Traders getting uppity. The usual. It's all packed away now." I stopped myself from babbling with sheer relief. "How are *you?* What's happened?"

"She's gone." A world of sadness in two words. "I'm coming home. Due in Tuesday at eleven P.M., I'm at the train station now."

Oh, thank God. "I'm so sorry." My breath caught. *He's coming home.* "You sound awful."

"Thanks." A dollop of wry humor lightening grief for just a moment. "She went peacefully. My aunts were there."

I listened to him breathe for a few endless moments. "I love you." Soft, high-pitched, as if I'd just been caught in the wrong bathroom in junior high.

It must have been the right thing to say. The rumble behind his breathing lessened. "I love you too, kitten. Pick me up?"

"With bells on." *Where am I going to find a car? Shit, I don't care. He's coming home.*

"You sure you're okay?" Now he sounded concerned. "You seem a little—"

"It's just been a long couple of days. And I miss you, and I feel bad for you." *And I almost lost my city. I almost didn't catch what was happening. I got lucky.*

Except hunters don't really believe in *luck*. Another reason to feel uneasy.

Like I needed one.

He didn't question it further, thank God. "All right. I've got to go, the train's boarding."

I squeezed my eyes shut even tighter. Yellow and faintly-blue stars danced under my eyelids. "Go on. I'll pick you up at the station. I love you."

"Love you too, kitten." A disembodied voice echoing behind him. Last call for boarding, probably. "See you soon."

It can't be soon enough for me. "See you."

He hung up. I listened to the dial tone for a little bit, then reluctantly put the phone in the charger and hauled myself up, paced back out to the barrel. The coals were back to glowing red. The formula and the sample were history. Apocalypse averted, again.

Saul's coming home. Thank God.

I made sure the barrel wasn't close to anything flammable and watched the last few dregs of light swirl out of the sky. When it was full dark, I shrugged into my trenchcoat and checked my ammo. I locked my home up safe and sound and headed out into the newborn night despite the stiffness in my legs and the aching in my heart.

He's coming home. He's on his way.

A thin fingernail-paring of waxing moon hung low in the sky. My city lay below, drowning out the night's lamps with streetlight shine. A field of electric-burning stars covering up holes of darkness, some Hell-made, some human.

And one more grave.

I went back to work.

Glossary

Arkeus: A roaming corruptor escaped from Hell.

Banefire: A cleansing sorcerous flame.

Black Mist: A roaming psychic contagion; a symbiotic parasite inhabiting the host's nervous system and bloodstream.

Chutsharak: Chaldean obscenity, loosely translated as "oh, *fuck.*"

Demon: Term loosely used to designate any nonhuman predator with sorcerous ability or a connection to Hell.

Exorcism: Tearing loose a psychic parasite from its host.

Hellbreed: Blanket term for a wide array of demons, half-demons, or other species escaped or sent from Hell.

Hellfire: The spectrum of sorcerous flame employed by hellbreed for a variety of uses.

Hunter: A trained human who keeps the balance between the nightside and regular humans; extrahuman law enforcement.

Imdarák: Shadowy former race who drove the Elder

Gods from the physical plane, also called the Lords of the Trees.

Martindale Squad: The FBI division responsible for tracking nightside crime across state lines and at the federal level, mostly staffed with hunters and Weres.

Middle Way: Worshippers of Chaos, Middle Way adepts are usually sociopathic and sorcerous loners. Occasionally covens of Middle Way adepts will come together to control a territory or for a specific purpose.

OtherSight: Second sight, the ability to see sorcerous energy. Can also mean precognition.

Possessor: An insubstantial, low-class demon specializing in occupying and controlling humans; the prime reason for exorcists.

Scurf: Also called *nosferatim,* a semi-psychic viral infection responsible for legends of blood-hungry corpses, vampires, or nosferatu. Also, someone infected by the scurf virus.

Sorrow: A worshipper of the Chaldean Elder Gods.

Sorrows House: A House inhabited by Sorrows, with a vault for invocation or evocation of Elder Gods.

Sorrows Mother: A high-ranking female of a Sorrows House.

Talyn: A hellbreed, higher in rank than an *arkeus* or Possessor, usually insubstantial due to the nature of the physical world.

Trader: A human who makes a "deal" with a hellbreed, usually for worldly gain or power.

Utt'huruk: A bird-headed demon.

Were: Blanket term for several species who shapeshift into animal (for example, cougar, wolf, or spider) or half-animal (wererat or *khentauri*) form.

extras

orbit

meet the author

LILITH SAINTCROW was born in New Mexico, bounced around the world as an Air Force brat, and fell in love with writing when she was ten years old. She currently lives in Vancouver, WA. Find her on the Web at: www.lilithsaintcrow.com.

introducing

If you enjoyed **REDEMPTION ALLEY**,
look out for

FLESH CIRCUS

Book 4 of the Jill Kismet series
by Lilith Saintcrow

*K*iss. A delight, as usual."

Don't call me that, Perry. I eyed the second one from the Cirque, a small, soft boyish Trader with huge dark eyes and a fine down on his round apple cheeks. My stomach turned over, hard. "Let's just get this over with." I sounded bored even to myself. "I have work to do tonight."

"As do we all." The Ringmaster's voice was a surprise—as hearty and jolly as he was thin and waspish. And under that, a buzz like chrome flies in chlorinated bottles.

The rumble of a different language. Helletöng.

"Always business." Perry shrugged, a loose easy movement, and I passed my eye down the small, doe-innocent Trader. He was thin and birdlike, and he made me uneasy.

Most of the time the bad is right out there where you can see it.

The Trader leaned in to the Ringmaster's side, and the 'breed put one stick-thin arm over him. A flick of the loose fingers, probably meant to be soothing, and the parody of parental posture almost made acid crawl up the back of my throat.

"This is Ikaros," the Ringmaster said. "Do you have the collar?"

I reached into a left-hand pocket, my trenchcoat rustling slightly. Cool metal resounded under my fingertips, and I had another serious run of thoughts about stepping back, turning on my heel, and heading for the Pontiac.

But you can't do that when the Cirque comes to town. The compact they live under is unbreakable. They serve a purpose, and any hunter on their worldwide circuit knows as much.

It just goes against every hunter instinct to let the fuckers keep breathing.

Perry rumbled something in Helletöng, the sound of freight trains painfully rubbing against each other at midnight.

I paused. My right hand ached for a gun. "English, Perry." *None of your goddamn rumblespeak here.*

"So rude of me. I was merely remarking on your beauty tonight, my dear."

Oh, for fuck's sake. I shouldn't have dignified it with a response. "The next time one of you hellspawn rumbles in töng, I'm going back to work, the Cirque can go down the line, and you, Perry, can go suck a few eggs."

"Charming." The Ringmaster's smile had dropped like a bad habit. "Is she always this way?"

"Oh, yes. Always a delight, our Kiss." Perry's slight smile hadn't changed, and the faint blue shine from his irises didn't waver either. He looked far too amused, and the scar was quiescent against my skin.

Usually he played with it, waves of pain or sick pleasure pouring up my arm. Fiddling with my internal thermostat, trying to make me respond.

My fingers curled around the metal and brought it out.

The collar was a serious piece of business, a spiked circle of silver, supple and deadly looking. Each spike was as long as my thumb from knuckle to fingertip, and wicked sharp. Blue sparks flowed under the surface of the metal, not quite breaking free in response to the contamination of two hellbreed and a Trader so close. My silver apprentice-ring, snug against my left third finger, *did* crack a single spark, and it was gratifying to see the little Trader shiver slightly.

I shook it a little, the hinges moving freely. It trembled like a live thing, the blue swirling hypnotically. "Rules." I had their attention. My right hand wanted to twitch for a knife so bad I almost did it, kept my fingers loose with an effort. The charms in my hair rattled. "Actually, just one rule. Don't fuck with my town. You're here on sufferance."

"Next she'll start in about blood atonement," Perry offered helpfully.

I held the Ringmaster's gaze. My smart eye—the left one, the blue one—was dry, but I didn't blink. He did—first one eye, then the other, slight lizardlike movements.

The Trader slid away from under his hand. Still, their auras swirled together, and I could almost see the thick spiraled rope of a blood bond between them. Ikaros took two steps toward me and paused, looking up with those big eyes.

The flat shine of the dusted lying over his irises was the same as every other Trader's. It was a reminder that this kid, however old he really was, had bargained with Hell. Traded away something essential in return for something else.

His lashes quivered. That was his first mistake.

The next was his hands, twisting together as if he was nervous. If the Ringmaster's hands were flaccid and delicate, the Trader's were broad farmboy's paws, at odds with the rest of his delicate beauty.

I wondered what he'd Traded for to end up here.

"We'll be good." His voice was a sweet piping, without the candysick corruption of a hellbreed's. He gave me a tremulous smile.

"Save it." I jingled the collar again, watched him flinch just a little. The hellbreed had gone still. "And get down on your knees."

"That isn't necessary." The Ringmaster's tone was a warning.

So was mine. "I'm the hunter here, hellspawn. *I* decide what's necessary. Get. Down on. Your knees."

The Trader sank down gracefully, but not before his fingers clenched for the barest second. Big, broad hands, and if they closed around my neck it might be a job and a half to pry them away.

He might have looked like a tchotchke doll old ladies like to put on their shelves, but he was *Trader*. If he looked innocent and harmless it was only the lure used to get someone close enough for those strong fingers. And that tremulous smile would be the last thing a victim ever saw.

I clipped the collar on, tested it. He smelled like sawdust and healthy young male, but the tang of sugared corruption riding it only made the sweetness of youth less appetizing. Like a hooker turning her face, and the light picking out damage under a screen of makeup. The stubble on his neck rasped and my knuckles brushed a different texture—the band of scar tissue resting just above his collarbone. It was all but invisible in the dimness, and I wondered what he'd look like in daylight.

I don't want to find out. I've had enough of this already, and we're only ten minutes in.

I stepped back. The collar glinted. My apprentice-ring thrummed with force, and I twitched my hand, experimentally.

The Trader let out a small sound, tipping forward as if pulled off-center. His knees ground into the dust. My stomach turned. It was just like having a dog on a leash.

I nodded. Let my hand drop. "You can get up now."

"Not just yet." Perry stepped forward, and little bits of cooling breeze lifted my hair. I didn't move, but every nerve in my body pulled itself tight as a drumhead and my pulse gave a nasty leap. They could hear it, of course, and if they thought it was a show of weakness things might get nasty.

Ikaros hunched, thin shoulders coming up.

My left hand touched a gun butt, cool metal under my fingertips. "That's close enough, Perry."

"Oh, not nearly." He shifted his weight, and the breeze freshened again. His aura deepened, like a bruise, and the scar woke to prickling, stinging life.

A whisper of sound, and I had the .45 level, the hammer cocked. "That's close *enough*." *Give me a reason. Dear God, just give me a reason.*

He shrugged, and remained where he was. The Ringmaster was smiling faintly, his thin lips closed over the tooth-ridges.

I backed up two steps. Did not holster the gun. Faint starlight gilded its metal. "The chain, Perry. Hurry up."

He smiled, a good-tempered grin with razorblades underneath. It was the type of smile that said he was contemplating a good piece of art or ass, something he could pick up with very little trouble. His eyes all but *danced*. A quick flicking motion with his fingers, the scar plucking, and a loop of darkness coiled in his hands, dipping down with a wrongly musical clashing. His left hand snapped forward, the darkness solidified, and the Trader jerked again, a small cry wrung out of him.

Ikaros's eyes rolled up into his head and he collapsed. Spidery lines of darkness crawled up every inch of pale exposed flesh, spiked writing marching in even rows as if a tattoo had come to life and started colonizing his skin.

Perry's hands dropped. The Trader lay in the dust, gasping.

The Ringmaster sighed, a short sound under the moan of freshening breeze. "He is your hostage." Now his cane had appeared, a slim black length with a round faceted crystal set atop it. He tapped the ground twice, paused, tapped a third time with the coppershod bottom. The crystal—it looked like an almighty big glass doorknob except for the sick greenish light in its depths—made a sound like billiard balls clicking together, underlining his words. "Should we break the Law, he will suffer, and through him, I will suffer. He is our pledge."

The Trader struggled up to his hands and knees. The collar sparked, once, a single point of blue light etching sharp shadows behind the pebbles and dirt underneath him. He coughed, dryly. Retched once.

Perry grinned. The greenish light from the Ringmaster's cane etched shadows on his face, exposing a breath of what lived under the mask of banal humanity. "May your efforts be fruitful, brother."

"No less than your own." The Ringmaster glanced at me. "Are you satisfied, hunter? May we pass?"

"Go on in." The words were bitter ash in my mouth. "Just behave yourselves."

Ikaros struggled to his feet. He moved slowly, as if it hurt. I finally lowered the gun, watching Perry. Who was grinning like he'd just discovered gold in his underpants.

The Ringmaster took the Trader's elbow and steered him away, back toward the convoy. Their engines roused one by one, and they pulled out, a creaking train of etheric bruising, tires shushing as they bounced up onto the hardtop from the access road and gained speed, heading for the well of light that was my city below.

Last of all went the limo. The Trader slumped against a back passenger-side window, and the inside of the vehicle crawled with green phosphorescence, shining out past the tinting. Its engine made a sound like chattering teeth and laughter, and its taillights flashed once as it hopped up onto the road and passed the city limits.

Jesus.

Perry stood, watching. I swallowed. Took another two steps back. The scar was still hard and hot against my wrist, like almost-burning metal clapped against cool skin.

I waited for him to do something. A conversational gambit, or a physical one, to make me react.

"Goodnight, sweetheart." He finally moved, turning on his heel and striding for the limousine.

It was amazing. It was probably the first time in years he hadn't fucked with me.

It rattled me more than it should. But then again, when the Cirque de Charnu comes to town, a hunter is right to feel a little rattled.